NIGHTCRAWLING

NIGHTCRAWLING

Leila Mottley

 ALFRED A. KNOPF · NEW YORK · 2022

THIS IS A BORZOI BOOK
PUBLISHED BY ALFRED A. KNOPF

www.aaknopf.com

Knopf, Borzoi Books, and the colophon
are registered trademarks of Penguin Random House LLC.

Library of Congress Cataloging-in-Publication Data
Names: Mottley, Leila, [date] author.
Title: Nightcrawling / by Leila Mottley.
Description: First edition. | New York : Alfred A. Knopf, [2022] |
"A Borzoi book."
Identifiers: LCCN 2021026295 (print) | LCCN 2021026296 (ebook) |
ISBN 9780593318935 (hardcover) | ISBN 9780593318942 (ebook) |
ISBN 9781524712204 (open market)
Subjects: LCGFT: Urban fiction. | Novels.
Classification: LCC PS3613.O8455 N54 2022 (print) |
LCC PS3613.O8455 (ebook) | DDC 813/.6—dc23
LC record available at https://lccn.loc.gov/2021026295
LC ebook record available at https://lccn.loc.gov/2021026296

Jacket image based on a photograph
by Mike Harrington / Stone / Getty Images
Jacket design by Michael Morris

Manufactured in the United States of America
First Edition

For Oakland and its girls

NIGHTCRAWLING

THE SWIMMING POOL is filled with dog shit and Dee's laughter mocks us at dawn. I've been telling her all week that she's looking like the crackhead she is, laughing at the same joke like it's gonna change. Dee didn't seem to mind that her boyfriend left her, didn't even seem to care when he showed up poolside after making his rounds to every dumpster in the neighborhood last Tuesday, finding feces wrapped up in plastic bags. We heard the splashes at three a.m., followed by his shouts about Dee's unfaithful ass. But mostly we heard Dee's cackles, reminding us how hard it is to sleep when you can't distinguish your own footsteps from your neighbor's.

None of us have ever set foot in the pool for as long as I've been here; maybe because Vernon, the landlord, has never once cleaned it, but mostly because nobody ever taught none of us how to delight in the water, how to swim without gasping for breath, how to love our hair when it is matted and chlorine-soaked. The idea of drowning doesn't bother me, though, since we're made of water anyway. It's kind of like your body overflowing with itself. I think I'd rather go that way than in some haze on the floor of a crusty apartment, my heart out-pumping itself and then stopping.

This morning is different. The way Dee's laugh swirls upward into a high-pitched sort of scream before it wanders into her bellow. When I open the door, she's standing there, by the railing, like always. Except today she faces toward the apartment door and the pool keeps her backlit so I can't see her face, can only see the way her cheekbones bob like apples in her hollow skin. I close the door before she sees me.

Some mornings I peek my head into Dee's unlocked door just to make sure she's still breathing, writhing in her sleep. In some ways I don't mind her neurotic laughing fits because they tell me she's alive, her lungs haven't quit on her yet. If Dee's still laughing, not everything has gone to shit.

The knock on our apartment is two fists, four pounds, and I should have known it was coming, but it still makes me jump back from the door. It ain't that I didn't see Vernon making his rounds or the flyer flipping up and drifting back into place on Dee's door as she stared at it, still cackling. I turn and look at my brother, Marcus, on the couch snoring, his nose squirming up to meet his brows.

He sleeps like a newborn, always making faces, his head tilting so I can see his profile, where the tattoo remains taut and smooth. Marcus has a tattoo of my fingerprint just below his left ear and, when he smiles, I find myself drawn right to it, like another eye. Not that either of us has been smiling lately, but the image of it—the memory of the freshly rippling ink below his grin—keeps me coming back to him. Keeps me hoping. Marcus's arms are lined in tattoos, but my fingerprint is the only one on his neck. He told me it was the most painful one he'd ever gotten.

He got the tattoo when I turned seventeen and it was the first day I ever thought he might just love me more than anything, more than his own skin. But now, three months from my eighteenth birthday, when I look at my quivering fingerprint on the edge of his jaw, I feel naked, known. If Marcus ended up bloodied in the street, it wouldn't take much to identify him by the traces of me on his body.

I reach for the doorknob, mumbling, "I got it," as if Marcus was ever actually gonna put feet to floor this early. On the other side of the wall, Dee's laughter seeps into my gums like salt water, absorbed right into the fleshy part of my mouth. I shake my head and turn back to the door, to my own slip of paper taped to the orange paint.

You don't have to read one of these papers to know what they say. Everyone been getting them, tossing them into the road as if they can *nah, nigga* themselves out of the harshness of it. The font is unrelenting, numbers frozen on the flyer, lingering in the scent of industrial printer ink, where it was inevitably pulled from a pile of papers just as toxic and slanted as this one and placed on the door of the studio apartment that's been in my family for decades. We all known Vernon was a sellout, wasn't gonna keep this place any longer than he had to when the pockets are roaming around Oakland, looking for the next lot of us to scrape out from the city's insides.

The number itself wouldn't seem so daunting if Dee wasn't cracking herself up over it, curling into a whole fit, cementing each zero into the pit of my belly. I whip my head toward her, shout out over the wind and the morning trucks, "Quit laughing or go back inside, Dee. Shit." She turns her head an inch or two to stare at me and smiles wide, opens her mouth until it's a complete oval, and continues her cackle. I rip the rent increase notice from the door and return to our apartment, where Marcus is serene and snoring on the couch.

He's lying there sleeping while this whole apartment collapses around me. We're barely getting by as is, a couple months behind in rent, and Marcus has no money coming in. I'm begging for shifts at the liquor store and counting the number of crackers left in the cupboard. We don't even own wallets, and looking at him, at the haze of his face, I know we won't make it out of this one like we did the last time our world fractured, with an empty photo frame where Mama used to be.

I shake my head at his figure, long and taking over the room, then place the rent increase notice in the center of his chest so it breathes with him. Up and down.

I don't hear Dee no more, so I pull on my jacket and slip outside, leaving Marcus to eventually wake to a crumpled paper and more worries than he'll try to handle. I walk along the railing lined in apartments and open Dee's door. She's there, somehow asleep and twitching on the mattress when just a few minutes ago she was roaring. Her son, Trevor, sits on a stool in the small kitchen eating off-brand Cheerios out of their box. He's nine and I've known him since he was born, watched him shoot up into the lanky boy he is now. He's munching on the cereal and waiting for his mother to wake up, even though it'll probably be hours before her eyes open and see him as more than a blur.

I step inside, quietly walking up to him, grabbing his backpack from the floor and handing it to him. He smiles at me, the gaps in his teeth filled in with soggy Cheerio bits.

"Boy, you gotta be getting to school. Don't worry 'bout your mama, c'mon, I'll take you."

Trevor and I emerge from the apartment, his hand in mine. His palms feel like butter, smooth and ready to melt in the heat of my hand. We walk together toward the metal stairwell, painted lime green and chipped, all the way down to the ground floor, past the shit pool, and through the metal gate that spits us right out onto High Street.

High Street is an illusion of cigarette butts and liquor stores, a winding trail to and from drugstores and adult playgrounds masquerading as street corners. It has a childlike kind of flair, like the perfect landscape for a scavenger hunt. Nobody ever knows when the hoods switch over, all the way up to the bridge, but I've never been up there so I can't tell you if it makes you want to skip like it does on our side. It is everything and nothing you'd expect with its funeral homes and gas stations, the street sprinkled in houses with yellow shining out the windows.

"Mama say Ricky don't come around no more, so I got the cereal all to myself."

Trevor lets go of my hand, slippery, sauntering ahead, his steps buoyant. Watching him, I don't think anybody but Trevor and me understand what it's like to feel ourselves moving, like really notice it. Sometimes I think this little kid might just save me from the swallow of our gray sky, but then I remember that Marcus used to be that small, too, and we're all outgrowing ourselves.

We take a left coming out of the Regal-Hi Apartments and keep walking. I follow Trevor, crossing behind him as he ignores the light and the rush of cars because he knows anyone would stop for him, for those glossy eyes and that sprint. His bus stop is on the side of the street we just crossed from, but he likes to walk on the side where our park is, the one where teenagers shoot hoops without nets every morning, colliding with each other on the court and falling into fits of coughs. Trevor slows, his eyes fixated on this morning's game. It looks like girls on boys and nobody is winning.

I grab Trevor's hand, pulling him forward. "You not gonna catch the bus if you don't move those feet."

Trevor drags, his head twisting to follow the ball spin up, down, squeaking between hands and hoops.

"Think they'd let me play?" Trevor's face wobbles as he sucks on the insides of his cheeks in awe.

"Not today. See, they don't got a bus to catch and your mama sure won't want you out here getting all cold missing school like that."

January in Oakland is a funny kind of cold. It's got a chill, but it really ain't no different from any other month, clouds covering all the blue, not cold enough to warrant a heavy coat, but too cold to show much skin. Trevor's arms are bare, so I shrug off my jacket, wrapping it around his shoulders. I grab his other hand and we continue to walk, beside each other now.

We hear the bus before we see it, coming around the corner, and I whip my head quick, see the number, the bulk of this big green thing rumbling toward us.

"Let's cross, come on, move those feet."

Ignoring the open road and the cars, we run across the street, the bus hurtling toward us and then pulling over to the bus stop. I nudge Trevor forward, into the line shuffling off the curb and into the mouth of the bus.

"You go on and read a book today, huh?" I call out to him as he climbs on.

He looks back at me, his small hand raising up just enough that it could be called a wave goodbye or a salute or a boy getting ready to wipe his nose. I watch him disappear, watch the bus tilt back up onto its feet, groan, and pull away.

A couple minutes later, my own bus creaks to a stop in front of me. A man standing near me wears sunglasses he doesn't need in this gloom, and I let him climb on first, then join, looking around and finding no seats because this is a Thursday morning and we all got places to be. I squeeze between bodies and find a pocket of space toward the back, standing and holding on to the metal pole as I wait for the vehicle to thrust me forward.

In the ten minutes it takes to get to the other side of East Oakland, I slip into the lull of the bus, the way it rocks me back and forth like I imagine a mother rocks a child when she is still patient enough to not start shaking. I wonder how many of these other people, their hair shoved into hats, with lines moving in all directions tracing their faces like a train station map, woke up this morning to a lurching world and a slip of paper that shouldn't mean more than a tree got cut down somewhere too far to give a shit about. I almost miss the moment to pull the wire and push open the doors to fresh Oakland air and the faint scent of oil and machinery from the construction site across the street from La Casa Taquería.

I get off the bus and approach the building, the blackout windows obscuring the inside from sight and its blue awning familiar. I grab the handle to the restaurant door, open it, and immediately smell something thundering and loud in the darkness of the shop. The chairs are turned over on the tables, but the place is alive.

"You don't turn the lights on for me no more?" I call out, knowing Alé is only a few feet away but she feels farther in the dark. She steps out from a doorway, her shadow groping for the light switch, and we are illuminated.

Alejandra's hair is silky and black, spilling from the bun on top of her head. Her skin is oily, slick with the sweat of the kitchen she has spent the past twenty minutes in. Her white T-shirt competes with Marcus's shirts for most oversized and inconspicuous, making her look boyish and cool in a way that I never could. Her tattoos peek out from all parts of her and sometimes I think she is art, but then she starts to move and I remember how bulky and awkward she is, her feet stepping big.

"You know I could kick you outta here real quick." Alé strides closer, looks like she's about to perform the black man's handshake, until she realizes I am not my brother and instead opens her arms. I am mesmerized by her, the way she fills up space in the room like she fills up that drooping shirt. Here, I settle into the most familiar place that I have ever lived, her chest against my ear, warm and thumping.

"You best have some food in there," I tell her, pulling away and turning to strut into the kitchen. I like to swing my hips when I walk around Alé, makes her call me her chava.

Alé watches me move and her eyes dart. She starts to run toward the kitchen door just as I rush there, racing, pushing each other to squeeze inside the doorway, laughing until we cry, spreading out on the floor as we step on each other's limbs and don't care about the bruises that'll paint us blue tomorrow. Alé beats me and stands at the stove scooping food into bowls while I'm on my knees heaving. She chuckles slyly as I get up and then hands me a bowl and spoon.

"Huevos rancheros," she says, sweat drip-dripping down her nose.

It is hot and fuming, deep red with eggs on top.

Alé cooks for me at least once a week and, when Marcus is with me, he always asks what it is, regardless of whether or not she's made it before. He likes fucking with her as much as he likes rapping off-beat and smooth-talking.

I hop onto the counter, feeling something seep into my jeans and ignoring it. Spooning the food into my mouth, I let the heat take over my tongue, while I watch Alé lean her back against the stove across from me, the steam from our bowls floating upward and forming a cloud around the ceiling.

"You found a job yet?" Alé asks, her mouth smeared in sauce like she's drawn outside the lines of her lips.

I shake my head, dip a finger into the bowl and lick it. "Been everywhere in this city but they all so hung up on the high school dropout shit that they won't even look at me."

Alé swallows and nods.

"Worst part is, Marcus won't even get off his ass and try."

She rolls her eyes, but doesn't say anything, as if I won't catch it.

"What?" I ask.

"It's just, he doing his best, you know, and it's only been a few months since he quit his job. He young too, can't blame him for not wanting to spend all his time working, and y'all are fine for now with you taking a shift at the liquor store a couple days a week. You don't gotta dig up this shit." She speaks with her mouth full, red sauce leaking from the corner.

I'm off the counter now, fully aware of how soaked the back of my jeans are. I slam my bowl on the table, hear it clink, and wish it would have shattered. She has stopped eating and watches me, twisting her chain around her finger.

Alé makes a small noise, like a gurgle in the throat that turns into a cough.

"Fuck you," I spit.

"Come on, Kiara. You don't gotta do this. It's funeral day, we should be twirling in the streets but you over here about to break a damn bowl 'cause you mad you ain't got no job? Most of us out here just tryna get some work. You ain't special."

I glance between her and the floor, her shirt glued to her skin with sweat. In these moments, I remember that Alé had her own world without me, that there was a before me and maybe there will be an after. Either way, I'm not about to stand in this steaming kitchen while the only person that got any right to say my name refuses to see how close I am to falling apart, to letting loose like Dee.

Alé steps forward, grabs my wrist, looks at me, like *Don't do this.* I'm already pushing out the door, my legs betraying my breath, moving quick. She is behind me, reaching out her hand and missing my sleeve, trying again, and finally grasping the fabric. I am being spun around, her face too close, looking at me with all the pity of an owned tongue looking at a caged one. I've let her save me more times than I've forgiven Marcus and I can almost see her slight shake under that shirt.

Her lips barely move as she says it. "It's funeral day."

Alé tells me this like it means shit when her fingernails are short and smell like coriander and mine are sharp and dangerous. But then the pit of her chin dimples and she is everything.

"You don't even get it," I say, thinking of the paper on our door this morning. Her face stitches together.

I shake my head and try to wipe off whatever look has imprinted on my face. "Whatever." I exhale and Alé frowns, but before she can continue to fight me on it, I reach up to the tender patch on her side and tickle her. She shrieks, laughs that surprising girly laugh she produces when she's afraid I'm gonna tickle her again, and I release her. "Now we gonna go or what?"

Alé swings one of her arms around my shoulder and pulls me with her out the door, toward the bus stop. We pass the construction and start to jog until we are suddenly sprinting, racing down the street, not stopping to check for cars as we cross, the singsong of horns trailing us.

J OY FUNERAL HOME is one of many death hotels in East Oakland. It sits on the corner of Seminary Avenue and some other street nobody bothers to learn the name of, welcoming in bodies and more bodies. Alé and I frequent it every couple months, when the employees turn over because they can't stomach another brushing of a corpse beside a plate of Safeway cheese. We've been to enough funerals in our lives to know nobody grieving wants no damn cheese.

Alé and I walk up to MacArthur Boulevard, where we catch the NL, hopping on with Clipper cards we stole from some elementary school lost and found. The bus is almost empty because we are young and foolish while everybody else is sitting at a desk in some tech building, staring at a screen and wishing they could taste the air when it is fresh and tranquil. We don't got nowhere to be and we like it like that.

Alé is one of the lucky ones. Her family's restaurant is a neighborhood staple, and even though they can't afford more than the one bedroom above the shop, she's never been hungry a day in her life. It's all degrees of being alive out here and every time I hug her or watch her skate down the sidewalk, I can feel how strong her heartbeat is. It doesn't matter how lucky you are, though, because you still gotta work day in and day out trying to stay alive while someone else falls through the cracks, ashes scattered in the bay.

Thursdays and Sundays are the only days Alé will come crawling around town with me. She normally stays to help her mom run the restaurant, standing over a stove or waitressing. When I'm lonely, I come watch her do this, observing the way she can sweat nonstop for hours without even moving.

I stare at Alé as she looks out her window, the bus shaking us into each other and away. We're at a red light when she nudges me.

"They really tryna replace Obama with that woman." She nods her head toward the poster pasted in some hardware store window with Hillary Clinton's face creased and smiling. We're more than a year away from the election, but it's already started, all the rumors and talk coinciding with rallies and protests and black men shot down. I shake my head, the bus moving again, before settling my eyes back on Alé.

"You not even wearing black, girl, what you doing?" I ask.

She's still in her white shirt and shorts.

"You ain't either."

When she says this, I look down at my own gray shirt and black jeans. "I'm halfway there."

Alé lets out a small laugh. "This a hood funeral, anyway. Nobody gonna question what we're wearing."

And suddenly we're both giggling because she's right and we must have known this, since we've never shown up to a funeral in anything but jeans and stained T-shirts, except for when Alé's abuelo died two years ago and we wore his shirts, ones that had yellowed from age and smelled only of cigarettes and clay from the deepest, most fertile part of the ground. No mortician ever interrogated the mourner's apparel just like they don't stop and ask about no stab wounds. I showed up to my own daddy's funeral in a neon-pink tank top and nobody said a word.

Mama blamed the prison for Daddy's death, which meant she blamed the people who made it possible for Daddy to have ended up there in the first place—which meant she blamed the streets. Daddy wasn't a hustler or a dealer and I only ever saw him high once, smoking a bowl while he sat by the shit pool with Uncle Ty. It didn't matter though, because Mama could only see the day Daddy got picked up, his friends' twitching mouths when the cops appeared and slammed them to the plaster walls. It didn't matter what they did or didn't do because Mama needed to blame someone, something, and her skin was too soft, too tender to handle blaming the world itself, the click of the handcuffs, the ease with which the cops slid them onto his wrists.

Daddy got sick when he was in San Quentin, started pissing blood and begged to see the doctor for weeks, the burn getting more persistent, until they finally let him. The doctor told him it was probably just the food, that sometimes it does that to you. He gave Daddy some painkillers and pills called alpha blockers to help him piss easier. It took the worst parts of it away, but I think Daddy still found blood in the toilet for years after he came home and never said nothing. Three years after he was released, his back started hurting so bad that he could barely walk to and from the 7-Eleven he worked at.

We took him to the doctor when his legs started swelling and they told us it was his prostate. The cancer was far enough along that there was really no shot at improvement, so Daddy refused when Mama begged him to do the chemo and the radiation therapy. He said he wasn't gonna leave her in no debt from his medical bills.

It was a quick death that felt slow. Marcus disappeared for most of it, off with Uncle Ty. I don't blame him for not wanting to watch. Mama and I witnessed the whole thing, spent hours every night wiping down his body with a cool rag and singing to him. It was a relief when it finally ended, four years after he was released from San Quentin, and we could stop waking up in the middle of the night thinking his body had gone cold. By the time the funeral came around, I was too exhausted to give a shit about wearing black and part of me wished I had stayed away like Marcus. Death is easier to live through unseen.

The bus rolls to a stop on Seminary and spits us out like the bay spits out salt. We hop from the bus to the curb and wait those few moments to watch it stand back up and continue on its path. The left tires fall into a series of potholes, coming back out again with a cough.

Alé puts her arm around me, pulling me close, and I remember how cold I've been without my jacket or her chest. My lips ache and I think they must be purple, nearing blue, but I pass a window of a liquor store and my reflection tells me they're still pink, the same color as Marcus's mouth was this morning, sucking in air and snoring. Alé and I walk together out of sync. She moves kinda like the Hulk with giant steps and each half of her body striding, leaving the other part behind, while I take small steps beside her. I lean on her and it don't matter how unbelievably mismatched we are because we are still moving.

We pause in front of Joy's, watch people in various shades of black, gray, blue, jeans, dresses, joggers, move sluggish through the doors, their heads slightly bent. The door to the funeral parlor is double-sided and dark, probably bullet-proof glass, and, when Alé looks at me, there's something that mimics guilt in her eyes. "Buffet or closet?" she asks, her mouth still close enough to me that I can see the way her tongue darts around in her mouth when she talks.

"Closet."

We both nod, copying all the others: heads down.

Alé squeezes my hand once and then walks inside ahead of me, disappearing behind the glass. I wait a few seconds and pull open the door.

The moment I enter the building, I'm met with two sets of eyes. A staple of most funerals, the blown-up photo of the bodies that lie in coffins some small number of feet away stares at me. There are two of them, but only one picture, like a miniature billboard. One is a woman, her eyelashes short ghosts framing her eyes as she stares at the child in her arms.

The child is not even large enough to be given the title of child. She is an infant, a small person bundled in what looks like a tablecloth but is actually a onesie: red and checkered. Neither of them smiles, drooling in the intoxication of a bond too intimate for me, a stranger, to watch. I want to look away, but the infant's nose keeps calling me back; it is small and pointed, brown but slightly red, like the baby has been outside for too long. I want to warm her, make her return to her color, but she is so far behind this cardboard and you cannot resurrect the dead, even when they have so much life left over.

I taste my tears before I feel them and this is funeral day: touching death and eating lunch. Pretending to cry until we are truly sobbing. Until we have shook hands with every ghost of this building and they have given us permission to wear their clothes like walking relics of their lives, or at least I would like to believe that those are the whispers that creep up my spine as the tears fall.

A hand touches my shoulder and I squirm.

"They were too young." The man behind me is maybe seventy or so, the silver in his beard appearing too bright in this room.

He is wearing a suit and tie while I shrink into my shirt.

"Yes." This is all I can think to say back, not knowing them past their faces and their names, which I don't even know how to pronounce.

I'm about to ask how it happened, how these beings got swept into a casket, but it doesn't matter. Some of us got restaurants and full-grown children and some of us got babies who won't never outgrow their onesies. The man leaves, his tie swinging, his handprint a cold spot on my shoulder.

I continue past the photo, through the corridor to the last door in the hallway, which opens up to racks of clothes and the scent of bleach and perfume.

It is a closet of death, welcoming me like it knows we are kindred. I weave through the line of fabric, dragging my hand across the clothes, moving toward the back row. A blazer has fallen off the hanger and sits on the floor, gathering dust. I pick it up, shake it a little, slip it on over my shirt. It's oversized in that way that makes you feel like the fabric is holding you, like two arms creeping around your chest, warm. I don't take it off.

Somewhere in this building, Alé is standing in a chapel for the public viewing, staring at the bodies, watching the service, crying. She's probably already in the back of the room with the food spread, grabbing a plate, some napkins, and beginning to pile it up, discreetly of course, masking her pain in a full belly. Soon she will slip out the back, exit Joy's, and wait for me at San Antonio Park.

I keep sifting through the racks, trying to find something that reminds me of her. I can't imagine Alé in nothing this formal, until I find a men's black sweater. There is a single hole in the wrist, an invitation for its taking, and it is softer than anything I have ever owned, plain in the way that everything Alé accessorizes herself with is plain. She doesn't need anything extra, with her ink and the intricacies of her face.

I've done my part now, gotten us the clothing I should've worn to my own father's funeral, but I don't want to leave. I don't want to walk out that door and pass by people with large hands who will touch me briefly and hum a sigh like we are sharing our own internal earthquakes, braving them together. I slide down to the floor, burrow into the racks of black where I'm encased in darkness. It is a relief to be removed from sight. Funeral day is a reckoning, when we mimic thieves and really just find excuses for our tears, then light up, eat until we have never felt fuller, and find somewhere to dance. Funeral day is the culmination of all our past selves, when we hold our own memorials for people we never buried right. The funeral always ends, though, and we all gotta get back to the hustle, so I breathe in one last whiff of this room, and get up.

When I make it outside, the sky is blinding. Everything is moving fast, cars and motorcycles stirring wind and dirt like they have forgotten how to stand still. Sometimes I don't remember how to move my legs, but my body always surprises me, moving anyway, moving without my permission. I start walking down the street toward the park that sits there, in the middle of the freeway and stop signs and small condos that house more people than they can fit.

Alé is sitting on one of the swings, a paper plate balancing on top of her knees, but she isn't eating. She's looking up at the sky, which is more of a fog than a cloud now, and I think she's smiling.

I walk up the slight hill to her and when I am close enough, I toss her the black sweater. It lands at her feet. Alé picks it up, that small smile morphing into a dance across her cheeks and this is funeral day, when we are free to own all the dead things, all the sweaters that were resigned to ghosthood revived.

"It was Sonny Rollins. On a loop," she says, and the smile is a familiar reflection of my own face. We always listen to what music they play during the wake, not because it says anything about the lost life, but because it says something about the people who were left behind.

"What song?" I ask her, wanting to hear it in my eardrums, the whine of the saxophone, the grainy sound of my daddy's stereo deep inside a memory with no edges, still pure.

"God Bless the Child." She shakes one of her knees a little as she tells me, the plate tipping slightly.

I sit down on the swing next to Alé's and she moves the plate of food from her knees to my lap. There's cheese and chips and celery that she has covered in peanut butter because she knows it's my favorite. We begin to stuff ourselves, shoveling food, crunching, jaws and tongues and swallows creating a chorus to Sonny's jazz tap that plays on repeat in my head as it must have in the funeral chapel. Alé and I both believe that funerals either have the most ingenious DJs or act as soundtracks for some hollow unwinding, a catalyst to sobs and suicide notes.

"Vernon's selling the Regal-Hi," I say, crunching on my last chip.

Alé's eyes are on me, waiting.

"They raising rent over double." I don't know how to look at her when I say it, feels like confronting myself. Like it might just be too real.

"Shit."

"Yeah." I look up into the sky. "That's why Marcus needs to get a job."

Alé reaches out for my hand and touches it lightly, at the wrist. I wonder if she can feel my pulse, if she's searching for it. "What you gonna do?"

"I don't know. But if we don't figure something out, we on the streets."

I begin to move my legs back and forth off-tempo, staying low to the ground. Alé pulls papers and a small jar with clumps of weed out of her pocket. I like watching her roll, the meditation of it and the smell when it's sweet and unassuming, kind of like if cinnamon was mixed with a redwood tree. I never figured out how to do it right, how to make sure the joint was tight enough to not unravel, but loose enough to breathe. Watching Alé is better, reminds me of the way my mama used to fold her clothes, so determined to make the crease just right.

She pauses to look over at me. "Don't worry, we'll figure it out."

She sprinkles weed from the jar onto a paper and I catch a hint of lavender. She calls the lavender-infused weed her Sunday Shoes and it don't even gotta make sense because when I suck it in, blow it out, I imagine my feet cased in something lavender calm and holy. She finishes, holding it up to inspect it, small smile, her lips almost pouting in their pride.

She pulls a lighter out and I cup my hand around the joint, a barrier from the wind. Alé's thumb presses on the lighter until it sparks and the base of the flame is the same shade of blue our pool was before all the shit. She guides the flame to the tip of the joint until it finally catches.

We pass the joint back and forth until it's too small to fit between our lips without crumbling. I've never really liked weed, but it makes me feel closer to Alé, so I light up with her and try to sink so deep into the high that it's all I feel.

Alé begins to swing her legs, me following her lead, going skyward. At the top, I think I might just enter one of those clouds. I look down, see a tent behind the basketball courts and an old man pissing by a tree, not bothering to look around and see who is watching. I aspire to be so reckless, so unassuming that I could take a piss in San Antonio Park at noon on a Thursday and not even look up.

"You know what I been thinking?" Alé asks me.

We're on opposite ends of the sky, swinging toward each other and missing, and for the first time all day I'm not thinking about the paper taped to our door, about Marcus's sleeping face, about how wide Dee's mouth opens.

"What you been thinking?"

"Don't nobody ever fix none of these damn roads."

She says it and I immediately begin to laugh, thinking she was about to tell me some philosophical wondering about the world.

"You don't even got a car, what you worried about?" I yell back to her, across the wind and the space between our swings.

Even as I say it, looking out at the streets that extend from the park like the legs of a spider, I see what she means. Chunks of road sit beside holes they left behind, where wheels of broken-down Volkswagens dip in and for a second I don't know if they're gonna pull back out until they do, the only remnant of distress left in the slight rattle of the bumper. All the holes in Oakland never seem to leave nobody stuck for long, an illusion of brokenness. Or maybe that's just for the cars.

"Don't you ever think about how none of the streets 'round here been redone for decades?" Alé, a skater to the core, spends more time dipping in and out of potholes than I ever have.

"Why it gotta matter? The roads ain't hurting nobody."

"Don't matter. I'm just saying it ain't like this nowhere else, you know? Why Broadway not this torn up? Or S.F.? 'Cause they putting their money in the city just like they putting their money into downtown. Don't you got a problem with that?" Alé's whole body has risen from its slouch and we're both slowing down now, returning from our sky.

"No. I don't got a problem with that, just like I don't got a problem with Uncle Ty buying a Maserati and a mansion down in L.A. and leaving us out here alone. Just like I don't got a problem with Marcus spitting rhymes in a studio while I'm just tryna pay our rent. It ain't my place to have a problem with somebody else's survival. If the city get they money from paying to smooth over the roads on some rich-ass street, then they should go ahead and do that. Lord knows I won't be thinking 'bout nobody else if someone offers me a wad of cash."

I wiggle my toes in my Sunday Shoes as the swing comes to a halt and I feel Alé's eyes on me, determined.

"I don't believe none of that," she says.

"What you mean you don't believe it?"

She shakes her head, her own high making her slow. "Nah, you got too much heart to be a sellout, Ki, you ain't cruel enough for none of that. I know you wouldn't go leaving Marcus or Trevor or me just to make bank."

I'd like to think she's wrong, but if she was then I would stay on these swings all day, get so high I don't have to think about nothing but Alé's tattoos and how the streets are fragmenting and will keep disintegrating until we are walking on dirt.

Instead, I think of Marcus, how we used to stand on street corners trying to sell paintings I made on cardboard. It barely made us enough to buy more paint, but Marcus and I were in it together, choosing each other. It's time I go tell him I can't be doing all the hard shit for him if he ain't gonna do nothing for me. Tell him it's time to put the mic down and face these streets like I've been for the last six months.

"I gotta go find Marcus," I say, hopping from the swing set and seeing the world fuzz, go in and out of focus, all of it sharp yet spinning. I leave her there, on the swings, a puff of smoke exiting her lips like she was holding it in this whole time, and she don't even have to look at me again because now this blazer smells like her Sunday Shoes and, today, on funeral day, that is all I need.

I T SOUNDS LIKE someone is giving birth. I descend the stairs to the recording studio cautiously, not sure if I'm about to find some strange woman with her thighs above her head, erupting.

Instead, the steps give way to the basement filled with Marcus's best friend's girlfriend—Shauna—moaning, throwing Taco Bell to-go cups into a trash can with more force than she needs to, and waiting for someone to ask her what's wrong. The remaining soda in the cups dribbles onto the beige rug and nobody asks Shauna nothing because Marcus is rapping in the next room and they're all trying to find a single word in his mouth's jumble.

After I left Alé at the park earlier today I went home to find Marcus, but he wasn't there. So I flipped through the yellow pages for hours planning where to go to ask for a job until it started to get dark and I knew I could find him at the studio. Now I'm preparing to enter the boys' sanctuary to see if I can get Marcus to hold me close again, like Alé does, and figure out how to escape this mess.

Marcus's best friend is Cole and his recording studio is hidden in the corner of his mom's basement, behind a closed door, the house stuffed on a deserted street in the Fruitvale district, a short walk from the Regal-Hi and East Oakland's own sort of downtown: always alive. The boys all pay Cole for studio hours, trading off nights of the week to record songs that never go further than SoundCloud.

Shauna's newborn lies sleeping in a crib in the center of the room while Shauna huffs, groans, tries to drown out Marcus's quick talking, but I'm the only one who really hears her. I reach the bottom of the stairs, the ceiling only seeming to get lower, competing voices filling up the empty space until the whole room is about to burst. The basement is smothering, but my brother's voice is the flat familiar that makes me remember why I stay down here, breathing this recycled Old Spice air and listening to Shauna's noises.

I enter the studio and I'm immediately thrust into a world of men and music that leaks into every corner of the room, some track Marcus is laying down in the booth. I see him there, behind the glass, eyes closed, wingspan stretching into some mythical version of my brother's embrace. Tupac might just be shivering in his grave because my brother don't know how to spit, and the only words I can hear in the mess of his tongue are *bitch* and *ho* and *this nigga got chains* and I wanna tell him this room knows how he hurled into our toilet for two weeks after Daddy died because his body cannot bear grief. This room knows how the only chains he got are from those machines that spit out plastic containers for fifty cents at the arcade. This room knows the only bitch he got is me and I'm shrinking back, trying to disappear myself into the doorway the way Marcus disappears us in his lyrics.

The studio isn't clean or expensive enough to be considered a recording studio by any professional standards, but my brother and his boys have made it into a haven and decided they are godly in this room, the same way I felt godly at the height of the swing with Alé, before reality hit. An illusion that just keeps feeding itself.

Marcus recedes into silence and the beat stops still, his eyes settling on me through the glass. The boys chorus my name, Tony standing up from the couch to put his arm around me, his body engulfing mine in its muscle mass and quiet. Marcus nods to me from behind the glass and I exit Tony's arms, pushing open the door to the recording booth, where I find my brother's warmth, his body beyond the beat.

My fist hits his stomach lightly, but all I feel is the tight push of his muscles. Marcus always flexing. "Hey, we gotta talk." I try to whisper so the boys won't have to hear, even though Cole can hear it all through his headphones anyway.

"Let's talk." Marcus's face tells me all I need to know. It's shut, every cavity of feeling closed down.

"Look, Mars, we don't got enough money for no rent increase. You over here without a job and I can't handle it no more, so—"

Like most days, the moment I try to speak, Marcus inserts himself. His voice fills up the whole room and it's like he's gone to war with the air, leaving me with nothing. Marcus pretending I am not standing here, that the paper I left him this morning ain't nothing but a lost cat flyer.

"Aight, Ki, don't be going on this *I don't got a job* bullshit. I got a job, so how 'bout you go on home and let me finish my track. Shit."

He doesn't even take a beat before he's rambling about his new verses, talking about how he's gonna make it big.

It didn't used to be like this.

About six months ago, Marcus was at a bar when he heard our uncle Ty's voice come on, rapping the same way he always has. Marcus looked him up and found out he had an album coming out, that he was signed with Dr. Dre's label and making bank in L.A. It unleashed something in Marcus and the next day he quit his job at Panda Express and started hanging with Cole every day, hell-bent on becoming Uncle Ty. I tried to give him his space, let him feel his rage, but it's been too long now and whether he likes it or not, he needs to start acting like a grown man again.

I look up at him, trying to search for a little bit of me in his face and finding nothing but a fingerprint beneath his ear.

He sighs. "It's fine, Ki."

"We don't got enough money to make rent every month as is. In two weeks when we out on our asses, pretty sure it ain't gonna be just fine." I slip my hands back into my pockets so he doesn't see the mess I've made of them, picking at them while his words stampede. "I'm out looking for jobs before you wake up every morning and all you ever do is hang out with Cole and Tony and pretend like it's getting you somewhere. You ain't even acting like my brother no more."

"Oh, we back on this shit." His eyes glaze over, stuck in the same place on the wall.

"Marcus, please." I don't want to beg him, not while Tony and Cole are on the other side of the glass, snickering and sipping on their beers.

For the first time today, Marcus looks right at me, stares, and finally his eyes are familiar. This time when he speaks, his voice shakes.

"You know when we were younger and Uncle Ty took us to that skate park and we'd go down and run at the wall, tryna climb back out? And you were smaller so you kept on tryin' but you couldn't reach the rim of the slope and you kept sliding back down and then you'd sit in the middle, all these skaters whipping in and out, flying around you, and you'd cry."

He doesn't say it like a question, but I know it is one. He's asking if I remember the burn on my palms or the fear throbbing behind my forehead.

"I remember."

Marcus hesitates, licking his lips, and continues. "I didn't help you get up and it ain't because I didn't care or I wanted to win, nah, it wasn't like that. I was just waiting for Uncle Ty to show me some tricks and if I helped you, waited for you, I woulda missed my shot. You get that, right?"

The air between us is thick. He is asking for my permission.

"I guess."

My mouth is dry, searching in the drought between us for something solid and full, before I look up at him and breathe in his crumpling face.

"It's okay, Mars." There's something about the way his eyes cave inward that makes me want to erase all of it, simply let it go. "I want you to shoot your shot or whatever. It's just . . ." I glance toward the other side of the glass where Tony is staring straight at us. "Never mind," I say. "Really." I look away from Marcus.

He waves the tension out of the recording booth. "Now can I get a beer or you gonna stand here sulkin'n shit?" His body straightens, the hurt disappearing and leaving only a tilted smirk. I nod, following him out of the booth to join the circle around the soundboard, where Marcus opens a can and chugs. I sit in between Marcus and Tony, across from Cole, trying to figure out if Cole's got a problem with his ears or something, why he don't respond to Shauna's bellows.

Cole is lengthy, his entire body appearing like it could stretch all the way to the ceiling if you pulled hard enough. His cheeks dip into his face and I know he's sucking them in, making them touch his grill. Cole is cocky in that way that might just be endearing because, in our crew, he has made it, can support his baby mama and afford a car, even if he's still living in his mama's house. He says it's by choice and the way his mama hugs him makes me believe it.

I catch Marcus staring at me, watching me sip the beer Tony gave me, and making sure I don't grab another can. He doesn't like when I drink. The minute I lock eyes with him, he looks away.

Marcus returns to the recording booth after he finishes his beer and we all watch his head nod, saliva flying out his lips, chest a bulk of muscle he worked harder for than anything else he's got. I'm alone with the boys and Tony's left arm hangs at his side. He reaches up to lift it around me a couple times and then retreats before patting my leg twice. His hand is heavy. When Tony speaks, his voice comes out with a hint of a growl, like a lion's been hiding deep inside his throat, attempting to claw its way out.

"You busy tonight?"

Tony makes the move, pulls his arm around my shoulders so I'm scrunched against his chest and my mouth is muffled by his denim jacket, his body heat suffocating. Tony taps my shoulder to the beat of the track and I feel like I can't escape, Marcus's verses sneaking up my spine. I shift my eyes toward Tony's and he's looking at me, always staring.

"You think you could talk to Marcus? Try to get him to look for a job?" I ask, acutely aware of Tony's hand slipping down my arm.

"You ain't even answered my question."

He smells like eggnog even though it's past Christmas and I'm not sure if I like it or not. Tony's had a thing for me for months, ever since he and Marcus became friends, and he's the only guy who has ever asked me a question and wanted to hear my answer. I let him try to hold my hand when he comes over, but I still don't understand him, why he can't seem to let me go when I've never given him a reason to hold on.

"I don't know if I'm busy, Tony, I got other shit to worry about."

I gaze into my lap, stare at my hands. Even with Marcus's belts gaining volume and Tony's stare carving into my face, his fingers tracing my arm, I can't seem to think about anything but my fingers. I used to keep my nails real long, pointed. I'd gnaw on them to make sure the tip was just right, like talons.

Now I'm itching to hide my hands or maybe sit on them, but I know that would make Tony nervous, make him think I was hiding from him, so instead I keep them in my lap. The nails are jagged, ripped along the edges. They look naked, defenseless, like the kind of nails six-year-olds have when they too busy playing cops and robbers to remember they gotta be ready for all the real cops and robbers.

"Okay," Tony says, his mouth close enough to my cheek that I can feel his breath. "I'll talk to Marcus if you come over tonight."

I tilt my head to look at Tony and his eyes are doe-like, hopeful. He is a hulk of something subtle and soft and I don't think nobody else in this room has ever listened to my breath like he does.

"I guess," I say, dipping out from under his arm. Cole opens his eyes at my movement and lifts his headphones from his ears.

"Where you goin', Ki? You tired of us already?" Cole shows his whole grill.

"You know I'm never tired of you." I smile at him. "Saw the baby, she real cute."

Cole sits up straighter against the couch, stops smiling and replaces the expression with a mellow kind of wonder, dreaming with his eyes open.

"Yeah, she beautiful."

Marcus comes back out from the recording booth to grab another beer, snickers, his eyebrows springing up. "If only yo girl could get it together and stop complaining."

Shauna's face flashes in my mind, her eye hunger and her moans. Cole emerges from his daze and lets out a noise, not a sound of agreement, but not a defense either. Marcus's tattoo is squirming again, trying to spring out of his skin. He looks toward me, the two of us the only ones standing.

"You leaving?" I'm not used to him all eyes on me like this, his lips puffing like a pre-tantrum child, like he don't want me to leave.

"Thinkin' about it," I tell him.

He tilts the can back and empties it into his throat. "Come here." He leads me back into the recording booth, turning to look at me. I watch him, my arms growing bumps, hair standing up, like they just remembered how bare they are behind the glass, without Tony's body heat.

"You don't gotta leave," he says.

"Why you care?" Sometimes, when I'm with Marcus, I revert to my ten-year-old little-sister self staring up at my big brother, to who I was before all our shit got messy, before my fingernails started ripping and Marcus decided he needed a beat more than he needed my hand to hold.

Marcus grimaces, his jaw winding up so it can unleash itself and suddenly my fingerprint is moving, roaring on his neck. "What you mean? I gotta care, Ki. I'm doing this 'cause I'm gonna get us a whole different life, like Uncle Ty. You just gotta trust me, aight? Give me one month to drop the album. You can handle one month, yeah?"

Marcus is better at talking than he's ever been at rapping and this is no different. My fingerprint has found legs and is moving quicker than his breath.

"One month."

I let him pull me into a hug that feels more like a choke than a goodbye.

On the other side of the glass, Tony and Cole are chuckling about something, punching each other and acting like they ain't been listening to us. Tony sees me and lights up.

"I gotta go," I say.

"You coming over later, though?" His height contrasts with the childlike demeanor, the boy waiting for his reward. I know it ain't right to let him keep doing this, hoping I'm ever going to lean into his chest for anything more than warmth. I start walking toward the door that leads back to Shauna, the stairs, the city.

"Maybe," I tell him, pausing to watch Marcus inside the glass for one last verse.

He's standing there, tilting side to side, beginning to rhyme, and I catch only one thing before I exit: *My bitches don't know nothing, don't know nothing.* I am trying to decipher the fallacies in that, the torn edges of memories that may belong to his words, but all I find is nothing, don't know nothing. Nothing.

Shauna is still moaning in the basement, leaning over to grab a breast pump from the floor. I don't say anything, but I bend over to pick up a pair of soiled boxers, making a pile for Cole's dirty clothes and moving the pillows from the floor back to the sinking couch. Shauna looks up at me and we make eye contact. There is something in her face that makes me think she's lonely, but I don't know what it is; maybe the way her forehead creases like she don't trust my hands. Maybe the way she stops moaning when I begin to help, like the only thing trying to push its way out of her body was stale breath.

"You don't gotta help," she says, her voice a steady monotone, only breaking with a slight drawl. I knew Shauna when we were more girls than women, shortly after she came out here from Memphis to live with her sister and her aunt, and I almost forgot the sweet home-sound that creeps out her lips.

"Don't got nothing else to do." I glance inside the crib, a small mound of cloth holding the infant. "How old?"

"She about to be two months."

I nod, not really sure what else there is to say about the baby's smallness. I think about the photo from the funeral home and wonder if Shauna ever thinks about how easy it is to stop breathing, to be something and then be gone, to love someone and disappear.

Shauna moves to pick up her child and walks to the couch, her sweatpants rolled down around her hips with her belly bulging. She sits, sinking in deeper until she's cocooned in the couch's soft red, like her baby is cocooned in her breasts. Shauna swiftly pulls her bra to the side and the child latches, sucking in deep like she was starving and is relearning how to be alive, how to feed. I think about looking away, but it doesn't seem like Shauna minds and the infant's lips are fascinating, the way they pulse. Shauna's eyes are still on her girl, sucking so hard I wonder how she isn't out of breath. Shauna's free nipple is dry and scabbed, but there is no evidence of this pain on her face, no worry of being cracked open.

"Kiara." I don't remember the last time she said my full name. I look at her, the lumps beneath her eyes heavy. "Don't get caught up in their shit."

She's still staring at her child, like the baby will choke if she looks away, so I'm not sure what she's talking about until the beat picks up and vibrates through my feet.

"You didn't have to have no baby."

Her head whips toward me. "You don't know nothing about what I've had to do. I'm just doing you a favor by telling you now not to give it all up for them." Her child stops suckling and begins to scream, and Shauna is on her feet, returning to her moaning, waiting for someone to ask, for one of the men to look at her, to wonder what's wrong.

Mama used to tell me that blood is everything, but I think we're all out here unlearning that sentiment, scraping our knees and asking strangers to patch us back up. I don't say goodbye to Shauna and she doesn't even turn around to watch me leave, to head back out to a sky that sunk into deep blue while my brother asked me to do the one thing I know I shouldn't, the one thing Shauna cared enough to warn me about: hollow myself out for another person who ain't gonna give a shit when I'm empty.

THE CAFÉ LADY sticks the pen behind her ear where her undercut fades from blue to hot pink and then blond, and she smiles the same way that the mean girls used to smile before they said I couldn't sit at their table in elementary school, like she's waiting for a punch or some kind of prize.

"We really can't do anything if you don't have a résumé."

A group of twenty-year-olds all wearing matching Converse swing in through the front door of the café and the undercut woman waves them in, grabbing menus from where she stands behind the cash register. Even the way she picks up the menus makes me want to slap the pen from behind her ear, her fingers pinching like the menus are too dirty for her to touch.

"I don't have nothing to put on a résumé, so don't really make sense for me to bring a blank page, do it?" My hands are resting on the glass counter, the sweet potato pie symmetrical and staring up at me, taunting.

The woman moves toward where the twenty-year-olds sit at a corner booth, handing them menus, returning to grab a water pitcher. The smile has faded, leaving only the grimace that comes before and after the mean girls tell you to get the fuck away. Funny how the playground follows us.

"Look, I don't have anything to give my manager and, honestly, I think it's highly unlikely we would hire someone with such limited experience." She pauses, pouts. "Maybe try Walgreens?"

When I step away, I make sure to make a fist and pound lightly on the glass display counter. Not hard enough to risk breaking it, but enough that the twenty-somethings look over at me with fear in their eyes before I swing out the door and back onto the street.

I tried Walgreens last week, CVS the week before. Even tried the MetroPCS that shares its building with the smoke shop nobody ever steps foot in unless they looking for a deal or a phone cheap enough to last them until they get out of town.

It always goes the same way: I ask to talk to the manager and either some man comes out from the back, huffing, red-faced and ready for me to leave before I even start talking or they say the manager ain't in and I try to negotiate with one of the employees. They start shaking their heads the minute I say I don't got a résumé and the bell hanging from the door rings like a timer on my way out, telling me I don't got much time before my world starts to crumble. It's hours of this, and it sinks something in me so I'm not even sure what I'm doing and then I realize I'm just wandering, that there is no destination.

Walking in downtown Oakland is like trying to find your footing on an ocean floor. Everything is big here, not like back home in East, where we keep our buildings low to the ground and our feet to the sidewalk. In downtown, it feels like everything is airborne or underground. Like if there was a compass, we'd all be levitating above directionality. Marcus and I spent a lot of time with Daddy downtown, before they inverted the buildings and sprinkled gold on the sidewalk. Before we were unrecognizable. Back then, it was a ghost town and the only people out here was the ones who slapped Daddy's back and offered us rides in the backseat of taxis they drove before Uber came in. Back then, we were royalty simply by association with Daddy, following him to his old friends' apartments, the ones nobody wanted 'cause they were crusted in dirt and dealing.

Now there are too many cafés on these streets, too many of the same faces bent at the neck because, in downtown, nobody gives a shit where they're walking, who they might bump into or stumble over. They've got their heads in a screen, their shoes laced so tight I bet their feet have gone numb.

The one thing downtown got that nowhere else in this city really does is a whole lot of bars, clubs, holes where people find themselves wasted and dancing. At two in the morning, somebody's always out here barbecuing right before the clubs shut down, the weed mixing with the smoke from their grills.

There's a strip club tucked underneath a yoga studio on the corner, its metal door painted a sparkling black. I can hear the faint sound of music and even though it's only five or so in the evening, they've got the door propped open. I walk into a room dimly lit by those lightbulbs that look sort of like candles, and a few lone people are propped up on stools or sitting at circular tables, lurking in the darkest patches of the place, the poles looming large in the center, one woman aerial and another bored.

I wander over to the bar, where a man stands with a rag in hand, wiping down the counter. He looks like every other bartender I've ever seen and it's sort of comforting how predictable downtown is, how it's changing in the kinds of ways that only propel more of the same, how every building seems to duplicate like this man's tattoos down his arm.

He looks up at me and I feel small in the expanse of dark. "Can I help you?"

I breathe in. I'm not sure I want a job like this or if I could get one anyway, but I'm desperate. "I'm looking for a job," I say, not even bothering to ask for the manager as if it will make a difference.

He nods, the gauge earring in his left ear glinting as he moves. "I can give your application to my boss if you want. He's always looking for more pretty girls."

"Don't got an application," I say, waiting for that familiar pity smile. "Or a résumé."

"Oh," he responds, tucking a piece of his hair back into his pony-tail. "I could give him your name and phone number, I guess." He grabs a pen and Post-it from behind the counter and bends over, getting ready to write. He looks up at me again and his nose wrinkles. "How old are you, sweetheart?"

I flinch at the name. "Seventeen."

He stands up from his bent position, the soft grimace finally making its way to his face. "We can't hire anyone under eighteen. Sorry, darling."

I nod, turning back around to where the light leaks in from the open door. I used to think the only thing you got from turning eighteen was the right to vote, but now it's clear you get more than just voting and I wish my birthday would come a little faster. Before I make my way out, I hear my name. I spin back around to see a woman materializing behind the bar, her face foreign until I squint hard enough and she is suddenly familiar.

"Kiara?"

"Lacy?"

She smiles at me, her eyebrows pointing inward just like I remember, before waving me back to the bar and then walking around to pull the stool out for me. I sit down and she pats my leg.

"What you up to, girl? I know you not old enough to be in here." She says it with that beam, the one that don't seem to stop.

I never really knew Lacy, at least not like Marcus did. She was his sidekick back at Skyline High and I never saw them apart, not for almost four years. Then both of them dropped out a few months before graduation because neither of them had nobody to push them into fighting the hallways for that diploma, stuff them into the cap and gown. School's got as many potholes as the streets, always chipping, always leaving us to trip.

"You know, living," I tell her, because I don't wanna lie like Marcus would, but it seems too intimate for this room to hear: how everything seems to be fraying.

"And your brother?" I watch her face turn inward, twist at the corners of her lips.

"You know, the same."

Marcus dropped Lacy the moment he found Cole, the moment he realized the real world don't hand us shit like he thought it would. Uncle Ty made Marcus believe that miracles would come to us and he seemed to think Cole was the way in, that staying with Lacy was a segue to a life of hoping without no reward. She got a job and was working forty-hour weeks and Marcus didn't want no part in it. All he got is half a dozen SoundCloud tracks and no paycheck and here we are: her with her hair tied up in two buns on top of her head, piercings lining her face, and looking like she owns the place. Like she don't need no light to see. And Marcus still out here waiting, like something's gonna change.

Lacy stands up abruptly. "You want a drink?" She's wearing the classic bartender black, but she still shines. "I won't tell." She winks and returns to the side of the bar where the man was. He slipped into the back at some point and even if he was to come back, something tells me Lacy's got more sway than him. Something about the way she moves: spine erect like redwood trees, like she'll just keep growing upward.

I nod. "Sure."

"What you want?"

"Surprise me?" I don't know how to order a drink for myself, not used to anybody asking me what I want. Usually, somebody just hands me a bottle or a plastic cup and I don't pause long enough to question it. Lacy grabs a bottle from behind the counter and then another one, pouring and shaking and stirring it all up into a glass with one of those straws that're so skinny I wonder how anything's supposed to get through them. She adds a cherry, one of the ones too sweet to believe they come from a tree, and pushes the glass toward me. The drink is a soft red, bordering on pink if it wasn't for the way the cherry draws out the color.

"What is it?" I ask her.

She leans forward. "It's a surprise. Don't worry, you gonna like it."

I bend my head down until my lips touch the straw and suck. It hits my tongue and it's euphoria spreading across my mouth, like all the flavor in the world combined into a brilliant heat. "Shit," I say after I swallow, looking up at Lacy.

She laughs. "You always loved something sweet."

"How long you been working here?" I ask.

"Started as a stripper around the time Marcus and I fell out, but money's a little more stable at the bar so been bartending the past few months." The door swings open again and a small group of men in ties comes in. Lacy straightens up. "Place about to fill up, but feel free to stay. Let me know if you want a refill. It's on me."

Lacy smiles and leaves to follow the men to a table right in front of the stage. One of them is wearing this polka dot tie that he's loosening and he's looking straight at me, the corner of his mouth tilted up. I don't know why, but his face is interesting to look at and part of me wants to touch it, feel if he has stubble, if his skin is soft enough that it would turn pink just from my fingertips. I return to focus on my drink and I wonder if I should stay, if being a young girl alone in a strip club with no money could make this night worse. But a free drink is a free drink and I'm tired of the endless walking and rejection from every employer in Oakland, so I take a sip. And another. And another. I slurp until the sugary red is gone and then ask Lacy to make me a new one.

Marcus can't stand nothing red after Mama. It's not like he was the only one who had to see it, but he was the one who tried to clot Mama's bleeding wrists, pick the razor up from the floor. He was the one who told them not to take me, his newly eighteen-year-old body lengthening as if his height could give him the ability to make it through the night without thinking about the color of the water. Since then, Marcus won't step foot in the bathroom. He showers at friends' places and pisses at the liquor store across the street.

The sirens that day left us sitting in the only unmarked spot of the apartment, the center of the rug behind the sofa, both Marcus and I staring at the neon tape signaling another spot of DNA, as if the whole apartment wasn't made up of us and our blood. The social worker left with the police, after an hour of questions following Mama and the ambulance. Marcus had his arm around my shoulders and every time I started shaking again, he'd scratch my arm to remind me he was still the same. I was two months from fifteen. He was the youngest adult I'd ever seen and it wasn't more than a week later that he dropped out of school. Marcus was determined to hustle for me, to be the man.

We settled in the patch of beige-turned-brown rug and Marcus whispered in my ear, "I got you." It was like the light finally found its way to Marcus's mouth because he was speaking sun into me and if Mama wasn't gonna be there no more, if Daddy was already no different than infertile dirt, then I needed my brother more than anything. He asked me what I wanted for dinner and when I told him I wasn't hungry, he found Mama's emergency fund in the pillowcase and ordered us three different kinds of pizza. He ate two slices of each, picked all the sausage off one of them, and left me his plate to wash up. Maybe I should've known it'd be like that, me washing up his dishes, cleaning up his ruins, but his arm around me, his whisper was enough for it not to matter. Marcus had claimed me. I was his.

I thought Marcus was gonna be everything I needed after that. He held my hand through Mama's trial, through Uncle Ty leaving town, through visits to Mama in the overcrowded Dublin prison. And then, two years later, he let it go. Marcus took off to Cole's, stopped looking me in the eye, left the newspapers he used to pore over in a pile by the door. I've been chasing him ever since, trying to get him to look at me.

By the time my fourth glass has emptied out to only ice, the club is full of crawling bodies, every stool and table occupied, the music thump-thumping even though I can't place a single distinct song. All three poles are in use and dollar bills make their way into the thong of each woman giving a lap dance. There's something about the buzz of the place that makes me feel alive, not like a girl barely scraping by but a woman free. The way the lights remain just the perfect mix of warm and not-quite-there. The way the music combines with the chatter to produce a chorus of muffled fuzz, like a melodic static. The way every time the door opens to let another cluster of bodies in, the Oakland outside seeps in: a drumbeat, somebody shouting about how we gotta beware the cracks in the sidewalk, a siren.

Lacy comes back from making her rounds with a tray of half-empty wineglasses and it don't make no sense to me why anyone would pay for something just to not drink it. I catch her eye and point to my glass, but I can't seem to locate the words to ask her for a refill.

She laughs. "I think you're done, Ki," she shouts.

I pout, spinning around on the barstool. Polka dot tie catches my eye again. He's talking to his suited friends but staring right at me. I come back from my spin to see Lacy mixing drinks and the room suddenly feels overcrowded, like every pocket of breath has disappeared in that single spin. I shout out to Lacy across the noise. "Gotta get out of here."

She raises her eyebrows, her figure even taller than I remember it being when her face elongates like that. "You sure you can make it home?"

I wave at her. Less at her and more at the outline of her, the figure that drags upward toward the ceiling. I lift myself off the stool and gather my footing, walking toward the door like it's hiding something glorious behind it. I swing it open and step out onto the street. I know almost immediately that it's gotta be after ten because Oakland's shut down, all the lights turned off. The only people on the streets are the ones who live there. That's what it's gonna be like for us—Marcus and me—pretty soon. No escaping the sidewalk.

The windchill enters my body, slips under my shirt right to my belly button. Sometimes I think about where my belly button might lead to. Like if it goes to the stomach, joins the slosh of cherry red up in there, or if it's connected to my womb.

The door to the club swings open behind me and Polka Dot is there, his hair loose from its gel in a way that looks more natural on him, like he wasn't meant to be that tied up.

"Hey." I'm not even sure he's talking to me until he says, "Gray shirt," and I have to look down at what I'm wearing to understand that he means me. I try to smile at him, but my mouth is buzzing and I think it turns up lopsided on my face, which he laughs at, a low laugh, one that never really reaches its climax.

"Yeah?" It's the only word my lips can form at this point, the only coherent sound.

I don't remember the last time a white man voluntarily talked to me, let alone followed me out onto the street, but I don't got enough space in my head or my stomach to question it because the red drink feels like it's overflowing in me.

He cracks another smile, just like he did in the sweat of the club. "Look, it's late and I don't want to have to pretend we aren't here for the same thing."

He's speaking, but the only thing that I can absorb is the way the wind keeps whipping his hair back. I don't know what he's referring to and I don't have enough energy to try to figure it out.

"I know a spot," he says.

"A spot?" My knees feel increasingly less reliable with the sloshing inside me.

I don't know if I follow him because it's cold and I think he might be taking me out of the line of wind or if the past couple days and the drinks have made me somehow want this man, a hunger for some warmth taking over every part of me that might still have had enough of a sense to step back, find a bus or a crowded street. Don't matter why I do it because the fact is, my feet keep on moving. I guess they're moving too slow, though, because Polka Dot takes hold of my hand and drags me toward a building.

The building is large and, when I look up, the top of it isn't even in sight. He leads me straight to the elevator and we get inside. I haven't been alone with a man other than Marcus since I was fourteen and a boy tried to teach me how to give him a hand job in a bathroom stall at school, but then our chemistry teacher's shoes appeared in the other stall and he couldn't get it up. When the elevator lifts us, the liquid does something at the base of my stomach, catapults upward, makes me feel like I swallowed the ocean.

The elevator dings and I'm expecting some office or maybe even this man's apartment, some place filled to the brim with cash. Instead, we step out and we are outside again. Except, this time, the sky is closer to us and there's a garden spread out, bordered in cement walls.

"Where?" I can only seem to make a singular word. He doesn't respond, but pulls me closer to the edge of the wall. The whole garden is deserted, trees branching out, a pond standing still in the center, and I think we might be on the rooftop of this never-ending building.

Close to the edge of the wall now, he pulls me in. When he kisses me and then comes up for air, his silhouette is an outline against the sky. I haven't been kissed in years and it is slimy, wet in a way that makes me wish he'd wipe his mouth.

He kisses me again and soon he has traded places with me, pushing me up against the cement so I am leaning against the sky, into it. He unbuttons my pants and the wind is suddenly holding me, along with his hands, clawing at my skin. He turns me around, bending me over, and my cheek is pressed to the cement, but if I look out the corner of my eye I can stare down at Oakland spread out in front of me, see a single siren light out there: too far to hear, but the neon flashing cannot be missed. Before I even realize it's happening, he pushes into me and the only thing I feel is the cherry liquid still filling me up, still drowning me in it. I'm not even participating, just letting the sky soothe me as it happens, and I don't know how this can be the first time I've felt a man's penis inside me and yet it's so dull I'm not even sure I'm here.

It doesn't take long before it's over and my pants are back up. He puts his belt back on and doesn't look at me again, just pats his pocket, and I think he's referring to his wallet.

"I've only got a couple hundred on me." A couple hundred. Bucks. This man trying to pay me. His fingers press a roll of money into the center of my palm and even though some part of me knows I probably shouldn't, I take it, close my fist, every inch of me shivering, teeth chattering, and he doesn't say anything else, but he reaches up and removes a scarf from his neck, placing it around mine instead. He doesn't even say goodbye, at least I don't hear it, before he has returned to the elevator and disappeared.

I need to piss. The ocean all swelled up inside me.

I stumble toward the pond, slipping out of my shoes and pulling my pants off, then wading in. I let it all out, my body streaming like all plugs been lifted with those bills, that red liquid coming out yellow into the pond and I don't know how bodies can consume one thing and produce another, but I guess tonight gifts us every kind of anomaly. I pull up my pants, slip my shoes back on, and make my way to the edge of the roof, looking out over the city to the way the fog parts just enough for me to see the bridge in the distance, all the hidden things showing themselves, and when I inhale, I don't smell piss or cigarette smoke or weed. I just smell remnants of the red drink still lingering on my breath.

I MET CAMILA the same night I met Polka Dot, when I was wandering home, trying to figure out how to get back to East Oakland when the buses weren't running no more. Marcus and Alé weren't answering their phones and I was freezing, lips cracking. I didn't know what I was doing, stumbling toward the sound of the freeway.

A car pulled over in front of me, black and shiny, and this woman climbed out from the backseat, removed her coat, leaned back into the car to give it to somebody I couldn't see, and shut the door before the car pulled away. Her extensions were bright pink and matched her outfit, the dress matte and tight. The way she walked made me think of the way you walk when the wind is pushing against you: determined, swaying.

I stood there in my gray shirt and that scarf still hanging from my neck, trying to pretend I wasn't staring, but Camila saw everything through those lashes, saw everything bordered in that kind of curiosity that crawls out the eyes and sucks you in. She strutted up to me, and said, "What you looking at?" I probably would have started punching or running if anybody else had said this to me, but the way she spoke wasn't enticing me to fight; it was like she thought it was funny, like I was standing in a crowd where I didn't speak the language and she was the first one to see my tongue.

"Nothing."

"You a baby ho, huh?" Camila's lips curled, revealing clear braces that I didn't catch before she was this close. "Listen, you ain't **gon'** make much just wandering the streets like this. Escorting where the real money at. I got me a pimp too, and I bet he'd take you on if I asked. Point is, nobody gonna take you serious out here like this and, I'm tellin' you right now, nobody gonna do shit if you get hurt. You hear?"

She was so radiant I couldn't find the words to tell her no, that I wasn't like her, that I didn't mean to do it, because what if I was her type of woman? Polka Dot's bills still stuffed into my pocket, my body still unsure how to make sense of that rooftop, that man.

Camila took my hand, her acrylics careful not to puncture my skin. She called a car for us, said she'd give me a ride on the way to her john's house. In the car, she told me about what I had to do to be like her, where to go, when, how to dress, and I thought maybe this is where girls go when they are tired. Maybe this is where I go to find my hum, make my body rumble big like Mama.

⸱   ⸱

I couldn't stop thinking about Polka Dot and Camila the next day, how easy it seemed for her. How many bills Polka Dot handed over to me for only a few minutes. I called three different escort agencies and phone sex companies, but they all told me my age was a liability, that I could give them a call when I was legal. They said I could try online, but we stopped paying for Wi-Fi last year and I don't have a smartphone or a computer. Camila said if I had to walk the streets, I should have somebody to make sure I was safe, that it wouldn't be quite so bad. Maybe I could do it a few more times while I tried to persuade Marcus to get a job. I've had sex now and I can do it again, nothing more than a body, I tell myself. Skin. I don't gotta make it more than that. Just till I get us out of our rent debt.

It didn't take much to convince Tony. I showed up at his door last night and he lit up like I was the surprise lotto ticket his mama bought him for Christmas. When I sat next to him on the couch, Tony tried to slip his arm around me smoothly, like his body mass could do anything that slick. I sat forward so his body couldn't collide with mine and turned to him, remembering what Camila said.

Tony could tell something was wrong and his skin wrinkled up on the bridge of his nose.

"Need you to do something for me," I said, twirling a loose thread from Polka Dot's scarf around my finger and pulling until my skin bulged.

"I talked to Marcus already," Tony said, unwinding the thread from my finger.

"Thought you weren't gonna do that unless I showed up."

He shrugged. "Changed my mind. Don't really matter though, he ain't listening to nothing I say."

I pulled the thread harder and more unraveled from the scarf. This time I wrapped it around my thumb, up and down, until it encased the whole thing in thread. "I got a different plan." I looked away from him because looking at Tony's kind of like looking into the barrel of a gun: too close.

"Yeah?"

"You probably ain't gonna like it, but it's what I'm doing so if you don't help I'm gonna do it anyway."

He chuckled. "You always do."

When I told him, he didn't respond for a while. Just sat there, one arm still around the back of the couch and his eyes planted on my thumb.

"Fuck that."

For somebody who don't say much, whenever Tony does talk, it is quick and gets right to the point. It's one of the things I like about Tony. That and how small I feel when I stand by him, like he could fold me into his arms and I wouldn't never have to find my way back out.

"You could come and make sure I don't end up down in a ditch. Or don't and I'll go by myself. Your choice." The best way to get a man to do what you want is by telling him he got a choice, got control, got the end of the thread.

"Your brother gonna kick my ass."

"Not while he living in my house." And then Tony grabbed the thread and unwound it from my thumb, ripping it apart at the base, leaving only the scarf and a frayed piece of something that could be thread, if you looked close enough.

· ·

This afternoon I meet Trevor at the bus stop after school. He takes hold of my hand, like usual, moves his head with every word as he tells me about how Ms. Cortez really don't seem to like him that much and today she even took away his basketball cards, the ones with each of the Warriors' faces on them, and wouldn't give them back until the end of the day. Everything feels so normal, even the way he looks at me, like he's soaking up my face to remember it in his sweetest dreams as we walk down High Street. I expected he would've been able to see it on me, see how everything has changed, but Trevor either doesn't seem to notice or maybe he just doesn't care. When I leave him at his apartment door, he wraps his arms around my neck in a hug and then pulls at my hair, stepping away from me and laughing, like he really got me. I laugh too, shoving him and his backpack through the door. The moment is so normal, I almost believe it's real, that there was no red, no piss, no man. I almost believe it will last.

Now it's evening and I'm out on the street, about five minutes away from that point where cold turns into numb. My skirt betrays me, lets it all inside, brushing against my skin like 7-Eleven slushies in the winter. I tried to dress like the mannequins lining Fruitvale Village shops, mesh and skirts so short the wind could meet every inch of skin. Out here, there's a kind of stillness that comes with having nowhere to go and the streets are still alive, so I survey the whole block, commit every person to memory.

Tony's across the street, looking at me. I try not to stare back, try to pretend I don't feel scared and nervous and that my bones are denser than they are, more resistant to breaking. As I move swiftly up and down International Boulevard, past the cosmetology school and the identical stores with overinflated ball gowns in the windows, Tony follows on the other side. I contain my smile, this big man attempting to hide in shadows of a street, pacing. If we were anywhere else, somebody would have called the cops on him, but nobody would dare invite the sirens onto International, where they'd say we're all some kind of criminal.

It's still light out, but already plenty of men are here, feasting on me. It is so much worse than Polka Dot, all of them together, knowing I am a girl who will offer herself up when I'm still not sure I want to. I wonder if Camila was right, if I should find some man online who just wants to lick in between my toes or if maybe I should've joined her and her pimp. Except I worry then I'd be too deep in to get out.

The men whistle.

"Ay, beautiful, come here."

"¡Mamí! ¡Ven aquí!"

"Why you out here like that? I'll get you nice and warm, baby."

They are relentless and grimy and Tony looks like he's about to shoot across the street and maul them every time there's a shout or a whistle. He's trying to protect me from the very thing I'm walking into.

"Kia!" The voice comes from behind me, slithers up. Camila's heels are a dangerous high, silver and sparkling, her arms out, and she's strutting toward me with her mouth open, like she is either going to sing or kiss me. Instead, she grabs my hands and begins to dance, shimmy really. "Why you here, hija?"

I lean into Camila, forgetting Tony, though I know he's watching. "You know," I say.

"What I tell you 'bout the streets? You got yourself a daddy?" Camila twirls me, towering over me with the extra inches her Cinderella shoes buy her.

I come back around from the spin. "Something like that."

Camila's tongue clicks in her mouth, her eyelashes big and heavy. "I got a john waiting on me."

Camila's breath is thick, full of all her loud. I can see it puff into the air and I know she been in this so long that her numb has transformed into a buzz, her body generating heat out of nothing. She's been in this game for so many years that I think she might just have the key, might just own it. Nobody shouts out to her. They all know she is not for their commenting, for their tongues or their teeth. Camila would cut anybody who is stupid enough to mess with her, leave them bleeding.

Her weave is adorned in blue extensions and her makeup is its own costume; she is ready for the runway, her voice coarse and magical. Camila waves those pointy fingers at me, says she'll see me around and, just like that, I'm alone again, except for the eyes: Tony, strangers, billboards advertising casinos I don't believe exist. I wish she'd return, make this feel like it is just another night, and I can still walk Trevor to the bus stop and eat stale chips with Alé on the swings.

Ever since the club a couple days ago, I've been avoiding Alé, dodging her texts and calls. I think she might look at me and see it, see this, and we'll never be able to smoke the same joint, look out over the city and see the same thing. Still, I wish she was here to make me laugh. Make the chill a little less sharp.

When the man appears in the street like he has materialized just for me, I wonder if I am being reckless, if I should go home, but then I think of the bill Vernon has drawn up. And I've got Tony here with me, so I'll be fine. It's just a body.

The man in front of me is small, barely my height with these shoes, and his mustache reeks of gasoline, which makes me believe he has been working on cars all day, somewhere oiled up and dirty. When Camila told me I needed a pimp, or at least some protection, I thought that meant I'd be picking up big men, ones with more muscles and cash than I ever knew existed in this city, on this boulevard. But, staring at this man, his eyes shallow, I think my body might make small men feel big. They grow an ego out their necks when they have me, spit out cash that probably should go to rent or their baby mama's diaper fund.

I try to collect myself, tell myself I am meant to stand in this street and this man is meant to pay me. I tell him a version of my name, Kia, and he asks how old I am.

Camila says the number one rule is don't reveal nothing about yourself.

"As old as you want me to be."

He doesn't ask more and I take note of this, how he doesn't want to know. Camila told me some of them would want to know my age, build up their little-girl fetish, that I could make more money if they knew. These are the men who sprout tears at the height of their pleasure, the ones who got flesh just soft enough to rip open.

"What you want me to call you?" I ask him. This is the first step. Camila says it tells you more than any of the other questions, so you know what you about to do.

The small man's shoulders drop, his throat stretching. He stumbles a little, coming up with a name. He tells me to call him Davon and I'm a little surprised, mostly because I expected something that reeks of acid and sex, something he'd be ashamed to say anywhere else.

"This your first time?" I ask him, taking his hand like I really got any idea what I'm doing. I glance across the street at Tony's shadow and I can almost trace the tense in his muscles, forming an outline from his body.

Davon shrugs, says he's got a car parked a block away, off Thirty-Seventh. I let him lead me, flit my eyes from him to Tony, who ambles in our direction from across the street, making sure everything is visible.

I don't know much about cars, but I know that Davon's is old and crumbling, probably has an engine that groans. He opens the back door for me and I crawl in. I'm hit again with this scent of oil, but now it's mixed with a sweetness, like vanilla has found its way into his car and made love to the machinery. He climbs in after me and we are sitting beside each other, two strangers waiting.

My chest starts to feel tight in the silence, so I speak. "Tell me what you want."

He hesitates, does not breathe a word, and takes my hand.

We continue to sit, only our hands intertwined, and I think I must have mistaken his loneliness for hunger. My panic is mounting and I'm not sure if I made a mistake, if I could exit this car and run back to Tony even if I wanted to. Before I have a chance to do anything, Davon's other hand creeps over to my waist and he pulls me closer to him, close enough that now I can smell the vanilla traced in his skin. I lean forward and kiss him almost like it means something. But he begins to move his hands quick, ripping and tearing at me. Skin to skin to the inside of skin and the slowness dissolves into the creaking of the car. I can feel the ripped leather of the seats on my back and his sweat, dripping.

There are no words, barely any sounds from either of us, but the car is talking. It squeaks and rumbles, like it is coming alive in the face of our bodies and I almost wish it would begin to drive itself, take me to the top of the hills and let me see the bay spread out farther than my eyes will ever be able to travel. The car stays in its spot, rocking slightly. Tony is a shadow out the window and I am a mass of limbs.

Davon hasn't looked at me since he let go of my hand. When he finishes, he stares back at me, but his eyes are a slick gloss, a floating body. He doesn't see me.

Climbing out of the car, I stumble, forgetting the height of these heels. I lean back into the car and he hands me a bundle of cash, sets it right into my palm, just like Polka Dot. I count it. It's only fifty bucks, not even close to what Polka Dot paid me.

"Where's the rest?"

"You ain't worth no more than that." He doesn't look at me, just gives a small grunt. "But you was good. I can give you some of my cousins' numbers, get you some more business."

Davon inputs new numbers into my phone and I straighten up, begin walking back to International. I tell myself I'll ask for the money up front next time, make sure I'm not getting ripped off. Now that it is over, everything feels muted. The windchill a little less cold, my heartbeat barely audible, my skin numb, asleep. Just a body. Just sex.

I cross the street to Tony's side and stop. He walks out of the shadows of a maple tree and his hands are stuffed into the pockets of his hoodie like a frustrated child. I take the cash out of my bra and hand it to Tony, knowing he loves me enough to watch me survive, to give him my everything without worrying about him running. If that ain't some shit my uncle would be ashamed of.

"Kiara, can I ask you something?" Tony's voice is a shudder in a tornado of quiet. His hoodie has the name of a college I've never heard of in blocked letters and I realize I don't even know if Tony been to college.

I nod to him because no is not an answer to this question.

His bottom lip moves side to side.

"If I, uh, got me a job—a real one, you know—and saved up for a while, would you let me take care of you? Like real talk take care of you, like a man takes care of a woman?"

He drifts into a mumble and I wobble on one of my heels, trying to balance, trying to find an escape. It don't make sense to me why he's asking this now, when I am still tender from Davon's thrusts, barely clothed and vulnerable.

"We both know it ain't like that. It ain't that simple. I got Marcus to think about." Marcus doesn't even realize how his life would dissolve without me paying for rent, his phone bill.

"Just 'cause it ain't simple don't mean it gotta be complicated."

"We talking blood, Tony."

"That ain't everything." His fingers start to grasp for mine and then still.

"When everything else goes to shit, he's all I got. And me and you can't never be that, you know?"

Tony don't even nod this time, don't say a word. Instead, he reaches into the pocket of his hoodie and pulls out the cash, pushes it back into the creases of my palms. He shadows himself until he's nothing but dark and I know he's not even there no more but I can't help thinking that he's watching, waiting. If Tony don't wait for me, then no one will.

I spin around, back to International, solo walking. And, God almighty, when it all goes to shit, Marcus better be my shadow. He better be my everything.

THE SOUND OF SPLASHING wakes me up at noon. It's foreign to me here, the water thrash noises both recognizable and out of place. Something's always waking me up in the height of my happy, right when my dream begins to dance. During last night's sleep, which really didn't start till four a.m., I dreamed up this meadow with flowers that exist in colors I've never seen in person. I could hear this melodic soundtrack, this Van Morrison kind of blues, and I couldn't figure out where it was coming from until I lay down in the flowers and realized it was coming straight from the sky. And then I was laughing because the sky was singing to me. God walked out the clouds like music. I was naked. I am always naked. And then there was a splash, bright midday through the shades, this empty apartment.

I stumble up from the mattress, swinging open the door and hanging my torso off the railing, so my body splits in two at the stomach: legs and breasts. Crust crumbles out my eyelids as I stare down into the pool, the scene materializing like a television turning from static to moving image. Trevor's head bobs up and down, in and out of the water. He's tall enough now to stand in the shallow end, but continues to dip his head under, moving it around; circles of boy turned fish.

"What you doing in there, boy? There's shit in that water," I call down to him. Though the brown of it has disappeared, probably through the filter, I swear I can still smell the feces lingering in the air. As far as I'm concerned, Dee's man's dog shit and the pool are interchangeable.

Trevor's head comes up, bends back to look at me. He has a birthmark on the top of his head, a dark spot in the shape of a spilling circle and I can see it as clearly now as I could the day he came out his mama. The whole apartment building went into labor with Dee when her moans found their way through the vents and out the windows. We all sweated with her, paced around and counted the minutes between each choke of her body. Mama was looking at the clock in our apartment, waiting for a couple hours until she turned to me and said, "It's time. Come on, chile," and just like that we were out the door and knocking on Dee's apartment, in a flock of women all joining the stampede of this birth, my eight-year-old shoulders shaking. Every woman in the Regal-Hi crammed into Dee's studio apartment, where she was splayed on the floor, gaping like the pocket of sky before the rain starts to pound, ready to bust open and release itself.

Dee kept saying, "Give it to me, please, just to get me through, Ronda."

She repeated this like a mantra between contractions, referring to the rock and pipe on the kitchen counter, ready for her. She said she had quit her habit after she found out about the pregnancy, but by quit she meant she used only on occasion, only when the morning sickness or the back cramping got real bad. Ronda, her childhood friend, refused to give Dee the crack, and a group of women stood in a line between the counter and Dee's body, guarding the child from its mother.

Mama pushed her way through the crowd, her arms long and spread out, me trailing behind her toward the center of the room, toward Dee's pounding.

"We got a little longer till he's out, alright, baby? It'll be over in about one hour. One more hour, one more hour." Mama repeated this, dropping to the floor by Dee and humming until the whole room was one rumble of my mama's lungs, intoxicating and heavenly, and I couldn't help but want to climb back into her body, feel those vibrations like my own breath.

Dee wailed and squeezed and trembled until my mama's hums drowned it all out and then the tribe of us saw the hair, saw the tiny round that crawled from her body, turning her inside out. The squeals began and the humming turned to chants and we all watched that child swim out his mama, head poking out more blood than hair, and my mama took him into her arms and laid him on Dee's breast and this was the sweetest, most whole thing to ever take place in our building, and the rain poured and poured and poured until Dee began to beg again and her birthmarked baby squirmed and Ronda gave up, passed Dee the pipe, and she faded into sky like she didn't hear her own baby crying. And Trevor cried and she smiled and we all hummed again.

Trevor splashes down below, looking up at me.

"Lost my ball," he calls.

"What you talkin' about? Why you not at school?"

"Mama not here and I woke up late and then I was gonna go but I dropped my keychain in the pool and if I don't got it, then the boys don't win the game and I lose my money."

I ask him, "What money?" but he simply dips back down into the water until the only thing distinctly him is that circular mark on his head, roaming. His pile of clothes is now wet from the splashing and when he emerges, small metal basketball keychain in hand, his boxers are slipping off him. I see the outline of his ribs like they been carved out of him and the rest of my day fades like a dream.

I walk toward the stairwell down to the pool and Trevor starts climbing up, pile of clothes a lump in his arms. We meet at the half-way point of the stairwell, Trevor a head shorter than me at age nine, with arms and legs that seem to stretch farther than he can control, but his face is still childlike.

"Go on and put some new clothes on," I tell him, beginning to guide him up the stairs.

"We goin' somewhere?" Trevor's teeth flash, always eager for the escape.

I grab the keychain out of his hand and look at it, taking in the way it shines like somebody been scrubbing it clean and tucking it into bed every night. "You wanna play ball so bad, let's go on and do it."

At that, little boy limbs fly straight up the stairs and into the apartment, just like they always have. His legs are longer and he knows more about what kind of life he has than he did when he was three and racing around the building, knocking on everyone's door, but he is still the same buoyant little man.

Dee tried to be his mother for the first few years of Trevor's life, at least enough that she was home half the time and she bought formula and bothered to make sure somebody was watching him when she went off to go get high in some other apartment. She used to leave Trevor with one of the women, sometimes Mama, any of the aunties who inherited all the Regal-Hi's children once theirs grew up. Then, between Daddy's death and Mama's arrest, all the aunties left. It was like something had come over the building and they all scattered, women disintegrating into nothing. Some chose to go and some got evicted, some passed away and some remarried, but all the women who had helped raise Marcus and me were gone by the time Trevor turned seven and then it was just us, motherless.

Trevor started to come around more often after that and then I was walking him to the bus, finding him some extra Doritos for after school. I was determined not to let nobody toss him away. So when the rent notice got posted, when Polka Dot came up to me and showed me what my body was worth, I thought maybe this was a ticket out for the both of us. Maybe this was how we got free.

I head back into my apartment and Marcus is awake, rubbing his eyes on the couch.

"Mornin'," he says.

I sit down next to him, thinking about how it felt to be in the second man's car last night, about Tony's back as he walked away. It was different when I was alone, the fear escalating and the grit so profound that when I got home last night I showered longer than I ever have before, didn't even worry about the water bill. I don't know if I can do it again, but I also don't know how to keep us alive if I don't.

"Marcus, I gotta ask you something."

He looks at me, rests his cheek in his hand, waits.

"I know I said I'd give you a month to work on the album, but I need you to get a job."

Marcus starts to nod slowly, looking at the carpet and then back up at me.

"Aight, Ki. I'll start looking."

I didn't expect him to say yes, so when he does, it's like there's suddenly more air in the room, his nod a solace that might make up for everything.

"I actually got a lead for you. I ran into Lacy a few days ago. She works at a strip club downtown and I bet she'd help you get a job there if you asked."

"You know Lacy and I ain't tight like that no more."

"You know you ain't gonna be able to get no other job." I pick at a scab forming on my knee. "Please."

Marcus nods again and I lean forward, wrap my arms around him like I've been wanting to since Polka Dot. He kisses the top of my head, murmurs something about needing to piss, and I think for the first time in months, we might just be okay.

Marcus leaves to go piss at the liquor store and I pull on a jacket and head back to the patio strip where all the apartments connect in a circle around the shit pool. Trevor still hasn't come out from his door and I decide to just head in anyways, opening the door to a scene of little boy blues, Trevor in his boxers dancing. Swing step, head bob.

The music floats out an old stereo on the floor mattress, half static and half disco song that I'm sure Trevor's never heard before in his life. And, still, like my dream, he dances. I run into the room, right toward him, and tackle him into a hug that fills with shrieks echoing a sort of happy that is all child before he pushes me away.

"Put them clothes on so we can go." I breathe heavy, my spine aligned with the stained rug that cushioned our fall. Trevor is blithe, speedy and awake, dressing in seconds. I stand and lead us out the door, into the daylight where it is just Trevor and me under the soft glare of sun.

* *

For early afternoon when all of us should really be sitting in some kind of classroom, the basketball court is alive with sweat and shuffles. Sneakers move quick enough that the asphalt seems to smoke and my eyes switch from flesh to flesh, everybody merging with sky. Trevor stands next to me with his basketball appearing oversized in front of his bony chest, just watching. Watching the way I watch Alé skateboard: so mesmerized I can't even begin to move.

We're standing on the edge of the court when a girl approaches us, basketball shorts clinging to her thighs with midday game sweat. She's got braids down to her waist, swooped into a ponytail, and she drips with salt, smells like the bay, can't be more than twelve but she is infinite.

"Never seen you two 'round here," she spits.

"Must not've been looking." I put my right hand on Trevor's shoulder so I might be able to tether us together, create a safety net.

Trevor steps forward. "Been betting for months on the morning game. Got a stack of money 'cause of you and your girls."

I've never seen Trevor like this, with a blade for a throat.

She twirls the ball in her hand and Trevor mirrors her with his. The balls are the same size but beside his body, his is massive.

"You been betting on me?" she asks.

"Against you, actually. Don't got money to waste on nobody who don't got no game."

The girl's salt stench gets thicker in her heat. "You ain't even know how to hold a ball so you best not go talking like that."

We all know what a challenge sounds like. We all looking for a fight without fists. This survival. Bay girl seems to expand her body, legs spread, like taking up more of this air might bring her some kind of victory. Trevor tells her the rules of the game, as if he's ever done more than watch it: two on two, eleven points wins, you foul and you out. Bay girl's teammate appears by her side like she's been listening in the whole time: she's smaller in frame but her arms are thick, coming out from her body and jiggling. Her sweat smells sweet, like jasmine, which probably means she stole her mama's perfume this morning.

"I ain't got all day," I tell them, holding out my hands for Trevor to pass me the ball. It spins right through the air and into my palms.

Jasmine girl tilts her heavy head, squints, and calls out to a boy across the court. The boy is older, maybe fourteen, and I think he might be too skinny for this sport. It'd be too easy to crack a bone, splinter each one of his ribs.

"Sean, come referee this shit."

Skinny boy saunters over and I look into Trevor's face, trying to catch a single glimpse of his terror. It's not there. Instead, there is a determination so fierce it has cemented into a scowl. Sometimes being this young unleashes the fury. I lick my lips, taste my own salt, and I'm ready to swallow the bay, extremities and all.

We separate onto our respective sides of the court, side by side, with Sean in the center. I toss him the ball.

"Y'all better not do some fuck shit. It too early for no fight." I expected his voice to be higher, but it is a deep pit in his throat, coming out mangled on his tongue.

"We ain't gonna start nothing," bay girl spits.

I mirror Trevor's scowl, nod. "Nah, we playing fair."

Trevor's fingers twitch at his sides, legs spread, boy ready to catapult into the game. I don't remember the last time I played ball, but if Trevor's gotta win, then I know I best be Steph Curry fourth quarter. I best be everything he ever wanted.

Sean starts the game real quick, throws the ball toward bay girl and she catches it, dips right, then left, then spears her body forward, too fast for Trevor and me to think long enough to stop her. She shoots and the ball swooshes right into the hoop like that's where it belongs. We stand, stunned, not ready for bay girl to have salt feet to match.

I step toward Trevor, lean into his ear. "It's all about the way you move. Don't think about it, just move."

The next play and Trevor fumbles again, bay girl's partner catching the ball and running with it. Trevor starts to shake his head and I almost think he's about to start crying, but when he looks at me, his eyes are fierce.

The ball, back in our possession, is heavier now. I toss it to Trevor, who catches it, bouncing and whirling across the court. Bay girl catches up to him just as he releases the sphere from the three-point line, jumping so high it's like he's weightless, the ball springing over our heads before it swooshes straight into the basket.

He comes back down from his jump panting, runs over to me, and we're both clapping hands and backs, trying to remain collected, but so elated we can barely handle it. Trevor bobs on the tips of his toes just like Alé used to when we were young and out here on this same court, bruising each other with elbows to the ribs and laughing about it later, when we started turning purple. We don't play no more, but not because we outgrew it or nothing. It's just that Alé couldn't stand to look at my skin like that and know her bones caused it to color in a way skin's not supposed to color. She used to touch the ones on my belly like you might touch a half-dead squirrel and even when I told her to stop that shit, she couldn't help herself. Sometimes she still looks at me like that.

Back on the court again, watching Trevor bounce side to side, I know the boy is fevered and confident the way winning makes you confident, hands gripping that ball like a godsend. Bay girl learns she likes us even less than she thought and, like a whirl, the game has turned into a beatdown, Trevor and I taking turns dodging their shoves and shooting. The sound of the ball making contact with the hoop is like a deep breath and pretty soon our lungs are full. By the end of the game, we're both slick with perspiration, hiding smiles as we nod to the girls, and walking off that court. I think Trevor is the most radiant boy I've ever laid eyes on: walking home with that ball slipped under his left arm.

It's almost like I can see the joy droop off him as we approach the gate to the Regal-Hi. The curves in his face dissipate into an angular pout and the only sign that his body was leaping through the air less than ten minutes ago is the sweat still trickling down his cheeks. I squeeze his shoulder as I unlatch the gate and Trevor still doesn't snap out of it, even when we're standing by the shit pool and the rest of High Street only exists in sound. I lean down so I'm looking him straight in the eyes. He tilts his head away from my gaze, so I cup the back of his head, which somehow is even more drenched in sweat, and hold it so that he has no choice but to look at me.

"What's wrong witchu?" I don't mean for it to come out harsh, but his eyes tell me it did. "You okay? You hurt?"

"No, I ain't hurt," he whispers, his voice still squeaky.

"Then what's up with you?"

I can see it happen. The ballooning inside him. I can see it pushing at all sides of his body, stretching him from the inside out like
bubbles on the surface of Lake Merritt, sitting there, pushing against
each other until one bursts, sprays, and returns the surface to the
shiny it was before. Trevor is on his way to bursting, his skin betraying him, sending waves of that heavy kind of lonely through the air.

"I just don't wanna leave." And it's like his own words rupture his
seams, tears flooding into his sweat.

I take him into me, hold him to my chest. The basketball falls out
of his hand and bounces across the pavement. "What you mean,
boy?" I whisper into his ear.

His response is half sobs and half words. "Mama ain't been home
and Mr. Vern keeps knocking on our door saying we gotta pay or
leave and I been hiding so he don't see me." Trevor says he's been
betting to make rent money, but he's been spending it all on lunch at
school, hiding half of his lunch to save for dinner. He trails into deep
heaves, and I grip him tighter, so tight I wonder if he's lost circulation
when he stops shaking, his body heavy against mine. His face is sunk
and he lets me lead him back up to his apartment, where I leave him
on the mattress looking like he's gonna either fall asleep or burst into
tears again.

The flying moments solidify inside my rib cage like a photo album
in the body. Trevor and I sweltering, jumping, always close to the sky.
Alé and her weed, that smile quick, Sunday Shoes, funeral day. For
these moments, I forget my body is a currency and none of the things
I did last night make any sense at all. Trevor's body, the way it fills up
with air and releases, reminds me how sacred it is to be young. These
moments when all I want is to have my mama hum me a lullaby I will
only remember in dreamland.

MARCUS HAS BEEN WORKING at the strip club for a week and he told me if I came by tonight, he'd get the cook to make me dinner. I step into the club and it looks different than it did the first time, more oily and less dark, like the lightbulbs finally started glowing right. Marcus sees me and comes out from behind the bar to hug me, holding my head to his chest like he used to when I was younger.

"Take a seat, Ki." Marcus returns to his side of the bar and I sit in the same seat I did when I was here last, glancing around the room to make sure Polka Dot isn't around. He isn't, but the memory still lingers where he used to be and my stomach churns. The club is full of its after-work crowd, everyone seated and the music still low and funky.

It's interesting to watch Marcus work, his black shirt clinging to his muscles, so much more passive than I'm used to seeing him. I didn't know he had the capacity to speak so different, even making his walk rigid and intentional. Marcus tells me my fries are on the way and then he pours me a club soda and leaves to take a new customer's order.

Lacy steps out from the back after about ten minutes, bringing with her my basket of fries.

"Heard these were for you," she says, placing them in front of me.

"Thanks." I smile. "Not just for the fries, but for helping us out."

Lacy nods. "Don't really matter how things ended with Marcus. You both family."

She pulls out her notepad and moves down the bar to take a young woman's order.

Marcus returns to behind the bar and steals a few of my fries.

"You look happy," I say.

"Don't mind it here." Marcus shrugs. "Would rather be in the studio, but this ain't so bad."

Both Marcus and Lacy continue to make their rounds, cycling from the kitchen to the bar to each table, always masterfully balancing ten things in two hands. Marcus brings me some kind of jalapeño poppers and I'm so absorbed with the taste of the food, I almost don't catch Marcus's slight tremors as he stands at a table by the stage where two men in suits are staring up at him, trying to hand him back a basket of chicken wings. Marcus shakes his head and takes the food and when he walks back to the bar, where Lacy is pouring drinks for a couple, his walk is slick and dramatic.

Marcus slams the basket down on the bar and growls. "These motherfuckers tryna tell me I ain't know what I'm talkin' 'bout." He's pacing, his mumbles getting louder until the whole club recedes to silence in the wake of his shouts.

Lacy tries to grab his arm. "What the hell are you doing?"

Marcus shoves her away.

"Marcus, stop," I say, and he looks at me, his snarl fully present in his mouth. He spits on the floor.

"I ain't gotta take nobody's orders." Marcus grabs the wings and walks back around the bar, dropping them in front of the suited men, wings and ranch flying everywhere. Marcus turns around in a circle, opening his arms wide, and shouts again. "Y'all motherfuckers gonna know my name real soon. I'm Marcus motherfucking Johnson and I ain't 'bout to be serving you shit, nah." He shakes his head more than he needs to before strutting straight out of the door, not even bothering to ask if I wanna come with.

· ·

Walking home tonight feels like walking underwater. Like everything is thick and cold and moving, but I can't really tell one block from the next. The way oceans make you glow until you remember that the glow is really just a reflection of your own skin and your fingers are wrinkled. It feels like that, walking tonight, the streets when it's only me.

I should've known Marcus couldn't handle it for long. He probably didn't even make enough to pay for our groceries, and I'm less angry that he doesn't know how to be a grown man than I am that I trusted he might actually try. I think he wanted to and I think that desire was mostly about me, but Marcus ain't figured out how to stifle his rage to get a job done. At the same time, I can't blame him. He's spent years bottling up every feeling to take care of us and ever since he learned Uncle Ty's made it big, he can't keep himself from erupting. He doesn't understand we don't got the luxury of fucking up, not right now.

I apologized to Lacy and took the bus home. The apartment was empty and I changed quickly, texting my small list of men to see who was willing to pay tonight. I tell myself I'll start looking for new job postings tomorrow, that this is what it's gotta be for now, the only way we gonna survive. It ain't that I'm not scared. I am. But I know we'll lose so much more if I don't keep us afloat, that suddenly Trevor won't have nobody to make sure he eats and Marcus won't have a couch to sleep on and I will be closer to my own funeral day than I ever have been.

One of Davon's friends picked me up around eight o'clock and parked his car on a side street. He pushed the passenger seat down so we were horizontal and had me lie on top of him, the windows steaming just enough with our body heat that when the sirens roared past, the lights shone through the haze and somehow it made them brighter. I stopped, like if I froze I could prevent them from seeing me, from getting out of that police car and tapping on the window. I know the stories of what happens when the blue-suits find someone like me doing something like this. The man beneath me asked me why I stopped and I didn't answer, still waiting for a cop to jump out and turn on his flashlight, blind me with it.

The sirens receded into the night, and nobody came tapping on the window, but I couldn't get the image out of my head of them zip-tying my wrists and shoving me into the backseat of their car, so I got off the man and he started throwing a fit and calling me a bitch and I thought he might try to hit me, so I opened the car door and fled.

Now I'm walking, the streetlamps looking like spotlights and I feel like I'm being followed, even though I know the ocean makes you believe things when it fills you up and tonight I am brimming.

Part of me hopes Alé might be out this late and run into me, find me on the streets, and take me home with her. I don't want her to have to see me like this; she probably wouldn't even look me in the eyes, but at least she'd take me somewhere safe. At least her arms would be warm. But Alé isn't gonna find me and since I haven't been answering her calls anyway, she probably wouldn't want to.

Alé's always dreamed big and lived small.

I met her when I tagged along with Marcus to the skate park and decided she was the only thing worth watching. Marcus and Alé hung out too, but then Marcus entered high school and suddenly she was too young to be his friend. Even in middle school, she was pointing out plot holes in every movie and questioning all her teachers, thinking beyond this city, but still living in it more fully than the rest of us. Alé's graduation was the most breathtaking and devastating day of my life, watching her do something Marcus and I didn't have the bandwidth or maybe the bravado to do. The entirety of last year I was waiting for her to tell me about whatever college she was gonna go to, bracing myself for her departure, but halfway through her senior year her mother had a small stroke and I think that stopped Alé in her tracks, made her stay when she probably shouldn't have.

Alé isn't unhappy, but I know she's still dreaming. She's always thinking about people, about how many of us been left in the dust. She secretly feeds families who don't got no food at home, letting them into the back entrance of the taquería and sending them out with bags of food she made with her own hands. I know she wants to do more than that, take her skateboard and set out into these streets, heal what she never could with me, with her sister.

Alé's sister went missing when she was twelve. Clara was two years older than Alé, just entering high school at Castlemont High. Alé says her sister was acting different those first months of school and then one day in November, Clara didn't show up for her after-school shift at La Casa. The family called the cops, who didn't say much beyond taking some basic information and entering Clara into some database. No news report, no AMBER Alert, just a cop who said she'd do her job.

After the first two days Clara was gone, their mama made posters that Alé and I uploaded onto Facebook and Myspace, then rode around the city taping them to poles and stop signs. Those first weeks after Clara disappeared felt like all the oxygen had run out in the city, like there wasn't enough room for us to breathe and we were waiting for our next puff. After a few months, when OPD still didn't have shit to say about Clara's case, we all started to realize she was gone, that her being gone meant more than her being dead because in this city, it's just as probable that she was stolen, that she's out there somewhere walking streets just like I am now.

Maybe it didn't make sense for me to leave tonight, when I've got money to make and it's still early. The things your body needs most don't usually make sense, though, so I let the air ripple my skin into a path right back to High Street, right back to the Regal-Hi. Sometimes when I walk, I look for Clara, try to find a glimpse of her in the shadows of these streets. I try to tell myself I'm nothing like her, that this is my choice and I'm old enough and I'm being smart. I'm starting to wonder if I even believe it at all.

I push the gate open to the pool greeting me like it hasn't been following me up and down the streets: same blue, same glow. The stairs are massive, never-ending in these heels, and each step makes my ankles click like the joints are trying to find a way out of the climb. When I reach the landing, I don't rush toward my apartment or even toward Trevor's. Instead, I walk slow enough, close enough to the doors that I can hear the muffled sounds calling out to me. A child's shriek. A stream of laughter. What sounds like the talking-to that comes right before the beating. A teakettle.

When I get to Trevor's door, I don't bother listening for a noise because there is none. Like Trevor said, Dee ain't been home in weeks and, as far as I know, Trevor's always in there sleeping or munching on another bowl of Cheerios.

Their door has an updated slip of paper taped to it: rent due in next 7 days or pending eviction. Vern keeps it sweet and simple, doesn't even bother signing it. I continue on down the line to my door, to the same slip of paper that I leave to soar upward with the wind when the door slams shut behind me. I toss my heels across the room, sinking into the couch next to a sleeping Marcus.

Marcus stirs from his sleep, blinking his eyes open, yawning and looking over so the faint trace of ink twists below his ear. "You good?"

I pause, holding my breath, looking down at my thighs, and part of me hopes he'll ask me where I've been. "No."

He doesn't move from his slouch. "Gonna be alright."

"No."

He shifts on the couch. "Look, I'm sorry, okay? I don't know how to do this either, Ki. But I got faith. Just go to sleep." He turns over so his face is pressed against the back cushion.

I stand up, slipping into the bathroom.

On my sixteenth birthday, Marcus told me he had a surprise for me. We were sitting in that same patch of carpet behind the couch, the place we spent most of our time together since Mama left, eating my cake out of the box with plastic forks. Marcus was always fucking around or at work, but he told me he was all mine for my birthday and he kept his promise. It was before I dropped out of school and I was taking a couple short shifts at Bottle Caps while Marcus worked at Panda Express. Together, we made it work, up until Marcus met Cole and Uncle Ty's album came out and Marcus stopped trying.

"What is it?" When Marcus told me he had a surprise for me, I assumed I wasn't gonna get nothing but his company, which was really all I wanted anyway.

His grin covered half his face and I could see his silver crown better than I had since the day he'd gotten it and proudly opened wide to show me. He got up from the floor and left the room, heading to the bathroom. He hadn't done that in over a year and I thought maybe I should go with him, hold his hand so he wouldn't panic if he saw flashes of dripping water spilling across the floor. I stayed put and he came back a minute later with a needle in his hand.

"You want me to sew your pants or some shit?"

"Nah, I'm gonna pierce your ears."

"What?"

"You always said you wanted your ears pierced. I ain't got no money to take you somewhere to do it, but I been watching videos about how and I even got Lacy to give me these." He grabbed his jacket slung across the couch and took out a pouch, shaking it into his hand. Two stud earrings fell out, leaf-shaped.

"You serious?"

His smile only grew. "Hell yeah, I'm serious. You ready?"

I sat on the carpet and Marcus kneeled next to me, a bowl of ice and a slice of apple in hand.

"You sure that needle's clean?" I'd never had any part of my body pierced, begged Mama for years, but she refused. "Is it gonna hurt?"

Marcus waved me off. "I cleaned it, quit asking these damn questions."

He stood up and went to the kitchen, turned the stove burner on, and dipped the needle in the fire before returning to me, tilting my head toward him. "What I say, Ki? I got you." He held my gaze and it was like I was nine again, following him into the trees by the lake and watching as he and his friends lit a bowl, the way he inhaled like some part of him had always known how to do it. Watching Marcus makes you want to join him, follow him anywhere.

"Do it." I squeezed my eyes shut and dug my nails into his shoulder as he slipped the apple behind my earlobe.

"Aight. I'm gonna count down from three."

I gripped his shoulder tighter on the three, squeezed more on the two, and screamed out on the one, even though he lied and pierced the needle through my skin on two. It wasn't nothing but a pinch. He pulled the needle out and slipped a piece of ice behind my ear as he fiddled with the stud and finally got it inside the hole, clasping the back on. He got a pan out from under the stove and held it up for me so I could see my ear, puffy and swelling with this tiny little leaf in the center. I looked up at him and beamed. It was perfect.

"Ready for the next one?"

I nodded and as I repositioned so my other ear was facing him, I caught Marcus look across the room to the little table set up between the kitchen and the door where the only Johnson family photo sat untouched, Mama in the center with her arms around all of us. Daddy stood there with his blazing teeth, like he was ready to pick up a saxophone and puff out a new tune. I hadn't seen Marcus look so doe-like and small in months and something about it relieved me.

But he didn't count this time and instead of that small pinch, my ear split into a raging burn, followed by a steady trickle of warmth leaking down my neck and Marcus's whispered *fuck*. I didn't scream, just looked at him, still holding the needle, bloody. The carpet still has a trail of blood spots and my earlobe still has a thin scar that only Marcus knows he is responsible for. Alé pierced that ear a couple days later, made sure to do it slow and careful.

Marcus brought me home a folded slip of notebook paper with his new lyrics every night for five days after my birthday. They weren't about me or nothing, but the sentiment was clear. Over a year after he had taken me in and he was still trying, at least enough to have any words for me at all. Sometimes I still see flashes of the brother who would give anything to reverse my hurt, like when he said he'd get a job for me, but he's becoming more and more unfamiliar.

I stare at the tub, unused with mold growing in each corner. Next thing I know I'm holding my phone to my ear like I'm really prepared for her to pick up. When the night nurse answers, I don't even have to beg for him to let me speak to Mama since apparently it's "free hour" and, moments later, she's on the phone. It's like the blood's been sucked out of my body with everything else, completely evaporated.

Even when every other memory disintegrates, there is no way to forget your mama's voice. Hers is so gravel, that Cassandra Wilson kind of deep, and it wraps around my waist, holds on tight.

I speak. "Mama?"

Mama don't miss a beat, says, "Hi, baby," and it feels like God climbing out her throat. Feels like every fear abandoned.

"I need you, Mama." My voice comes out mumbled and I wonder if she can hear me at all.

Mama coughs. "Whatchu need, child?" That gravel voice fills up with her pride and I know my call satisfied all her hoping.

"I don't know what I'm doing out here."

"Don't know nobody who does." Mama doesn't speak for a moment. I think maybe I should talk again. Or just hang up and forget I ever called her in the first place. Then her voice comes back and I let myself sink into it. "I've been thinking about you. Was telling one of the girls in here last week about how you used to draw those pictures for me, remember? The ones that you'd always do in the same damn color and I told you they must got more than just a red marker in that school of yours but you kept on saying you liked the red."

"Yeah." I don't remember much about the actual pictures, but I remember how my teacher used to hide the red markers from me so I didn't make another one like that, how I had to get one of the other kids to let me have theirs in exchange for some other prize I don't remember giving.

"Your brother taking good care of you?" Mama asks.

"He quit his job today."

"Why don't you get one, then? I know I didn't raise no incompetent child." Mama dares to heighten her voice into that same octave she used to use pre-lecture.

"It ain't that easy," I say. "Got a gig but it don't pay much and they raising our rent."

Mama laughs.

"What?"

Her voice is too bright. "It just makes more sense why my girl decided to call for the first time now. Baby needs some money."

"I'm not stupid, I know you ain't got no money," I spit back.

"Don't mean I don't know people who do."

I scoff. "I don't want none of your prison friends' cash."

"You know your uncle got money."

"Also know he left the minute you did."

"I still got his number," she says, and I can feel the grin pasted on her face. "Family keeps each other safe, yeah?"

Ironic how she keeps on preaching family values, like she did not destroy this one. Our family started and ended with Mama, with the same voice that's telling me how we keep each other safe when she never could. Sometimes it feels like Daddy was the only one she ever loved.

There's nothing coincidental about their love story.

For someone so fixated on destiny and God's plan, Mama always knew how to get up in everybody's business and make something happen. Daddy had just joined the Panthers in 1977, late to the movement at nineteen but still in a honeymoon phase with the revolution, used *comrade* in every sentence, and wore black even in ninety-degree weather. He mostly just sold the party newspaper and helped out with filing, but every chance he had to get in on the action, he took.

A fight had broken out on Seventh Street in West Oakland. Daddy was on his way to work with a couple friends, rifles resting on their shoulders, berets on. Covered in leather. Daddy always described it as an attack; cops just sauntered up and started berating them. Pretty soon, Daddy was cuffed and in the backseat of a patrol car, charged with resisting arrest.

Daddy said his friend Willie was the one who started it, wrote a letter about Daddy and his case and released it to every chapter of the Panthers in the country. Got everyone in every city on the streets, signs up, fists pointed. Daddy never said it, but I think he was proud of the arrest; of having Elaine Brown's right-hand man say his name and visit him in jail.

Mama was living in Boston with her cousin Loretta that summer. Loretta said she had some business to attend to out in California and thirteen-year-old Mama came right along with her. When they hit Oakland streets, Mama saw Daddy's face plastered on signs and posters all over town. Said he looked like Louisiana bayous tasted: rich and overgrown; that skin a whole muggy river. Scrawny and pre-pubescent girl that she was, she said she was gonna make that man hers, make him show her where the water flowed in Oakland.

The Oakland Police Department decided not to press charges once *The New York Times* picked up the story, and Daddy was released two weeks post-arrest. Some of the Panthers threw him a release party in the streets, then had a barbecue at a West Oakland park. It was Mama's last day in town and she begged her cousin to take her.

Mama went straight up to Daddy and said, *"Hi. I'm Cheyenne, it's a pleasure to meet you."*

Daddy didn't pay her no mind, but Mama watched him all day. Watched the way he spread out his arms when he laughed. Watched him sing with that perfect mouth oval. Watched him dance with a pretty woman twice her age when the jazz came on.

Mama didn't mind waiting. Went back to Louisiana, grew up, worked almost ten years in a hospital answering calls, and saved up enough to move out to Oakland. Then Mama went looking for Daddy, twelve years after she first met him in that park. She eventually found him bartending in a little pub off MacArthur Boulevard in 1989, when downtown was full of crackheads and abandoned buildings and cops who still liked to mess with Daddy, the lead-up to his eventual lockup.

Mama knew she was that kind of beautiful that seemed to have just walked out of a painting. Her hair was teased into a faux mohawk like she was starring in a Whitney Houston music video and she was a graceful tall, took these huge steps when she walked. Mama wore wide-leg red pants to go fall in love with Daddy and kept them even after they tore at the seams. This time, when Mama strutted up to him, he was so mesmerized he almost dropped a bottle of whiskey. Not by the way she looked but by the way she existed. Mama was like woman grown out a seed, arms twisting, fruit and breasts and all things hard to resist. Daddy wanted to wrap his arms around her trunk and Mama knew he would.

An orchestrated love is almost more precious than a natural one; harder to give up something you spent that long making.

Mama married Daddy and they moved into the Regal-Hi by the time Marcus was born. When Mama looked at Daddy, she saw posters of a lightning boy's face. She didn't never see the way Daddy fogged up in the winter or how he would save a dollar bill before he'd ever save a family photo. I only ever saw Daddy and his music: dancing in the kitchen. Daddy was away in San Quentin from ages six to nine for me and I barely remember him not there. Marcus don't feel that way, though. Used to throw a tantrum every time Daddy tried to touch him post-lockup. Mama used to tell him, *"You lucky yo daddy got out 'fore you even grown a single hair on that face."*

And she was right: we were lucky that everyone knew Daddy's name, until the day when suddenly we weren't so lucky, and Mama's trunk splintered.

"You'd really give me Uncle Ty's number?" I ask.

Mama coughs again on the end of the line. "Course I would. Just want my babies to come see me out here first." She says it and it sticks onto the insides of my stomach, the way Mama makes everything into a deal.

"Mama, we ain't gonna try to get you out again or nothing. Can't do it even if I wanted to. You in a halfway house now, you should be happy about that. And you know Marcus not going nowhere for you." My teeth grind and I don't know why she always makes me say it, crush all the parts of me that just want her to hold me and hum.

"You gotta talk to him, Kiara, really talk to him. I know you ain't been trying like that and it's okay, baby, I just need you to come here. Give me an hour and I'll give you all your uncle's shit. We got visiting hours Saturday morning. I know I'll see my babies there. You be there."

And Mama repeats this, goes on about all the things we're gonna do together. I don't say nothing else because her voice is here, breathing into me. I sit down on the tile floor, close my eyes, lean back against the wall, let the phone send her voice right to me, let the heat melt me away. Mama hangs up at some point, the bathroom lightbulb goes out at some point, and I drip into sleep at some point. The night blurs together into a stream of Mama's voice.

THE BUS RIDE UP TO MAMA is loud. The windows don't open and the whole vehicle is a fever of noise and muck and bodies without destinations. I didn't even know there was a bus to Stockton, but I looked it up and got on the first one this morning straight out of Oakland right through Dublin to Mama. When I boarded the bus, I already knew it would be hours of waiting to escape. I have a window seat, but this woman with three trash bags full of clothes decided to sit next to me and I swear those bags smell like the section of West Oakland right by the wastewater treatment plant.

Yesterday I went to the studio looking for Marcus and found him where he always is, rapping some nonsense. I begged him to come visit Mama with me, but he refused, over and over again, no matter how many of my tears escaped, said he'd already tried working at the club for me, that he needed space to record his album.

Not long after I left Marcus, Alé called and asked if I wanted to share a washer at the laundromat down the street with her. I haven't seen Alé in a while, but after everything with Marcus I couldn't imagine sitting and waiting in the apartment for night to come, so I said yes. Still, when I went to the apartment to fill a pillowcase with my dirty clothes, the only ones I could find were Marcus's. So I took

Marcus's laundry to meet Alé and when I poured it into her basket, she looked up at me like a bloody knife had fallen in there with all the clothes.

"What?"

"These ain't even your clothes."

Instead of laughing at me or hollering or going over to one of the girls sitting in the line of the lavandería chairs and telling them, *Look at this girl, she don't even wash her own clothes,* Alé hugged me. Came right up to me and enveloped me into the damp sweat of her shirt.

We sat there watching the water flood in on the fabrics, turning them all a darker color and then taking them for a spin. Alé tried asking me what was going on, why I haven't been around, what's up with our rent, but I kept my eyes on the suds of soap collecting on the glass. She dropped it and stared with me until it was time to change the load.

I get off the bus in Stockton, which looks like the desert has found its way to Northern California, reminding me of what it was like up in Marin County the day we reunited with Daddy. The dust in the air gets in my eyes and I hope Mama's got enough heart left in her to disregard Marcus's absence.

The day Daddy got released from San Quentin, Mama borrowed Uncle Ty's dusty Honda and drove Marcus and me to Marin to pick him up. Marcus didn't wanna come. Mama threatened him with everything she could think of until finally, when she said she'd take away his time with Uncle Ty, he said he'd go. We were sitting in the back of the car while Mama paced around the parking lot in front of us, the buildings uniform and cream-colored and industrial. I watched Marcus's twelve-year-old fingers search the cracks separating the middle seat, coming up with cracker crumbs, remnants of weed, and a broken pencil.

Daddy walked out of those doors with his arms spread up, hands facing the sky, teeth so dazzlingly white I thought he must've been using whitening strips inside, but Daddy said it was just God keeping them clean so he'd look nice for his babies. His face was so unfamiliar, I didn't even realize it was him until Marcus huffed beside me and Mama took off running across the parking lot toward him. She ran fast, sprinted into him, and he stumbled back, but held on to her waist. Mama gripped her hand inside his short 'fro, speckled silver, and we could see her shaking from afar.

After a while, they walked hand in hand toward us. Mama motioned for us to get on out the car, but Marcus told me to stay put. He gripped my hand. When the two of them climbed into the car, Mama looked back at us, strained her eyelids as wide open as they would get, and said, "You say hi to your daddy now."

I squeaked out a "hi" and Marcus stayed silent beside me, his hand tightening around mine like he was worried I'd slip away.

"You ready to go home?" Mama's voice was a wash of relief, her smile so wide all her teeth showed through.

Daddy shook his head. "Nah, baby, I can't be going back inside yet. Let's go to the lake, yeah? What you say, kids?" He looked back at us and, even though this strange man still didn't feel like my father, the way his face spread open and lit up from the gums made me want to belong to him.

"Yeah, Mama, the lake!" I nodded.

Marcus shook his head, but when Daddy asked if he'd be alright with us going on an adventure, he said, "I go where Ki goes," and even now I don't think he's ever said nothing about me that made me feel more special.

Mama drove back to Oakland and parked on a side street near Grand Avenue. We heard the sounds as we started walking to the lake. Daddy had his arm around Mama when he steered her toward the pergola, Marcus and I holding hands and following, the drums chorusing our arrival.

We should have known Daddy would hear the drum circle and

gravitate right into it. Daddy sauntered up to one of the drummers and pulled him into a clap-back hug, mumbled to him in his sweet talk till the man handed his drum right over to Daddy, who joined the group's rhythm like he was born into it.

Daddy always knew how to enter the music, his hands slapping, chin tilting in every direction. This newly free man bobbing like he hadn't seen the things he'd seen. Mama stood straight and still, faintly swaying, and I could tell she was waiting for something to happen. Waiting for Daddy to collapse. But he didn't. He just kept on slapping that drum, grinning at us. Eventually, he gave the man his drum back and Daddy went over to Mama and whispered in her ear until, finally, Mama's mouth opened wide and the melody came out like it had just been uncaged. Daddy separated from her and started clapping, looking at everyone around him like *Damn, that's my woman, look at her sing.*

Next, Daddy locked eyes with me and strutted right over to where Marcus and I had our hands locked together, watching.

"My little girl know how to dance, huh?" He leaned down and reached a hand out to me. I took it, but Marcus's tug on my other arm pulled me back. I looked up at him and he shook his head, so I let go of Daddy's hand.

Daddy turned to Marcus. "I hear you got some talent of your own, son. How 'bout you show us some of these rhymes?"

Marcus glared at first. Daddy turned around and shouted out to the drum circle, "Y'all ready for some rhymes?" The chorus came back loud, unanimous, more people from the street gathering under the pergola, contorting their bodies into dance, and joining the music.

Marcus hadn't ever heard nobody want to listen to him like that and I could see the smile itch at him. I let go of his hand and he stepped forward, busted out into bars I had heard a million times when he was memorizing them in the bathroom while he thought we were asleep. Daddy beatboxed for him and the drummers staggered into his rhythm, which seemed to change every couple verses. Still, when Marcus was done, Daddy applauded and clapped his back and Marcus nodded, not objecting when Daddy pulled me onto his feet and waltzed me around. I don't think Marcus ever forgave Daddy, but he accepted him after that. We walked around the lake and when Daddy asked him how school was, Marcus responded.

There's not a thing Daddy could've done that would've made me hate him. When he died, I thought maybe it was a consequence of not resenting him more, not playing into karma like Marcus had so the world wouldn't have had to kill him to keep the good-evil balance in check. That was before I learned that life won't give you reasons for none of it, that sometimes fathers disappear and little girls don't make it to another birthday and mothers forget to be mothers.

. .

Every time I leave Oakland I miss the trees. Out here in Stockton, the gray sky is bright. It stings my eyes, stings like my childhood burns when Alé tried to make me frijoles and spilled the whole bowl of boiling beans right down my shirt. My stomach still has lines that Alé traces with her finger whenever I let her. Sometimes it feels like she's still trying to make up for my burns, my bruises.

I hit Blooming Hope Halfway House after walking for only four or five minutes. The name only makes its appearance more ironic: all the flowers out front are dying and the building looks like it was built three centuries ago and hasn't been renovated since. I swear the roof just about sags and that porch might as well call itself a burial ground because it's covered in dirt from God knows where and, still, as I approach, I see a gathering of people out front who could not be beaming wider. Maybe anything is better than a cell.

If you look up Blooming Hope, they'd tell you it was a "facility supporting the rehabilitation of compromised persons," but really it's just a mandatory halfway house where the security guards wear jeans and everyone has their own wardrobe and their own ankle bracelets. Mama is lucky to be here, I guess, especially for what she did, but I still can't shake how dead the place feels, a prison without the bars.

When I get close enough for them to realize I plan on coming inside, the three people stop talking and turn toward me.

The man, beard long enough to hide an entire pipe, removes his cigarette from his lips and calls out to me, "You here for visiting?"

I nod, dipping my head under the overgrowth of what used to be a beautiful floral entryway and is now rotting leaves and branches that just keep extending. A series of steps lead up to where the three are standing. One of the women is short, has red hair and piercings lining the entirety of her bottom lip. She smiles faintly at me. The other woman has hands so massive I bet they could cover Trevor's whole basketball or hold Shauna's baby in just one palm. They don't match the rest of her body, which isn't small, but isn't large enough to warrant the size of her hands. She has bantu knots all over her head and each one has a single flower tucked into the base.

The redhead speaks next. "Go inside and the visiting room is on your left."

I nod again and it's like my throat has stopped working: clogged up with all this air and the trail of Mama's voice and how lonely this is without Marcus.

The door creaks just like I expect it to. Houses give away all their secrets at the door. Dee's is full of scratches. Mine doesn't even have a working lock no more.

Immediately I'm encased in sound. Not like on the bus, though. This time, the sound is harmonies of shrieks and crying and laughter that rolls into rambling and there are too many voices to discern a single word, but I know the room is joy. When I think about Mama, I think anything but joy.

The room is chaos in its most raw form: bodies on bodies. Bodies beside each other on couches, in chairs. Bodies embracing. Bodies sipping coffee. Bodies sobbing and clinging and smiling. I don't see Mama, but I hear her. "Oh please, Miranda." Mama's voice is booming, but her laugh is chill, almost robotic.

I move toward it, through the clutter of people whose limbs cement in my vision, but never their faces. Their lips blur with their noses and they are just bodies. Bodies on bodies. And Mama.

Mama sits on a green couch in the back corner, her bare feet resting on a coffee table, head tilted upward in a laugh that doesn't even seem to produce sound at this point, just a jaw opening and shaking slightly. I watch her: this woman whose skin I crawled out of.

Her body has blown up, so now Mama is soft where she used to be all collarbone. The woman seated next to her, Miranda, is a dwarf of Mama with gray jumbo box braids and lips that curl straight down into a pout. She is huddled on the couch, resting her head on its edge when she sees me. Mama's face erupts outward from her mouth, quivering around her tongue. Then her eyebrows twitch. Then Mama lets out a single shriek that sounds more like a gurgle and stands.

"Kiara," she shouts across the room. The sound gets lost somewhere in the muddle of the room's noise. I walk toward Mama until we are close enough to touch and then she pulls me into her arms and squeezes. For such a familiar voice, her arms could not feel like less of a home, the way the flesh cushions me. I don't remember Mama ever feeling this safe, like a barrier to the sound.

When the embrace ends, Mama drags me back to the couch and plops me into the green of it, right in between her and Miranda, who seems to sink into the cushions. Mama keeps hold of my hands and fiddles with my fingers, moving the tips of hers along the base of each of my nails. I can't help but look at her, just fixate my eyes on that face I've been trying to remember for so many years. Something is strange about it, like her skin has a purple tint beneath the surface, like she is glowing.

Mama don't even pause to really look at me. She's got things to say, always got things to say. "So happy to see my baby's face all grown up. How old you now, nineteen? Twenty? So grown. You know I looked just like you at that age, pretty and shit. Time really do fly, child, just like your grandma used to say. Where my Marcus? You tell him like I said you gotta tell him?"

I don't know how she keeps on talking, how she's got enough breath for that.

I blink a couple times and try to remember all the things she asked. "I'm seventeen, eighteen in a couple months. And yeah I told him, but I don't got control of him, so I don't think he's coming. Listen, I came down here 'cause I need Uncle Ty's number and I know you wanted Marcus too, but I'm what you got. Okay?" I'm still staring at her, at her cheeks, at the purple underneath.

Mama's smile doesn't waver and she goes on like I didn't say nothing at all. "I'm getting outta here soon. I'm comin' home, just a couple more months—year at the most—and I'll be cleared."

Mama home. The thought never even crossed my mind, her back in our apartment.

Miranda speaks for the first time. "Yeah, Chey got real lucky her parole officer likes her ass."

"That's nice, Mama. I really gotta get Uncle Ty's number though—"

"You know yo uncle always had a thing for me? Yo daddy didn't wanna see it, but that man sure did want me."

I shake my head, fuzzy from what could be heat or noise or the way Mama's voice seeps into every canal of my body. "No, you not listening, Mama, I—"

"Nah, don't you tell me I'm not listening, chile. All I ever done is listen to you. You ain't got no ground to stand on, baby. We talked about this when I first went in there—Mama made a mistake. When I was just trying to support you, feed that mouth. Don't mean I ain't still yo mama." Mama takes her thumb and pats my bottom lip.

I open my mouth again to talk, but Mama has stood, pulling me up with her and through the maze. As Mama leads me out of the room, my feet buzz in their shoes and I realize I might just be a little scared of my mother. As a child, I was never scared of Mama. She was a sacred figure and even when she was about to give us a spanking, I knew she'd rub our red skin after.

We head out into a hallway, up a stairwell, and into a room that must be hers because there are Prince posters lining the walls, and if there is one thing that could never change about my mama it would be her love for Prince. She used to break out into his songs on our Sunday morning walks to church and even though she'd go off on runs and belts that made them unrecognizable, I didn't want Mama to stop, wanted to worship her voice.

"You sit on the bed." Mama lets go of my hand and I stumble toward the twin-size bed, feet still buzzing. There are three other beds in the room, one in each corner, and each section of the room has been fingerprinted in portraits and photos and posters. It looks kind of like a child's bedroom, but I can tell Mama is proud. She stands at a dresser now, rummaging through drawers, finally pulling out a hairbrush and spray bottle full of something that isn't water.

"Remember Mama's special potion?"

I didn't. I do now, though, almost the moment she says it, memories of sitting on the floor, scalp bruises, Mama saying she's putting a spell on my head gonna make me so pretty. Or maybe I don't remember any of this because Mama is reciting these stories and memory is really just the things we trust to be ours and I guess I want this to be a story of Mama and me, so it is.

I expect Mama to come sit next to me on the bed and ask to brush my hair, but instead she sits on the ground right in front of my feet and hands me the brush and bottle.

"Got so many knots in there, thought you might wanna help me while we catch up." Mama leans her head down so her neck is visible.

Mama's neck is five different shades of brown and black and purple
and I can't tell whether it looks like she been beat up or like her body
is a whole galaxy.

Spraying her hair, I'm hit with the concoction's scent of lavender
and shea butter. When we were little, Mama would take us into the
shower with her and soap us up with soap she said she made, but
neither of us never saw her making it. Her soap smelled like a mix of
new shoes and forest.

When we got out of the shower, she'd rub her entire body in shea
butter that she bought from the West African shop down the street
and then she'd sit us in her lap one at a time, her naked, smooth
thighs a sweet comfort even in her boniness, and rub us down in it
too, so we were soft, shining babies. Sometimes we'd dance to Prince
or Mama would let us listen to Daddy's old CDs and we'd be nothing
but skin. We stopped all that after Daddy came home and I think
Marcus never let Mama close to him again, blamed her for Daddy's
return and his death, for Uncle Ty, for what she did. I blamed her too,
for some of it at least, but I also needed her. She was the only one
who knew what it felt like to watch Daddy dissolve from our lives,
and I didn't have an Uncle Ty to take me away. I only had Mama's
hums.

"Now how 'bout you tell Mama what's going on?" Her voice is so
smooth, lulls me back into all the lullabies she used to sing.

I sniff. "They raising our rent so high and I didn't have no choice,
so I been out on the streets and, I don't know, Mama, I'm just scared."

Mama reaches back and rubs my knee with her fingers. "And now
you want Mama to help you."

I can hear how hopeful this whole thing makes her, giddy to be
needed.

"Thought with Uncle Ty's number and everything, you might be
able to." My voice is so small now, it gets swallowed by the sound of
her breathing. Mama's hair still looks the same as it always did and,

watching each curl soak in potion, I don't understand how my mama could have done what she did and still kept her hair, kept her voice. "Why did you do it?"

"Do what, baby?"

"Fuck over our whole family."

Mama doesn't pause, says, "No point in losing sleep over something none of us can change. Like I said, was survival."

I pull the brush once through her hair, knowing how it's gonna hurt. Mama don't make a sound.

"We been trying to survive every day since then and I ain't been locked up."

"You call me when that changes. There are consequences to surviving out here, just 'cause you too young to know it yet don't mean I gotta apologize for the truth. I spent every day for years apologizing, praying up some heaven that might forgive me. I don't got no breath left for that."

Mama holds her hands up and I look at them from behind her hair, which is less kinky than both mine and Marcus's, and the creases in her hands are pale, with a trace of lavender, color that shouldn't exist in a palm.

Looking at Mama's hands, I remember a time when Alé was fourteen and I was thirteen and she decided that she was gonna learn how to read palms. She used my hands to practice, trying to distract me from Daddy's approaching death. She would point to the line running vertically up from my wrist and say, "See how it splits right there? Means you got two caminos de la vida, you know, ways shit might go down." Then she would look down at the palm-reading book from the library resting in her lap. "And you gotta make a choice someday."

Mama's line doesn't split like mine does. It veers left, toward her thumb, like it got sidetracked on the way up.

"I'm coming home. You hear that?" Mama's hand waves backward to pat my arm, shake me into getting it. "We gonna go back to normal."

I brush faster, move the bristles in and out of each individual lock and coil.

"I really just want you to give me Uncle Ty's number, Mama. Please."

Mama huffs. "You always wanting. Don't do nobody no good to want."

I think about the way Trevor chases a basketball, his feet bouncing on the court. How it always ends. How the ball always comes back down.

"You right, Mama," I say. Her hair, which is normally jumping up out of her roots, falls limp, matted. "You gonna give me Uncle Ty's number or not? 'Cause I ain't gonna sit around here waiting. Wanting don't do nobody no good, right?"

Mama don't even seem to register anything I'm saying. "Did I ever tell you about that time yo daddy brought me my favorite flowers?" The swarm of her voice is closing in on me, like poison dripping out her mouth, and she can't seem to ever look at me and tell me what I need to hear.

I don't know how she can talk about Daddy and not about the only thing that matters now, how when Daddy died, Soraya was already halfway to full-grown inside her. A late surprise in Mama's mid-forties. A last remnant of Daddy she ruined.

"Mama," I say. Her tongue keeps rolling.

"Anyway, they was the nicest flowers. Thinking I'll get some for the apartment once I get out of this place. Speaking of, I need you to do something for me, baby. Parole officer needs some letters of recommendation for my release. Seems like you could use Mama at home with you, helping out."

I close my eyes because this had to come at some point and Mama's mask peels eventually and here we are, her between my knees asking me to fix her up when I'm the one who came here to be held. Here we are, Mama asking me to wring myself dry of everything I got while she sits perfect, full.

I can't do it no more.

I try again, louder now. "Mama." She don't stop talking. This time, I let it thunder. "Mama." She pauses mid-sentence. "I knew coming here wasn't a good idea, but you really gonna ask me to get you out of this place when you can't even say Soraya's name? You don't never change."

Mama swallows, smacks her lips. "That happened a long time ago."

The smell of Mama's potion keeps me dizzy, but still talking, all of it swirling together. "Three years last week."

"No."

"She was my sister, Mama. I know when she died and it was February 16, 2012. That's three years from last Monday."

Mama's head is shaking. "No."

"Yes."

Her head shakes faster, hair flying out the roots.

I nod. "Marcus and I came home from school and the door to the apartment was open. Same apartment Daddy brought them flowers to." Her head is tilted up toward me and I look right at her, right into the pupil blown up so there ain't no other color in them. "We walked in and her crib was empty and we thought you wasn't home, thought you might've gone to the store, but then we went to the bathroom and there you was, in the tub, just staring at the ceiling, bleeding. And we was so scared, Mama."

I'm shaking now, earthquake in the body.

"And we kept asking you where Soraya was, but you wouldn't answer, so I left the room and started looking for her and I remembered the door was open, so I went outside and downstairs and I didn't see her at first, but then I heard Marcus scream from the balcony and I looked in the water and there she was. Floating.

"I dove in and scooped her out and held her, but she wouldn't wake up and her body was cold and she was so small, Mama. She was so small.

"I kept saying, 'Soraya,' and Marcus came down and saw her head hang to the side and he started hurling all over the ground and I called 911 and when they showed up, I was holding her still, just looking at her eyes and they was just like glass, didn't have no spirit and when they came in with their boots, they didn't even rush her to no hospital. They put that sheet over her and I kept saying her name 'cause they had to know her name but they didn't pay no mind to it and they asked where you was and Marcus told them in the tub and then they went and got you and they took you 'cause your wrists was bleeding and you told them how you thought you locked the door but you knew the lock was broken and you saw the sheet and you screamed, but you the one who did it. And you didn't look at us, didn't say nothing to us, and we was there, alone. Marcus just turned eighteen and they let us stay, but we didn't know how to do nothing and you was gone, Mama."

Mama's body seems to slip down to the floor both gradually and all at once, until she's suddenly sprawled across the carpet, her hair still dripping.

After that, Uncle Ty paid Mama's bail and we thought we'd all recover, but she didn't even come home. She went out partying until she got picked up again and we still went to her trial. We still testified for her, so she would get off on negligence and end up out here in a halfway house after a couple years instead of locked up for the rest of her life.

My teeth are chattering now and I gotta take a minute to slow down the words so she can hear them, really hear them.

I set my feet on the floor, lean down so my face is at her level, right at her ear. "We done kept ourselves alive. Without you. So now I come here asking for one thing—one thing, Mama—and you don't even give enough of a shit to remember the day you killed her? Bet you wouldn't give two fucks if I died too, huh? What about Marcus? That why you ain't helping?"

I curl my lips, every word a deep cut. "So you know what, Mama? You sit there and you say her name. You say, 'I killed Soraya three years ago from Monday.' You say that and then you can have your fucking letter and I'll get on up and go home 'cause Lord knows you ain't gonna help me. Do you even have Uncle Ty's number?"

She's still in the same position, shakes her head once, all that hair and color, rumbling. Mama lifts her head up, stares right at me. Her eyes are gushing and, I swear, her tears come out violet.

"She died three years ago." Mama's voice isn't the same, has shifted into a guttural grind.

I crouch on the floor next to her. "No. 'I killed Soraya three years ago from Monday.'"

Mama's face cracks into shards, watering, eyes big and pooling. "I killed her three—"

"Her name, Mama. Say her name. Your name mean more than anything." I've got tears to match, voice gone from thunder to blade.

She nods, one swift movement of the head, opens her mouth. "I killed Soraya three years ago from Monday."

At the end of her sentence, Mama lets out a sob straight from her gut and I don't even flinch. I stand, not bothering to retrieve Mama from the ground, and the moment I shut the door, I hear the muffled sounds of her singing "Pink Cashmere," then wailing.

STRUT, FLY, GALLOP. There are so many ways to walk a street, but none of them will make you bulletproof. I got back from Mama's and found myself stuck between street and gutter, Trevor knocking on the door early Sunday morning saying Vern been by again telling them they out if they don't pay in three days. I know my knock isn't far off. I gave Vernon every dime I got after Davon and the others, but it's not nearly enough to make up for Dee's rent debt or mine, and it doesn't come close to the way they're raising it after the sale. It was Trevor's face staring up at me this morning that did it. Pulled me right out of the pit Mama made of me.

I have a body and a family that needs me, so I resigned to what I have to do to keep us whole, back on this blue street. I'm tilted, half walking, half stumbling. All up and down International: no music, no Tony, just me and a stomach full of tequila.

I'm shuffling and skipping and trying to warm hands in a sky that only breeds cold and real quick my heel snaps off the sole of shoes I stole from the Salvation Army and sidewalk meets cheek. Stings. Glass inside the cut. Blood spill. Blood clot. Voice.

"Lemme help you, mama." He reaches down, pulling me up.

His eyes are rimmed in gray like he is aging only in the iris and his hand, too smooth, picks glass out of my cheek and throws it away. He doesn't ask me shit about whether or not I'm okay, but I don't expect him to. I don't expect much of anything. He asks me to hand him the intact shoe and I do, watching him break the heel off and throw it. It tumbles into the street right as a car speeds through, crushing it into pieces of persona. I am four inches less of a woman. He is so tall.

The man gives me back my other shoe and I slip it on. He's towering over me, his mouth showing a grill that is some kind of trophy color, but it isn't gold.

"Thanks," I tell him, the cut in my cheek beginning to itch the way cuts do when they are trying to remember how to heal.

He nods. "Now that I helped you out, can I have some of your time?" He asks this like it is a question, like he isn't still holding on to one of my hands. I look down and see traces of my blood on his finger.

"Yeah." This is what my lips say. This is what my breath says.

He doesn't tell me his name and, for some reason, I don't think to ask. I just follow him, let him lead me like a child in a foreign place. He waits until we are on Thirty-Fourth, closer to Foothill Boulevard than International, and then leans me against a building. It's cold out and I thought he was leading me to a car, but sometimes the body has no shelter for its animal and here we are, here he is, outside. He pushes me against the brick. He doesn't kiss me and part of me is relieved to not taste whatever metal makes up his mouth, but part of me wants a reason to believe this stranger might care about my scabbing.

I try to get out from under him, telling him I don't do it like this, that I need money up front, that I need a house or a car. He pushes me back, continues, unbuckles his belt, running his hands under my skirt, pressing into me. He pins my arms to the side and with a shove, the back of my skull digs into a protruding brick. I can feel every crack in the brick as easily as I can feel every crack in my skull. I squirm, mumbling that my head hurts. He continues to push. He continues to grunt. My body says what my breath does not. He is so tall. The soles of my feet are blistering. My cheek stings, skull sharp pain. He pushes. He pushes. He is all metal.

Siren.

It isn't that the car startles me, but it is loud. That echo-in-an-empty-room loud and if you could call a street empty, this would be it. St. Catherine's Church stands to my left: the statue of her standing witness to the car, to the man, to the metal.

The passenger-side door of the cop car swings open, and a man steps out belt first. If this ain't every horror movie come to life. Us, street, too many fractures to be afraid and still my breath is a shallow squeal. If this ain't my daddy's worst nightmare.

"Stand back." Cop puts hand to gun and I'm lucky the metal man believes in a trigger because he steps back, lets me remove my skull from the brick's dagger. Everything is still spinning.

Cop approaches metal man like he himself is weapon and, in one swift movement, metal man has his hands clasped behind his back by Cop's fist and Cop's mouth spits right into metal man's ear.

"I don't wanna see you around here again, you hear?"

Cop's hair is thick and dark. He is nothing unusual, just a uniform and a mannequin.

Metal man spits right out his grill, nods once. Cop pushes him, makes him stumble into a run back to where the light is. I watch him, think about how he fixed my shoe, think about how small I am.

It is me and Cop and car now. Ain't it funny to be so scared of being saved? Cop approaches me, still has his hand on the gun.

"What are you doing out here? You know it's late."

I think about responding but I can feel a pool of blood in the back of my head and my hair will probably be crusted red tomorrow and there is no answer to something that is not a question.

"You know prostitution is a misdemeanor." He smirks, licks his lips. "We're gonna have to take you in, for your own good."

The mannequin is saying things and Saint Catherine must be responding because I am not, I am silent, I am two funeral days past forgetting.

Cop comes up and grabs my arm, fits his fingers into the bruises metal man's imprints made on my body. Catherine's statue waves to me with a missing nail as Cop drags me into the backseat and climbs in after. Another officer sits in the front seat and Cop says something to him about keeping the streets safe before laughing, and the driving man is tapping his fingers on something I can't see and singing country music real soft to himself and Cop is on me, Cop is digging at my flesh and ain't this everything they said it would be and ain't I so sad to be familiar. Ain't this just another night.

So many ways to walk a street and I am still just girl with skin.

Hotel rooms taste like chalk. The air filling up in decades of sweat and semen, smoke gathering from where one of the men is lighting up by the window, all of us assembled at the table, one of their hands on each of my thighs. When they brought out the deck of cards, the men placed their badges in front of them, like plaques with their names engraved, marking their territory. They just finished playing Texas Hold'em, and the winner of each round won the two spots beside me. Now they're onto blackjack and Officer 220's fingers are climbing up toward my shorts; 81 has his hand closer to my knee than my thigh, trying not to look at me.

I've never wanted to reverse a decision more than I want to right now. Say no when Cop from the alley asked for my number, when he asked to give my number to a few of his friends, when those friends invited me to their cars, when I got in them. Last week they told me they wanted me to be their entertainment at this party. They told me they needed me, that I would be compensated for this post-work relief session with ten OPD cops and no escape, and I wish I had said anything but okay.

What choice did I have, though. The officers say they ain't gonna hurt me, that they'll pay me and, at least half the time, they do. Their guns and tasers have a bigger presence in this room than their bodies and even when I try to say no, they just laugh. They like that I'm young, that I don't know what I'm doing, and I keep on telling myself it's only for a while, that they'll let me stop when I want to. Except I know they care more about their badges than me, that I am nothing more than a reward in their game.

The cops got a suite in a run-down motel everyone calls the Whore Hotel off the freeway. The king bed looms on the other side of the room from our table. It's probably close to midnight now and they're all wasted, getting sloppier with their eye contact and where they let their gaze go. I know it's gonna happen soon.

The difference between the cops and street men is that the cops like to make it a game. They wait to fuck me, instead watching me, salivating, trying to figure out how to make me just scared enough that the fear swallows me and leaves a body worth getting on top of, hands to clasp behind my head, fear to lick away. Most of them are like that and then there are a few like 81, with his neatly trimmed beard and shy smile, or 612 across from me, with the red curls and eyes that linger on the table. Not that they won't find the thing in them that wants to lie on top of me and shove a finger or two in my mouth. It's reliable work, though, and it's done more for us in the past week than my job at Bottle Caps has in the past year. I've already made enough to pay Vernon half of what I owe so he won't evict us.

It's 220's turn and he's got a jack of spades and a facedown card in front of him. He squeezes my thigh and slams his palm on the table.

"Hit me."

The dealer flips a card over in front of him: a six of hearts. He's three points away from winning me, six points away from losing it all. The game's been going for a few rounds and there's gotta be at least three grand in the pile. Three of them have already folded and they're all watching as 220 jitters, preparing himself to turn over the last card.

He leans closer to me and whispers in my ear, "You think you're my good luck charm, darling?" 220 flips it over and a three of diamonds sits on the table, his arms raising as he shouts, "It's mine, motherfuckers," and pulls the cash toward him.

The other men cuss and slip their hands in their pockets as 220 rises, grabbing my hand so I'm pulled up with him.

"Don't mind if I take my prize." His hair hangs limply, swinging as he nods at each man, who forget their losses and holler, their eyes lingering as he leads me to the bed, undresses me so the calluses on his fingertips meet bare skin.

He pushes me onto the mattress and reaches down for his belt and I think he's gonna take it off until he goes straight to his holster and unleashes his handgun. Black metal so sleek I can see his fingerprints all over it. He unzips his pants but doesn't remove them, climbing onto the bed so he's hovering over me. 220 glances behind him at the rest of them and smiles, refocuses on me to place the mouth of his gun to my temple.

"You like that?" His voice is a growl.

I feel the tears find their way to my eyes and I want him off me. I find somewhere inside me that still believes in a god and I am praying for an ending. He's on top of me, his penis inside me, his hands all rough and the barrel of the gun cold and threatening above my eye, where I can only feel it, only hear his grunts and the snickers from the men behind him. I pray that it will end, that I will stop all of this and go back to being broke, to begging Marcus to find a job. Anything for the gun to go back in its holster.

I can tell that part of what he likes is knowing the others are watching. Ones like 81 and 612 avert their eyes at first, but eventually they all stare, waiting to see what 220 will do next. The only thing worse than them watching is when they get bored, start chatting about the upcoming championship game or whose wife won't get off their ass about the dishes. 220 still has his gun pointing at my head while he thrusts and none of them even seem to notice, listening to my body wilting just a few feet away.

They take turns and sex feels no different from an insistent punch to my gut. The cops believe they are invincible. They want me only to show themselves they can have me, that there will be no consequence to putting a gun to my head, to taking me. They want me to feel small so they can feel big and, in this moment, they have succeeded.

After they've all had a turn, they don't even let me catch my breath. One of them throws my clothes at me while another pulls some cash out of his pocket, not even giving me enough time to count it before they're shoving me through the motel door and leaving me to walk home, feeling more naked than I did lying in that bed. That's when I count the bills, when I realize they paid me less than a fraction of what 220 made tonight, and I can't do nothing about it. Even if I tried to fight them, these are not the men who would care. These are the men who load their guns and point them with a grin, who find a girl in an alley and decide she is theirs.

.   .

The cops continue to call me, asking me to go to one thing or another, and there is a jerk in the socket above my stomach, a repulsion that has me tasting bile, but I take my thumb and make circles on my abdomen, gulp down a drink to wash the taste away, and find a way to say yes. It reminds me of our yearly decision about whether or not we're gonna pay our taxes, how I sit down with whatever pay stubs Marcus or I got and I stare at those numbers and the pure desire to get away boils up and I have to swallow it and make a choice because if I pay those taxes, then I forgo rent or new shoes or bus money. Even when I know the IRS could come after me, I would rather have a well of fear in my stomach from some unsigned documents than no way to survive the tax month. So most of the time I don't pay the taxes and most of the time when the cops call, I agree to join them, despite the disgust and the shame and the undeniable urge to run away.

The parties always take place at night, a revolving door of badges and men who take turns and then hand me envelopes full of their protection. Usually there are a few other girls or women, different rooms they keep us in so we don't get to talk to each other. Sometimes they don't even pay me, say they're keeping me safe from the next raid. Tell me about the stings, the next time all the uniforms unleash themselves, like it's gonna pay for breakfast, for Trevor's rent and mine. Like it's gonna make what I'm doing feel like anything but dirt shoved beneath fingernails, something I can't figure out how to get out of.

I was able to give Vernon enough for him to not evict Dee either, told Trevor to hand Vernon my envelope of cash next time he came knocking, but April is approaching and more and more of them are trading some kind of protection for my body, saying I don't need their cash when it is all I need.

This my job, my roof, the clothes on Trevor's back. This every night now, a full ring of them, my own clan of men, and I don't worry so much about not having enough to pay for hot water. Instead, I worry about bruises and guns and what Marcus thinks. Stopped telling myself it's just sex, just skin, because it has become so much more than that; there is the sex and then there is the terror, the fear, the marble white of their eyes.

Once I paid March's rent, I bought Trevor a new ball, the ones that are so fancy they paint them black. Gave me a little hope back when he sprung right off the soles of his shoes and it looked like he might've just been happy enough to dunk his whole body back into the shit pool. His smile makes it easier to tell myself it's worth it when I hear a siren and a new part of my body knots; a whole rope wrapping around each of my ribs, like my bones preparing to be broken. Lately, the only way I can get through a night with the men is by taking shots and trying to sink into the dizziness of it, so I don't see what they're doing, so my body doesn't know what's going on enough to fear it. I don't know if it works, but I know that when I wake up the next morning, I'm still alive and Trevor is still waiting for me to walk him to the bus stop and, at this point, that's enough.

Tony keeps trying to apologize for his brooding and talk me out of doing what I'm doing, like I have that much of a choice. Funeral day would be a reminder of the bloodstains in the backseat of all their cars, when they're just a little too rough, and I can't handle standing next to Alé in a funeral home I know I am edging closer to never leaving. Alé can't make me remember what it was like before the statues started moving, before I was the girl who wore a man's skin and not just his clothes.

On the days when none of the uniformed men call, during the stretches of time when I start to think I am free, eating a meal that doesn't send me right back into the nausea, I start planning a way to live without cops or sex, maybe returning to Bottle Caps and begging Ruth to give me just a couple hours of work.

This is one of those days. Actually, it's the seventh day they haven't called and I don't have any more money in reserve. My insides are starting to slosh again and I know I gotta find a way to make more money, cops or not. Today, I swing by La Casa Taquería on the way to Bottle Caps. It's not quite lunchtime yet and the place is sprinkled with folks. I spot Alé at a table taking an order and when she looks up and sees me, I catch the way her eyes widen. I stick my hands in the pockets of Daddy's old corduroy jacket, the only one that Uncle Ty didn't take with him, and walk up to Alé.

She finishes the order and takes me into her arms. "Hey," she whispers in my ear, mid-hug, and it's so simple, but there's something about it that warms me up.

"Hey." I haven't seen Alé since the first cop found me and I don't know how to stand in front of her like this without feeling like I've got a layer of shame on me, like when she looks at me she can't possibly see anything but their handprints.

"What you doing here? Been a minute."

I nod.

"On my way to Bottle Caps and thought you might wanna walk with me?"

She looks at the floor, smiling, then back up at me. "Yeah, okay." She begins to nod, glancing around the room and flagging down one of her aunts to tell them she's heading out. "Lemme grab my board," she says to me, squeezing my arm.

Alé comes racing back down the stairs a couple minutes later, her forehead glowing and damp. "Let's go," she says, following me out.

Alé loops her arm around my shoulders and pulls me in, lifting her skateboard into the air and sighing. "Ain't it beautiful?" she shouts into the open air, and I twist my head around to take it all in. The construction still lines the alley, bang-banging wood into more wood, and I swear it's like the city is spiraling around us, skyline popping up a glorious portrait of windows and wheels that don't gotta be as large as they are. Alé's arm around me makes me wanna skip, lift my knees to the sky, the way we sway together.

Oakland doesn't operate on a grid. We wind here. The streets pulling us closer to the bay, to where salt melts with street, and bikes turn to trucks that moan and thrust forward at every light. Then they push us back toward the buildings, where shouts line the perimeter of the sidewalks and, with Alé here, I don't bother trying to decipher what they're saying or who they're saying it to. Just let the noises scatter, like chunks of asphalt out the road. I find my favorite murals, new swirls added to the backgrounds, bordered in tags.

"I been missing you," Alé says.

"Yeah, me too. Been busy."

She looks at me and I can see the worry welling up, but she doesn't push. She never pushes.

"While you work, I'm gonna skate for a minute," Alé says, gripping her skateboard to the other side of her body, but still holding on to my shoulders as we approach the corner of MacArthur and Eighty-Eighth, right around Castlemont High. Bottle Caps is painted bright orange like a life jacket or the way the sun looks in a dream.

Alé releases me from her arm and waves to me, heading off to the skate park the Castlemont kids use across the street. Alé graduated from Castlemont. That brought us this far east when the rest of us were up at Skyline for school. Marcus took me to the skate park a couple times when he was in middle school and the minute I saw Alé, this girl whipping in and out of slopes and then taking my brother in for a handshake and a pat on the back, I wanted to know her, know her real deep.

Back when I was still in high school, we all used to come out to Bottle Caps after school, gather around in front of the store after buying a pack of sodas or some chips. We'd bring a speaker and start the music going, and Ruth wouldn't mind having us out there 'cause we never did nothing wrong. We was just living. Ruth even gave us discounts sometimes and, one time, when Lacy's younger sister fell and split her chin open on the concrete, Ruth closed down Bottle Caps to take her to the hospital so her mama wouldn't have to pay for the ambulance bill.

I open the door to Bottle Caps and I'm met with that familiar ding-dong beep that every liquor store makes upon entry. I head straight for the counter, where this man is looking up at the mini-television hanging on the wall. Cartoons are on, *South Park,* I think, and the man is laughing so hard his locs are bouncing.

"Hey," I say, calling his attention to me.

He seems irritated to pull his eyes away from the screen. "You buyin' something?"

"I'm looking for Ruth," I tell him, and the moment I say her name, I know something ain't right. His lips separate but no sound comes out.

"Um," he starts. "She ain't around no more."

"What you mean?"

"Ruth died last week."

It's not that I didn't know the moment his face pulled downward, but hearing it always hits a little different, digs a little pit somewhere in the body to bury her in. "What she die of?" I ask.

"Does it matter?"

He turns the volume up on the TV, but I don't move.

"You gonna buy something or not?" He clearly wants me to get the fuck out, but all I can seem to think is *How the hell am I gonna pay the bills?* Maybe that's a shitty thing to be thinking when this woman who gave me a steady gig when I had nothing else is suddenly gone, but it's the truth.

"I used to work here," I tell him, and he raises his eyebrows like he doesn't believe me or maybe just like he don't give a shit. "Ruth been giving me a shift when I need one."

"Well, Ruth don't own the place no more. And we can't afford to be paying no one extra. Sorry." He turns the volume up so it's blasting so loud I don't think he'd be able to hear me even if he tried. I pat the counter with my palm and retreat back out the door, back into the light.

Feels like I'm flushed with memories, like every cell in my body switched on and won't stop moving. Trevor bouncing that ball. Our swimming pool. Mornings sitting at the counter shoveling cereal into our faces. Breathing. All of it so temporary that it feels like I'm edging closer to some future nowhere place, where I don't even exist in this body. Without Bottle Caps, without cops, without Marcus, what choices do I have? I wander toward the skate park, but my body doesn't even seem to be following where I tell it to go. My feet sway, zigzag toward the sound of wheels to concrete.

When I make it, Alé is in the air, returning back to the slope, doing it again; her hand gripping the front of the board as her torso twists before she comes down. I sit on the edge of the slope, feet hanging, and she slides backward on the board when she sees me, flying off onto her back and skidding. She groans at the bottom and stands, shaking her arms out before climbing back up to me.

When Alé started high school and I was in eighth grade, she began dating a girl with this violently blond hair, the kind of blond that didn't match her skin or her face and just made her look majestic, in this artificial kind of way I couldn't understand. The girl and I would sit together on the edge of the slopes watching Alé and I remember trying to stare harder, make my gaze so concrete and powerful that Alé would know I saw her more than her girlfriend ever could. After a couple months, the blond girl stopped coming around and when I asked Alé why they broke up, she just shrugged.

Alé places her skateboard down on the concrete and sits beside me, dangling her legs into the slope.

"You scared me," she says. "What's up? Why you ain't working?"

"Ruth's dead," I say. Seems wrong to complicate it with any extra words, to make death more than it is. I picture Ruth's photo etched into cardboard in the lobby of some funeral home, her body coated in powder, but cold. The scent of cheese nobody wanna eat.

Alé looks out at the skaters and then back at me. "Shit."

"Yeah."

"You okay?"

"No."

"She knew you loved her."

Alé pulls me into her, but I shake my head and move back out of the side hug. I wish I could tell Alé how fucked this whole thing is, how I'm sitting here thinking about money when this woman's dead, when Alé just wants to hold me.

We sit like this, not touching, for a while. Watching the couple other skaters out here flipping and falling, rubbing their shoulders, and beginning again.

We're facing the street, close enough to see everyone slinking by, but the faces are hard to distinguish from a distance. That's why, when I see her, I try to convince myself it ain't her. That someone else is out here walking in that blue, sparkling like her, hair adorned in what looks like the hottest part of the fire. But, as she comes closer, her face solidifies, and I know it's her. Camila walking toward me, seeing me, lifting her hand up in the air, shouting the only name she knows me by. Kia. The slope stands between us, and Camila takes these giant heeled steps all the way around its perimeter until she's standing above Alé and me.

"You gonna stand up and give me a hug, girl?" Camila reaches her hands down to help pull me up and I take them, but she doesn't put any effort into pulling me, just stands there, so I lift myself up. She wraps her arms around me loosely, careful not to mess up her eye shadow on my cheek, and then releases. She cups her talon hands around my face and takes a thorough survey of me, like she's looking for scars. "How you doing?"

Her hands on my face make it difficult to speak, but I try anyway, my words getting swallowed. I'm acutely aware of Alé sitting and watching us, staring right at my back. "Good, you know."

"Uh-uh, don't you try to fool me." Camila clicks her tongue at me. "Tell me what really going on behind that pretty little face."

Part of me wonders if Camila knows about the cops, if she's been at their parties too, but it still feels like a secret I'm not supposed to tell, so I give her an answer close enough to the truth to satisfy her, one that won't give much away to Alé. "Ain't been getting much work lately, that's all."

"I told you, honey, you need you a daddy. Listen, I been telling my man about you and he's interested. Name's Demond. He's throwing a party next weekend and he wants to meet you, get you set up so you don't gotta be out here worrying about nothing. How that sound?"

"I don't know—"

"Oh, c'mon, Kia, just come to the party. Next Saturday night, 120 Thirty-Eighth Avenue."

"I—"

Camila lets go of my face and waves her fingers. "I ain't hearing it. I'll see you next weekend." And, just like that, Camila has twirled back around and is walking the outline of the slope like she owns it, back to the street, fading into a blue form that could be her or could be fire or something in between.

I stand still, facing the empty space that used to be Camila, and I know Alé's teeth are grinding, her jaw locked. I can almost feel it boiling in her: all the questions, her eyes on my back. Maybe, if I'm still for long enough, I will fade into the sky and she will forget I ever existed, that I ever walked into La Casa Taquería today. Maybe she'll forget how she fell from that board at the sight of me, how she skidded onto her back, how she'll ache tomorrow morning.

I shut my eyes and still don't disappear. A couple minutes pass and she speaks.

"Guess I shoulda known you got into some shit." Her voice comes straight from the throat, like she's holding so much more that she's not letting out.

I turn around and look down at her.

"Were you gonna tell me?" she asks, her jaw moving side to side now, like if she moves it enough it will release all the hurt that I can see coming up out of her.

"I don't know," I tell her, and I really don't. Telling her would have been like saying this is my life now, like committing to the streets. Letting the streets have you is like planning your own funeral. I wanted the streetlight brights, the money in the morning, not the back alleys. Not the sirens. But, here we are. Streets always find you in the daylight, when you least expect them to. Night crawling up to me when the sun's out.

"I just don't get it, Ki. You know what happened with Clara, so why you being so stupid?" She shakes her head, looks out at the two boys still trying to do some trick on the railing across the slope from us. "Why you doin' this?"

"Don't got no other choice," I say.

"Nah." Alé's head shake increases until it's a full swing and she gets up, grabbing her skateboard, her whole body shaking. She stands in front of me now and says, "Nah," one more time with her body tremors before setting her board down on the cement, climbing on, pushing forward again and again until she's halfway down the block and I'm standing above a skate park slope with nowhere left to go.

I STARTED WALKING HOME from the skate park after a group of teenage boys showed up with their boards and hollered at me. It's different walking in the city midday alone. Makes me feel like I have to sprout eyes in every direction and learn how to walk with more leg, less hip. I end up on a bus after a couple blocks and now I'm being dropped off right by the Regal-Hi, which is an off-putting color at this time of day, so close to white I'm not sure if I've been tricking myself into thinking it was blue this whole time.

Almost immediately after I get inside the apartment, my phone starts ringing. I pull it out of my pocket as quick as I can, thinking maybe it's Alé. Instead, the phone flashes SHAUNA and I pick up, even though every cell of my body says not to.

"Kiara." Her voice sounds tired, and I can't tell if it's that new-mother kind of fatigue or if there's something else mixed in with it.

"Yeah?"

"I don't know what shit they on, but last week they showed up with new equipment and now Cole talking about some type of deal and how they real close to making it and I don't know, girl, I don't want no life like that."

"What you talking about?"

"I don't know what's going on, but they getting themselves into some shit and I don't think this the kind they can get out of. You gotta help me out." Shauna's voice escalates in pitch.

I sigh. I know what getting caught up in the streets can do to you, but I don't know how to get out of it, how to help no one, especially Marcus. "Look, I don't know what I can do about none of that." I tell her I gotta go, that somebody's at the door even though they're not, and I hang up when she's mid-sentence, the whole apartment going silent.

We're always trying to own men we don't got no control of. I'm tired of it. Tired of having to be out here thinking about all these people, all these things to keep me alive, keep them alive. I don't got no air left for none of it. Maybe Camila's right, maybe it's time to let go, to let one of them take over, take care of me. But I can't stop thinking about Shauna's call, if Marcus is alright, if maybe he's got enough money to help us out. Part of me is still angry at him for not coming to see Mama with me, but with Alé not speaking to me, I need him.

It's two p.m. now and even though it's only early spring, the heat has found its way to us, an unexpected warm day among the cold. It's still afternoon when the door to the apartment swings open and Marcus steps through, turning to look at me with the most glorious smile on his face, my fingerprint scrunched beneath the grin. Marcus comes right up to me and picks me up from the waist, does a spin. Coming down, I'm dizzy, don't remember the last time he spun me like that, like I'm his little sister and we might still be young.

"What you do that for?" I laugh, swatting at his chest. He seems taller today.

Those eyes stare at me and they got the smile in them too, lit up.

"I been missing my lil sis, what you talkin' bout?" He looks like he might just pick me up again. "I got something to show you."

In seconds, Marcus has taken my hand, grabbed a backpack and his skateboard from the closet, and is leading us back out the door.

Marcus pulls my wrist a little harder and it almost feels like I'm imagining it. He seems to have forgotten all the shit that's built up between us in the past couple months. And I guess since he ain't really been home much, maybe he hasn't seen me scramble to fill the envelope with next month's rent or felt the way the chlorine and feces have become part of the air, the natural scent of the apartment. I wonder if he knows where I've been, what I've done.

I grab my scraper bike, the one Marcus and I made out of duct tape and junkyard scraps, from its spot on the rack by the pool. We ride them proud all over East Oakland, our wheels neon and brighter than the sky. I mount my bike and follow him out onto the road. Marcus winds us through streets I don't remember being on before, which is funny because I swear I've walked every inch of this city. Maybe I never looked up. Maybe I've been too busy searching.

I call out to him, "Where the hell you taking me, Marcus?"

"Don't worry about it, we almost there."

Maybe this is how he's gonna tell me he's got some extra cash for us, even if Shauna's right and he been doing something he shouldn't to get it. Street money's still money. I can hear the cars on the freeway now and we're still in East, so 880 must be close, but I don't see it yet. Sometimes you can hear things, feel things, that will never manifest in sight. That is Mama's voice in my head: an unseen thing.

Under an overpass, Marcus stops abruptly. It is so unexpected that I almost lose control of the pedals and run into him. I skid, brake, hop off. It's dark under the overpass and entirely empty except for two tents, a mini city. This is where we'll be soon if Marcus don't help me; sleeping in tents, my hips leaving me gaping when no zipper can keep me safe. Not even Marcus's ego could salvage my body from the coldest nights out here in the tents, and nothing could hide us during fire season, when the smoke catches up to us.

"What we doing here?" I ask Marcus, leaning my bike on the wall.

He doesn't respond. Marcus removes his backpack, crouches

down, and unzips it. Inside are cans and cans of spray paint, that expensive kind that sometimes we rack from Home Depot when we're feeling real invincible. He starts to line them up on the ground: a whole rainbow.

"Where you get these?"

"Don't worry about it. Look, I got you a lil present and I'll even be your assistant. You got a whole wall. Go crazy with it. You tell me what to paint and I'll paint it. This your day, Ki." Marcus stares up at me, beaming from his crouch.

Part of me wonders if I should object, if I should question him, but instead, I smile back at him, grab the green paint first, and tell Marcus to start with the yellow. I begin the outline, directing him. Marcus never does anything I say, but today he traces my lines and follows me. Today he is my brother.

When I paint, I close my eyes. Marcus and Alé both laugh when I do this. They think you gotta see to paint, but sight is just a distraction from what it really takes to translate image to art. I let it float out my fingers, escape out my breath, and I don't need to see when my body is an entire vision.

I've been tagging since I was thirteen. Back then I wouldn't have even called it tagging because I just had some Sharpies and a will to have my name on every block. Then, Alé bought me a can of blue spray paint for my fourteenth birthday and I spent a month going wild with it before I shook it one day and it was empty. It became a tradition; a new color for every birthday since.

Marcus was the one who took me on bike rides and told me that there really ain't no difference between the murals and swirling tags we'd pass, that art is the way we imprint ourselves onto the world so there is no way to erase us. He says that's what his lyrics are for.

When I was fifteen, in the first months when it was just the two of us, we'd bike to pick up the cheapest groceries, shove them into backpacks, and bring them back to the apartment. I'd always be the one to cook, if we bought anything worth cooking. Marcus would take his Skittles to the couch.

One day, about a month into belonging to Marcus, he decided that we were gonna have to be innovative if we wanted to make enough to afford the Farmer Joe's type of groceries and not the Grocery Outlet type of groceries. He decided we'd start selling our art. He hadn't met Cole yet, so he didn't have a way to record his music, which meant that I would be the one to start us out by painting cardboard with paint we picked up for a dollar per tube at the East Bay Depot for Creative Reuse. It's the only reason we ever bothered riding into Temescal, a neighborhood that boasts its pistachio ice cream like they aren't settling the land and calling it entrepreneurship.

I started coming home from school and finding Marcus sitting in our spot on the carpet with my cardboard and secondhand paint spread out in front of him, ready to hand me a brush. It was the best thing Marcus could've done for me, giving me the colors. Sometimes I even dared to think I could be more than his sister, could be the kind of artist who had a frame for her art.

We started taking my paintings out on the weekends, offering them at twenty bucks each. Marcus said this was the going rate, but nobody was buying them. Weekend after weekend, we stood exposed in the sun, bartering the price down until finally a couple old women took pity on us and bought a few paintings at five dollars each. I apologized to Marcus and he kept saying it was fine even though I knew it wasn't. He spent a couple nights at Lacy's and came back with a tight smile. I haven't really painted since then, not more than a swirling tag on a bus stop or portraits of Alé with my birthday paint.

I raise the green up to the wall, far enough away I can see it spray through the air for that millisecond before it makes contact with the cement. It sounds like the ocean if it was manufactured, if we could control a wave. Holding it, the metal can starting to boil in this early spring heat flash, I have never felt more like I belonged somewhere.

I paint my recurring dream: the one where I'm in the meadow, where everything's ripe and it's like every cell in each blade of grass has come alive. I tell Marcus to paint the flowers: yellow, petals on petals on petals until you cannot separate one from the other.

On top of the grass, inside of the grass, really, I start to paint the girl. I shake my can and hold it to the wall, then think again. I switch the can to my other hand, getting closer to the wall, and trace the outline of the girl who is me and isn't. This girl is younger and her mouth is open, wide open.

I tell Marcus to paint the girl a yellow dress too. I want her to look like she's melting into the flowers. My closet is void of anything this kind of vibrant, but my dream tells me that this is the color I will be buried in, mouth gaping. My hands are a mess of green and brown and yellow and now I add blue, moving the can farther from the wall. I'm not tall enough to reach as far up as I need to, but Marcus lifts me from the legs so I am taller than even he is, making sky on an overpass wall.

Behind us, one of the tents unzips. Marcus puts me down at the sound and we turn to two young women climbing out of their shelter. I stand with my hands up, paint as blood.

"What you doin' out there?" one of them asks, and I realize the cloth draped across her body is a sling and not a scarf. A small child whines softly.

"Ain't mean no harm. We just painting," Marcus calls out, putting his stained hands out in front of him. We always showing people our hands like it's proof we're human.

The other woman's eyes squint and I don't know if that's directed at us or if the sun's just too bright. "You finish that and don't come around here no more, waking the baby up and shit."

Marcus and I mumble apologies and turn back to the wall. It feels sort of tainted now, us invading a space that isn't ours.

"C'mon, let's finish," Marcus says to me in a half whisper.

He lifts me up again and I fill in the rest so that the wall is a whole sky. Marcus takes my body back to ground and I catch the eyes of the mother sitting in the tent. She's smiling, faint, but smiling as she zips the tent back up and disappears.

"Yo, Ki, it cool if I add something?" Marcus brings my attention back to the wall. He's standing, staring at it.

I nod and he grabs a can of black and reaches his arm all the way up to the sky. He draws a single music note. Then moves his hand lower and adds another. And another. Marcus paints a sequence of music all the way down to the girl's mouth so that there is a treble clef hanging on to her lip. It looks like it's about to trickle down her throat and the wall is the only thing keeping it in place.

"Yeah?" Marcus turns around, eyebrows raised, his face on pause, and I can't help but think he looks a little like Daddy.

I nod. "It's beautiful," I say, and that is the most honest thing I have told Marcus since Mama left.

Marcus and I stand back together and look at the mural.

I think maybe today is the day I've been waiting for. The day when Marcus decides he will straighten his spine and learn how to hold up a little of this life again. The day he'll put his head in my lap and let me cradle him. He might even hold my hand or ask me why there are bruises tracing my chest. Some days it feels like I'm stuck between mother and child. Some days it feels like I'm nowhere.

I've got something to say to him. I promised myself I would and I don't remember most things Mama taught us, but she always said we stick to our word. Not just Mama. This whole city knows the one thing you don't do is break a promise. Just like you don't take the last piece of chicken without asking every person old enough to be your mama if they want it first. Maybe it's southern manners that traveled. Maybe it's Oakland etiquette. Maybe it's just learning from our mistakes.

If Marcus could just be with me, on my side for real and not just in words, I might be able to get out of this mess with all of us intact enough to love right. I open my mouth to speak, but heat finds its way down my throat until the last thing I want to do is make a sound. I swallow.

"Mars."

"You ain't called me that in a while."

My voice comes out soft enough to be called a whisper. "Ain't been around for me to call you much of anything."

He sighs, tilts his head away from the mural to look at me. "Neither have you."

I stare at him, watch those eyes stare back when normally they look away. I turn to the wall. He doesn't say anything for a while and neither do I.

"Where you been, Ki?"

I've been waiting so long for him to ask me. Ask me what I need. Tell me he's ready to help me.

"Streets." I respond. The sky in the mural is void of anything but music notes and blue and it seems like there's no end to the blue, like blue is falling from the sky with the music, coming in closer. "Didn't know where else to go."

I see Marcus shake his head from the corner of my eye. "So you thought you'd go around fucking random guys like some whore? Tony told me, but I didn't wanna believe none of that. Fuck, Kiara."

"You don't got no right to judge me. I been out there for *you*, because you over here living a fucking fantasy. You told me one month for the album and I gave you it. Actually, I gave you almost nine months of fucking around, but it's been too long, Marcus, and we still in the same place."

Marcus's eyes are solid, sharp. "So you thought you'd pimp yoself out?"

"I done what I had to do while you been sitting on your ass. I wouldn't have to be doing none of it if you helped me and stopped fooling around," I say.

"You said you were cool with me shooting my shot." Somehow his voice is only getting higher. "You think I didn't try? I been trying to keep you safe since before Mama fucked up. Hell, I'm the only one that ever really cared about you. Can you blame me for wanting something for myself?"

"No, I can't. But we not living in Uncle Ty's world right now and it don't do nothing to pretend we are. Pretty soon, neither one of us gonna have a place to sleep and at least I'm trying."

"That's why I thought I'd take you out today, you know, make up for it." His forehead is a twist of lines staring down at me. He really thinks some paint can erase all this. My eyes fuzz and I realize I'm crying: soft, slow, but crying.

"Paint can't pay our rent, Marcus. I don't know what you want me to do, say I forgive you? Don't really matter if I forgive you when we don't got no food to eat."

"What you want me to do about that? I already tried with a job. Twice."

I sigh, trying to wipe the blur out my eyes. "I went to see Mama. She don't have Uncle Ty's number, but he always liked you best." I feel him seize, his body tightening. "Help me, Mars. I don't give a shit what you gotta do, but I need you to try something. Find Ty or another job or anything. Please."

"Fuck that." Marcus kicks the ground with his unlaced sneaker. "You know he's not helping us do shit."

"Best plan I got."

When Marcus turned thirteen, after Daddy came back home, he started skipping school to go hang out with Uncle Ty. This was before Uncle Ty left town, before he got signed to a major record label and bought his Maserati. He was just Daddy's little brother, the baby of the family, our only connection to something bigger.

Uncle Ty's the kind of person you wanna get as close to as you can, magnetic really. He don't even need to speak. It's almost like you can see the thoughts fly through him, the intensity of every belief, the way his eyes set on something and don't look away. As kids, we thought Uncle Ty was magic and Mama thought it'd be best we didn't talk to him much. Stopped coming to Christmas when I turned nine. Marcus cried that whole first Christmas without him, rolled on the floor of our apartment clutching his stomach like the distance bred physical pain. Maybe it did.

None of us knew Marcus was cutting class to spend time with Uncle Ty until the truancy notice came in the mail. For an entire semester, they spent most days together. When our uncle skipped town on us after Mama's arrest, Marcus went around the apartment breaking whatever shit reminded him of Uncle Ty.

After Marcus heard Uncle Ty's song at the club last year, found out about his fame, he came home drunk and teary and stroked my forehead, telling me about what they spent all that time doing. Besides bringing Marcus to the skate park, Uncle Ty was meeting up with lots of big men with bigger chains, getting high, talking shit, playing them his music. Marcus would sit in the corner, inhaling the smoke and waiting for Uncle Ty to take him back to the skate park. He said sometimes they'd go to these nice houses where rich dudes would offer him cigars and Uncle Ty would tell Marcus to try one out. Marcus would inhale when you really ain't supposed to breathe in cigar smoke and end up vomiting in the bathroom. Even when Uncle Ty only brought Marcus grief, he loved our uncle more than anything. Worshipped him, really.

Marcus shakes his head. "You on your own."

"Really? You can't do this one thing for me?"

Marcus looks at me with that same scared look he gave me when Daddy tried to take my hand at the drum circle. He shakes his head. "I'm sorry."

I reach for my bike and all I can think about is getting somewhere that's not so blue.

I've made the decision before I've even registered it in words, looking at Marcus still shaking his head. "Daddy would be real disappointed in what you've become. Feel free to go shoot your shot, Marcus, but I ain't gonna give you a bed when you come home empty after all that big-boy shit. You wanna be on your own? Go live somewhere else. If you wanna stay with me, you figure your shit out and help me."

I climb onto my bike, the seat still warm, and I start to pedal, harder, harder, until my legs are a blur of muscle and woman and sweat. I know I've sliced into something between us, ripped apart the treaty that was our apartment by saying this right after something so sacred. Maybe the mural will memorialize this day, take us back to before, back to each other.

O AKLAND'S SUN faded to its usual mild hum. Alé hasn't answered the phone since the skate park and I'm too scared to ask her if she still loves me like she used to. Every day I don't see her, it feels like we are getting further from recognizable. I bet she has some new tattoos now. Maybe she even smells different.

Marcus is gone. It's officially been a week since the mural and yesterday he picked up the clothes I washed for him. He must be staying with one of his boys, and I feel like the last survivor in our family, the only one left in this apartment.

I can't stop thinking about the party Camila invited me to, about a disco. There probably won't even be no disco, but the flash makes me wanna go, just to see if the shining would make me dizzy or if maybe this is the life for me. Maybe I can hold Camila's hand every night, make enough money that Trevor never has a worry in his life, give up comfort for something stable and harsh.

I meet Trevor at the bus stop after school most days and we go to the court, got a whole lineup of bets. After we beat bay girl, she told all her middle school friends that somebody best show up this little boy and his grown babysitter. Thought she was talking shit, but turns out they young enough to waste all their cash on bets we already know we're gonna win. It made us enough to help cover the March rent, along with some money from the cops.

Trevor and I practice late at night sometimes, when Dee comes back and starts wilding out with her laughing. He knocks on the door to my apartment and we take the ball out, do dribbles around the pool. Sometimes I imagine him showing up at my door and knocking when I'm not there, waiting when there's never gonna be an answer.

It's getting close to dark and the party starts the second the sun disappears. I get ready, slip on the only dress I own, which is more of a nightgown than anything. It was a gift from one of the cops, and it reminds me how I've lived a whole century in the span of these months. Time moves in so many directions.

In the bathroom, I stare straight into the mirror. I am all shades of brown. My hair has remnants of red in it from the one time I tried to dye it auburn, and I paint my face in watered-down mascara and eyeliner I don't really know how to use. Eventually, I look like a grown version of myself: more angular. I got more sharpness in my face than I used to, and my shoulders make the bareness of the dress more stark with the way my skeleton shines through. I'm not really that skinny, but my shoulders seem to think I am. The rest of me has a soft cushion, keeps my organs insulated, safe.

It's ten now and I slip on my new heels. These ones are silver and the stiletto is two inches shorter than the old ones that metal man threw into the street. I don't take a jacket because I know how humid whatever house or shack or warehouse this party is in will be, and the only thing worse than a chill is the sweat from inescapable heat.

When Camila gave me the address, I don't think it even crossed her mind that I'm on my own out here, don't got a car, don't even got a bus pass after the ones Alé and I stole ran out of money. I mapped the directions to the place before I left, but standing on High Street, that two-mile walk feels like a marathon my feet can't handle.

When there is no choice, the only thing you have left to do is walk. The soles of my feet ache in that familiar way that tells me I'm not only gonna have blisters in the morning, my feet are gonna bruise themselves into a purple that looks closer to my mama's neck than flesh should.

I think about each step and repeat to myself: *heel, toe, heel, toe.* Makes it easier. The honks from assholes in cars accompany each step, but I don't pay no mind until one pulls over. Window down. I tense before I look close enough to realize it's a woman. She's got her speakers blasting to Kehlani and her eyelashes are adorned in blue sparkles.

"Need a ride?" she asks.

I nod, then look into the backseat. It's a full circus in there, only the middle seat in the back row empty. They swing the back door open for me and the girl closest to me slides over. They're clearly heading to a party, got dresses with barely more fabric than mine.

I close the door.

"Where you going?" the driver asks, turning to look at me.

I tell her the address and the girl next to me leans toward the driver. "Ain't that Demond's place?" She tries to whisper but it comes out loud enough for the whole car to hear, even over the boom of the stereo.

The driver nods slightly and then calls back to me, "I'm Sam. You know what kinda house you walking into, yeah?"

"Know all I need to know," I call back to her. "I'm Kia."

We spend the rest of the ride in silence except for the music. When they let me out in front of the house, Sam turns around and touches my knee.

"If Demond tries to give you some shit, don't take it." Her blue eyelashes flap up and down and then she turns back to the wheel and the door swings open. The girl next to me shoves a little and I tumble out onto the sidewalk, gaining my footing despite how stilettos make me feel like I'm walking on stilts. The house reminds me of the way cartoons animate a house party: the building looks like it's bouncing up and down, strobe lights shining through the windows, people lingering on the front steps. The rest of the street is dark, all the way up to the cul-de-sac, and if it wasn't for the rager going on inside, I would've thought some kids lived up in the house, picket fence and shit.

I watch the circus car pull away.

"Ay, you one of Demond's girls?" one of the men smoking a Backwoods on the front steps calls out to me.

"No, just pulling up for Camila," I call back, walking toward them.

Fear don't do nothing but paint red across the neck, tell them all how easy it is to split you open.

The man nods and his friend joins in, taking a hit of the blunt. "Camila." He draws out her name, chuckles a little. "She been in the game so long, bet she got some fine tricks." I don't know who he's talking to because he's looking at the sky like he expects it to talk back.

The man next to him is shirtless and looks me in the eye. "Yeah, cost one damn pretty penny too."

Sky man turns to him. "You ain't been with her?"

"No man never been with Camila and lived to tell no one about it. You got that kind of money, you also got a hit out on your ass." He focuses back on me. "Guessing you one of Camila's new girls. She knows how to pick 'em."

His eyes gaze over every part of my body and I feel as naked as I do right out of the shower, before the shea butter has absorbed into my skin.

"If you'll excuse me, I got somewhere to be," I tell them, maneuvering between their bodies up the steps toward the front door and the blasting trap music. Shirtless yells after me, "Imma find you later, girl." And I know that is exactly what I came here for, but needles still course up my spine like a warning.

Inside, the heat of the room pushes down from the ceiling and this is a different kind of bodies on bodies: these ones grind and, instead of joy, there is so much wanting, everything Mama says not to do. We're all wanting something, though; most of us replacing what we really want with skin, which works until you wake up and the mirror is a blur of time twisting around the throat.

I make my way through the first room, then the second. Someone is dancing on a counter in the kitchen and every corner of the house is occupied by half-clothed people. I head toward the table and the scent of spilled vodka. Looking for the cleanest bottle, I find tequila and pour it into a plastic cup. I tip it back and the moment it touches my lips, I am hit with a sweetness that shouldn't accompany hard liquor but I'm too tired to care where it might have come from. I drink more than I should, hoping it's enough to last me even after I've danced and sweated half of it out, hoping it will kick in quick so the paranoia will fade.

When the warmth has made its way into my chest, I turn back to the chaos. There are so many eyes in the room and I go in and out of locking with them, receiving every wink and second glance but responding with nothing but a cold stare. I'm looking for her, know she will be taller than most of the room with whatever sparkling shoes she has mounted the length of her onto.

She's standing on the patio, arms above her head, twisting her body to the sound of some other music that probably doesn't exist in this universe. Camila is more radiant than the bassline of this track can handle. I swerve toward her, slide past a short man who looks like he is standing guard at the patio door. Camila sees me and pauses the glide of her neck toward her shoulder, swings both hands up, and squeals. "¡Mija!"

And I really do feel like hers.

Camila takes me into her arms and today she is orange, head to toe. I didn't think orange was a color that could be worn without it looking like Alé's cheap quinceañera dress, but Camila wears it flawlessly. She has shorts and a tube top on, both shimmering a deep blood orange. It's like the juice of it drips down to her feet, which are adorned in neon boots that get darker and more saturated in color as they make their way up her thighs.

"How you doin'? You got a drink?"

I nod and Camila turns to tell the semicircle of people gathered around her, "This is one of my lil hoes, Kia. Don't nobody mess with her if you don't got the cash to back it up. My girls run expensive."

Most of the people around Camila nod or murmur hellos, but all their eyes remain locked on her. They don't even look at her ass or her tits. Camila's face is enough to send any room into a frenzy: dimpled chin emphasizing every other dip in her face, she is angles with a sweet curve on every edge. Her eyes are endless in their brown, and Camila wears her eyelashes like they are accessories in themselves.

"You met Demond yet?" she asks.

I shake my head. Camila tells me I gotta learn how to talk a little more and I laugh.

She notifies everyone on the patio that she'll be back and brings me inside, through the kitchen to a closed door that she opens like this might as well be her house.

The moment we step into the room, I'm hit with smoke. They're hotboxing and I swear there ain't no air left to breathe. The bed is the central focus in the room, gotta be king-size, and about ten people sit and lie scattered on it. They're all girls except for the man in the middle, who is wearing sunglasses and has the most delicate designs shaved into his head. He is skinny, but longer than any man I've met in real life. His feet reach the end of the bed. I don't know where he's looking under those sunglasses, but I feel watched.

Camila leads me toward the corner of the room to a couch I didn't even notice was there under the fog of smoke, and we sit down in between two girls.

"Demond, this my girl Kia. The one I was telling you about."

Demond slides his sunglasses down to the bridge of his nose and I can finally see his eyes, even through the mist of smoke. They look like grease has saturated the eyeball, slick and slippery. They are black but there's something else behind the black, edge-of-the-knife silver flashes. He twirls his nose ring around a couple times, then coughs.

"She special." His voice is a penetrating croak, rings out across the room.

Camila swirls patterns on the back of my hand, her legs crossed, leaning toward Demond. "And she don't got no daddy."

I shift on the couch, the leather sticking to the back of my thighs, uncomfortable, and I'm not sure what Camila thinks she's doing, selling me off like this.

"Doing fine on my own," I say, and every head in the room swings to stare at me, all the girls' eyes blazing.

Demond sits up, pushing one of the girls off him, setting his feet on the floor. He clasps his hands together and stares at me. We can't be more than five feet from each other now, but the haze is still so thick.

"Baby, I can take you to a whole new level." His breath is a mix of peppermint and weed, flows out with the husk of his voice.

Camila turns to me, whispers in my ear, "Just listen to him. You don't gotta make no choices tonight. Give him ten minutes, then come find me."

Her torso rolls back up and she is standing, removing her fingers from my hand, orange and radiant and leaving me. I watch her disappear through the smoke and out the door until it is just me, Demond, and a coven of girls.

Demond reaches for the hand Camila has left unoccupied and pulls it toward him. He opens each of my fingers from the fist and stares at it, palm up, like he's reading it.

"You young." He isn't asking. "I don't mind 'em young but I can tell you gon' be trouble, that right?" The bones in each of his fingers poke at me.

"Just don't like being told what to do," I respond in a deep voice to mask the chill that has migrated to my stomach.

He laughs at this and within seconds the girls have made a whole chorus of giggles. The moment he stops, they do too.

I remove my hand from his grasp, lean back into the couch. "Don't wanna be your little bitch, laughing at shit that ain't funny." Only way to make it out this room is to talk as big as he does. I try to make my voice guttural now. I thought I might have wanted this before I came, but now, looking at him, I know he won't protect me, won't make things any easier, even if I do make more money. I'd be giving up my chance at anything close to freedom, at a life outside the night world.

"You really is Camila's girl." He mimics me, leaning back. "How many nights you out on the streets? Five? Six?" I don't respond, but he can see the collapse, the fatigue in me, keeps talking. "My girls only out there two, maybe three nights a week and they raking in over two grand each. Lexi'll tell you about it, won't you?"

He's talking to the girl directly beside me. I didn't concentrate on her through the smoke until now, but the moment I focus on her, I want to edge away.

Lexi is small, under five feet, and she can't be much older than fifteen. Her hair looks just like mine did when I was a little girl and Mama took care of it, tight coils framing her round face. You can tell she tried to paint her face, contour herself a woman, but she still looks so young. Her hands grasp her handbag tightly and she's fidgeting with the strap.

"Hi," she says to me, and I don't think she's trying to whisper, but her voice is shallow. She's about to say something else when the door to the room opens and a man steps in.

"Yo, Demond, some niggas out here tryna take your shit." It's the same man who stood guard at the patio door, short and wide.

Demond stands and he's even taller than I expected, close to the ceiling. "Fuck, man." He takes two large steps and is out the door, slamming it shut.

It's just me and the girls now. I watch them as they look around, like they're trying to figure out where they are, like they ain't had a moment to breathe and see it. I realize none of them have moved since I entered the room. Now a couple of them stand and start to walk around, picking up photos on the shelf or whispering to each other.

"One of Demond's boys take you too? This your first stop?" Lexi's voice is a little louder now, but it still sounds like she's underwater, the sound floating out.

I look at her again, the smoke fading, and I don't get it until I see the way she fiddles with the strap and her eyes shift wild around the room.

"I ain't one of his girls. Nobody took me."

When this comes out my mouth, something in her face droops, and a hope I didn't notice was there disappears.

I scramble, thinking of Alé and Clara. "You got a phone? I can try to help you out, give you a place to stay and you can call somebody to come get you . . ." I fumble for my purse to get my phone, but Lexi's fleshy hand reaches out to stop me.

"Ain't nobody looking for me." And she smiles this brutal, hollow smile that doesn't belong to her face, and she continues to fondle the strap to her bag, not looking at me anymore.

The room has gone from musty to suffocating and all I gotta do is get out, get back to Camila. I stand and, again, all eyes in the room rest on me as I make my way out the door, leaving it a crack open so they might be able to breathe again.

After I found Camila, shirtless man from the front steps came looking for me, brought me out to the shed behind Demond's house. When he asked me *how much*, I gave him a higher number than I've ever asked for from one man and he didn't even flinch, just retrieved the bills from his pocket and pulled his zipper down. When I asked him what he wanted me to call him, he said I didn't need to call him nothing, said he didn't like no talking.

After shirtless left, his friend—sky man—entered the shed, asked for a turn. I didn't even ask him what he wanted to be called because in my head he was just sky man and the moment you place a name to that, the fantasy of it dissipates.

I slip the dress back on, alone in the shed now, and climb back into my heels. My feet have swollen over the course of the night and I have to squeeze just to fit back into them. I exit the shed and the first image I see is Camila and her orange, shaking—this time to the actual music—but still she moves more graceful than I ever have.

I climb the steps up to the patio and the moment Camila sees me, she pulls me into her dance. I've had a couple more shots and I let the buzz crawl across my chest, bring me into the looseness of Camila, and we are in the music. The thump in my chest, belly swing side to side, hips roll, her body pressed on mine.

At first, I think the buzz is coming from my chest, another wave of tequila or something. But the beat of it is too linear, too compact to be produced from me or the dance. I fumble for my purse, removing myself from Camila to lean over the edge of the patio and answer my phone. I haven't even spoken yet before the voice does. I know who it is without him having to tell me. I don't forget any of their voices.

"Just got a call that you're at a party. Two of us are undercover in there, gonna shut it down and do a whole roundup in maybe an hour. I'm parked around the corner. Be outside in five."

He hangs up without a response. I don't know his name, but I know his badge number: 612. That's what I call him, what he told me to call him.

None of them have ever called me like that before and suddenly I'm looking around at all the bodies in the house, trying to figure out who is undercover. I place my phone in my bag and turn around to Camila, still twisting, grooving, shaking. Her eyes are closed and everyone around her is in a trance just watching her. What 612 said is finally registering and I tap her shoulder, but she doesn't open her eyes. Trying again, I shake her lightly until she finally looks at me. Leaning into her ear, I tell her, "You gotta get outta here, this a sting."

"Whatchu talkin' 'bout, Kia?" She laughs, throws her arms up. "Relax."

I try to tell her again, but I think the beat has entered her head because she isn't moving, just opens her mouth and lets a laugh out so melodic it might as well be music.

Eventually, I leave her there: on the patio, dancing. Looking back at the image, I realize the people standing around her aren't watching her, they're guarding her, and something about my image of Camila suddenly appears so false. She's a woman tricking herself into thinking she's in control, but what if she tried to leave with me? Men would find her and take her back, just like any of those other girls in Demond's room. Trapped.

I weave through the house and I swear it has only gotten more crowded and loud as we edge closer to two a.m. The eyes are a ravenous wanting now, like the night has swallowed them and spit out only desire. Out the door and down the steps, someone shouts something, but I don't really hear it through the buzz and the relief of breathable air.

I look around for some sirens, flashes of color, a car. Across the street, a deep blue Prius rolls down the window and there he is, just like I remember: ginger hair and splotches of red on his cheeks. I cross the street toward him and the passenger-side door swings open for me. I climb in.

"This your car?"

He chuckles, no uniform, no badge, just jeans. "You know we have lives outside the station, right?"

I try to laugh with him, but no sound comes out, kind of like how Mama opened her mouth and let her jaw move, detached from the noise erupting from it.

He pulls away from the house and I take one last look at it, think of Lexi with her purse strap, Camila turning her body into a spiral.

"Where we going?" I ask 612, staring out the window. He's one of the ones who's hard to look at because part of me wishes this wasn't him, that he was at home somewhere, reading a book to some redheaded child and not out here, with me. The way he grips the steering wheel makes me nervous, like he can't hold it tight enough, like he's about to rip it open.

He coughs. "It's late, I'm taking you back to my place."

I used to have these dreams about Mama leaving me in the grocery store. Whenever we went shopping, she'd have to go figure out how much money she had left on our EBT card, receding to a corner to call customer service, because she inevitably lost the last receipt. I'd go wandering around the store, sometimes with Marcus and sometimes on my own. I'd pick up everything I wanted: boxes and boxes of that fancy cereal and the pizzas that TV families throw in the oven and then eat around their oak dining room tables. Then I'd walk a few aisles and leave them somewhere they didn't belong, hoping they'd still be waiting there when I got back a couple weeks later. They never were.

In the dreams, I am sitting in the middle of an aisle, looking around, waiting for the aisle walls to morph and reveal my mama. I don't think you can feel more trapped than in the center of food you're not allowed to eat, waiting to go home, and not knowing if anyone will remember your existence.

I feel that kind of confined now, sitting in the car, watching 612's fingernails rip slowly into the steering wheel. I wonder how long it will take Marcus to forget about me, if the only time he'll think about me is when he looks in the mirror and sees my fingerprint.

When you don't got much, a fingerprint is everything.

I don't think 612 is gonna murder me or nothing. Actually, as far as they go, he is kind, has this nervous lather that makes the whole thing feel sticky. He is nothing to fear, everything to pity.

Nobody's ever taken me home before. Not the street men, who ain't rich enough to have places of their own worth taking me to and prefer to drag me to their cars or motel rooms. Not the cops, who got women at home and like to keep me separate, like to take me in groups. Not the boyfriend I had when I was fourteen and still try-ing to live out childhood: clean sneakers and basketball practice. Alé don't even take me to her place. It's really just been my apartment, Cole's basement studio, and the streets. Haven't even thought much about how the world extends beyond that, how they all go home and pull their sheets up, dream a little.

"Don't worry, it's empty, just a little dirty."

I nod, turn back to the window, and smile. He's concerned about how dirty his bedroom is. Us, in this car, two a.m., and he don't want me to judge his dirty-ass apartment.

I expect to drive for longer, but it isn't more than ten minutes before he pulls into a driveway. I thought he'd bring me to some little apartment, bigger than mine, but fit for him and his loneliness. Enough room for him and his badge. Instead, a house stares down at us: gray and freshly painted, with a porch swing. I don't think I've ever wanted to sit on a porch swing before, but it almost invites me into it and I have to shake off the urge to just start swinging like I am back in the park with Alé.

He fumbles for his keys in the dark, even though his whole street is lit up in streetlamps. Perks of living rich, I guess. Didn't realize cops made this much until 612 and 220 and 48 pulled out their wallets. This big gray house trumps it all, though.

612 opens the door and lets me walk through first, almost like a gentleman would. For such a gigantic place, there is barely any furniture. He walks me through the hallway and each room has a chair, maybe a coffee table, but nothing bigger than that rocking chair from *Goodnight Moon*, which Marcus used to read to me when he was six and still needed to sound out the letters, waiting for Mama and Daddy to come home from work.

"Want some water or something?" 612 stands in the doorway to what must be the kitchen, awkwardly rolling his neck until it cracks.

"Got anything harder? Whiskey or something?" I know people say not to mix drinks, but I like the way they swirl together in me and, if I'm going to make it through whatever happens next, I need something to make it feel fuzzy, give me a chance at not remembering tomorrow.

He nods, turns around, and goes into the kitchen. I stay in the hallway, not even sure I can handle another step. The only thing I want is to remove the heels from my feet and sleep. I try to blink enough that I'll remember I'm on the clock, that this man has red hair and an appetite I will only fill for the remainder of the next couple hours, if that. He returns a couple minutes later sipping a cup of water, hands me a glass of amber liquor, and leads me down another hallway to a room with a bed. The bed has a quilt that looks like something

Daddy used to try to make when he was sick and gave up on halfway through.

"Can I sit?" I ask 612, desperate to peel the plastic from my toes.

His words tumble out, "Of course, please," and I sit on the edge of the bed. The lights in the room are still off and I say a silent prayer that he won't try to illuminate the room. Don't wanna look at the way the red spreads across his cheeks.

Shoes off, I climb farther onto the bed. My dress is sticky and I'm almost glad 612 starts removing it. My back rests on the quilt and it's itchier than I expected it to be, a violent stench coming from it. When he gets on top of me, I can tell he's trying not to put his whole weight on me. I place my hands on both sides of his shoulders and pull down a little, so he presses harder. It's not that I want all his weight on me or nothing, I just don't like the feeling of him trying to restrain himself. Only thing worse than a man untamed is a man on the edge of it.

612 moans like he ain't never fucked before. That whole body release, he twists his head and scrunches his eyes together: lion mid-roar. I grab on to the fabric of the pillowcase, focus on the sound of the mattress springs. I don't even sleep on a bed at home, never heard the scratch of wood frame and mattress bounce at the same time.

He finishes quick, just like I remember, and immediately reaches over to his bedside table to turn on the lamp. I wish he wouldn't. His face is flushed an even deeper red and I reach up to cross my arms over my chest like it even matters. I move to grab my dress from the floor, but 612 takes it from me before I even begin to lift it over my torso.

"That shit is nasty. Here." He tosses me the shirt he was wearing, sweat stains and all, as if it's any better. I put it on and it doesn't reach below the top of my thighs, wide and sagging on my chest.

"You gonna pay me?" I ask him, reaching down for my heels and already dreading the walk home.

He laughs from across the room, putting on a new shirt, clean and gray, like the house.

"Already paid you. Told you about the sting, didn't I?" He turns around to look through a drawer, shaking his head.

I stop, mid-motion. "Didn't ask you to do that. Need my money."

I'm fully aware of his uniform laid out on a chair in the corner of the room, handgun and all. I know I should have asked for the money before the sex, but I also know it wouldn't have made a difference.

He looks back at me, traces of eyebrows rising. Just stares. Like a ghost might up and spill out my mouth. Maybe I'm just that magical or maybe he is plotting how he's gonna explain my arrest or my death or why that pretty girl don't come around no more.

And then he smiles and those red cheeks just get redder. "How 'bout this: you stay the night and I'll pay you in the morning? Couple more hours, place to rest your little head. That work for you?"

The thought of lying back in that bed, smelling the mold grown between stitches of his quilt, remnants of someone else's perfume, makes me want to climb back into my shoes and walk another five miles. But I'm not about to waste the past hour of soaking up his splotches and leave without my payment.

"Okay," I tell 612.

This time, when he gets into the bed, he lies beside me, pulls the quilt up over both of us. I stay propped up in the bed until 612 pulls at my arm to get me to slide down to his level. I do. He drags his arm over my body and pulls so I am pressed against him. He's asleep in minutes, snoring into my ear, and his breath smells like mint been living in it. I don't know how his body lets him fall asleep like that: so effortlessly, like he's never had a nightmare before.

I stare at the ceiling until the sun paints it this glorious too-early-for-eyes orange, reminds me of Camila before the house collapsed like I know it did. I don't sleep, but something behind my eyes rolls over, climbs into itself, and emerges like a newborn baby.

TREVOR IS STANDING on the counter in my apartment, reaching up to the top cupboard and opening it, closing it again. He does this a couple times, as if something might appear in place of its emptiness.

"You really ain't got no oil?" he asks.

I'm standing over the only large bowl I own, stirring with every muscle in my arm, making a whirlwind out of the chocolate.

My right hand starts tensing up, so I switch to my left. "Thought it'd come with some. Shit, why I gotta do everything? Buy it from a box for a reason."

It's my birthday.

Normally, Marcus and I take a bus down to San Leandro and go to this bakery Daddy's childhood friend owns and buy this huge-ass fancy cake with the edible flowers on top. This year, though, Marcus and I ain't speaking and I don't have enough money in my pillowcase for no flowered cake. After a night perspiring under the heat of 612's arm, I watched him finally wake up and turn to me, spitting at me that I had to get out of his house. I asked again for my money and he said he already paid me, let me sleep in his bed.

I've been out on the streets for the past two weeks and still haven't seen Camila. There's something in the air, in the way all the johns been staring me down that tells me when it's time to go home. I'm surviving off sky man and shirtless and whatever savings I have hidden behind the mirror in the bathroom.

Trevor asked me if he could sleep in my apartment last week and he hasn't gone back to Dee's place since. We moved all his clothes into my place and now I'm not as worried about paying his rent, except if Vernon evicts Dee, then Trevor can't be seen around no more. I like having him with me, sleeping on my mattress, especially since Marcus is gone.

Trevor said he'd help me bake a cake after I told him I wasn't gonna have a birthday cake or presents or nothing. Said everybody gotta have cake on their birthday. I don't remember Dee ever making him no cake on his, but I wouldn't be surprised if she showed up at midnight on his birthday with a three-tier chocolate cake and didn't even remember who made it. She's ethereal like that, appears out of nowhere and might just open her mouth and turn the whole city to laughter, make everything sweet.

I tell Trevor to look in the other cupboard and he climbs down, opening it and muttering some joke about how I don't know how to clean, then pulling out a bottle of syrup from the back of the cabinet.

"Guess we making a pancake cake." He brings it over to me at the counter and I swear he's grown another inch in the span of the last month because he's nearing my height and can stare into the bowl without shifting his weight to the balls of his feet.

"How much you gonna put in?" I ask him.

He screws open the top of the bottle. "All of it. Gotta be real sweet, Ki."

The bottle is about halfway full and I know this cake's gonna taste like Aunt Jemima exploded all over our kitchen. I let him pour it all in anyway.

Trevor finishes stirring and I pick up the bowl, pour the batter into a pan we got from Dee's cupboard. The pan is shaped like a heart and I bet Dee got it one year for Valentine's Day and forgot about it because it is rusted and unused. Trevor opens the oven door for me and I slide the cake in.

"How long it gonna take?"

"Box said twenty minutes. Go on and grab your ball and we can practice your dribble or something."

Trevor runs toward the mattress and starts throwing blankets and clothes aside, looking for his ball. He comes back and tosses it right at me. We go outside, scrimmage along the row of doors until the ball falls down to the pool area. I chase Trevor down the stairs and my legs might be longer, but the boy knows how to turn his body into a bolt.

I slow down when it looks like he's gonna beat me.

"Now I get the first piece of cake, right?" he calls out to me.

I try to keep my mouth a thin line, but it spreads into a smile. "Better get your ass back up there before the cake burns."

Today is my eighteenth birthday, the one I've been waiting for. I'm letting today be just about me and Trevor, our cake, and *Sesame Street* reruns on TV. Trevor and his ball sprint up the stairs and I hear the door of the apartment slam closed before I'm even on the landing. Maybe adulthood makes you slower. Feels like it.

Trevor has already wrapped his hand in a rag and is reaching into the oven and pulling out the pan. He drops it on the counter and the aroma is a sharp punch of overwhelming saccharine.

"Don't it smell good?" Trevor rests his head in his arms beside the cake and breathes in, eyes wide and waiting.

I laugh. "Smells like you dropped a whole bottle of syrup in it. Gotta cool now, might as well go do something else. Whatchu wanna do?"

I wrap my arms around his stomach and pick him up, then set him back on the ground.

"Can we go swimming?" he asks.

"Told you I ain't going in no shit pool."

Trevor stops in the doorway, turns to look at me. His face cradles his eyes like they are fragile and ready to roll.

"Please."

Trevor takes one of my hands and laces his fingers through it, tugs on me lightly.

"Don't even know how to tread no water," I tell him.

His whole face lights up, cheeks rising. "I'll teach you."

I never said yes, but Trevor knows my ability to refuse him is waning and he drags me out the door, down the stairs. I try to pull back, but all that basketball has Trevor's stringy arms building enough muscle to fight against me.

Down by the pool, I tell him I don't got a swimsuit.

"Nobody swims in no swimsuit." And before I can even argue, he's taking off his shirt and shorts, standing there in his boxers, looking like a mix of bony child and growing muscles.

The things I do for this kid.

I take my shirt off, then my jeans, leaving only a sports bra and underwear.

"It's best if you just jump in, makes it a little easier." Trevor reaches out for my hand again and we stand together at the edge of the pool. "Count to three."

I don't count, but Trevor does it for the both of us. On three, we jump, and I feel like I've been catapulted straight into the ocean. All I can think is *There's shit in this pool*. Still, I haven't showered in a couple days and the water is a cool relief. We jumped into the shallow end, so I find my footing on the floor of the pool and stand, wiping my eyes. Trevor is already above the surface, grinning so big I think his cheeks might pop out his face and start dancing.

"Now what?" I ask him, spitting out water.

"Move your arms like this, like you a frog." Trevor swims to the deep end, cups his hands, and fans his body out, back and forth, like a snow angel in reverse.

After a couple minutes, he turns around and swims back to me.

"Don't know how you expect me to stay up like that."

He reaches for my arm and pulls me into the deep end. "Now start moving, I'll hold you up."

Trevor holds on to one of my hands, keeping me tethered, and I try to make my other arm move like his did, coordinated and frog-like. It's not listening to me, though, flapping around in the water aimlessly.

"Don't be afraid of the water. It ain't gonna hurt you." Trevor's hand stays in mine.

I let my head submerge into the water and then come up for air. It's really not so bad when you breathe into it. I like the sound of my breath when I'm under, a gurgle that floats off into nothing. If this was the bay, I'm sure every sea creature would hear my sounds travel through the molecules. Nothing got an end in the water.

Pretty soon, my arm is moving kinda like Trevor's, except there's a lot more splashing and my feet don't follow in sync. My free arm is flapping while my feet swirl the water in violent half circles. Trevor lets go of my other hand and I'm staying above water, at least for a moment.

I panic and the rhythm of my arms dissolves into whatever move-ment will keep me from drowning. I start to swim until I reach the end of the pool and then pivot around. My feet touch the edge of the pool and I push off, glide through the water, feel like I'm flying. I start my hand motions again, coming up for air and trying to blink the water off my eyelashes before I dive back under. Can't see much of anything. Except a flash of shoes. Back beneath the surface. A pocket of deep blue. Water submerges. Trevor's eyes spinning.

My feet hit pool bottom and I stand to the sight of uniforms that shouldn't be this familiar and Trevor standing waist-deep in the pool, looking down at his stomach like he's waiting for blood to gush out an invisible wound.

I've never been this close to a woman cop before, but she is the one kneeling down at the edge of the pool. She is the one that looks at me like I best put some clothes on. As much as I want to sink back into the water, I know I gotta get Trevor in some clothes and safe before they start asking him about where his mama is. We don't got no space to deal with Child Protective Services too.

"C'mon, Trev. Go on and get some new clothes and a couple towels." He looks at me, at the lady cop staring at us, then back at me, and I can see the short convulsions of his chest. I nod at him, make my eyelids lift up like I don't got no worries.

Trevor puts both hands on the pool edge and lifts his body out, boxers soggy and trying to drip off him. He holds them up with both hands and starts jogging toward the stairs, up them, back to the apartment.

"We'll give you a minute," lady cop says, standing and walking back to the man cop behind her. Her hair is pulled into a bun so tight, I wonder if she's got a headache.

Trevor comes back a few minutes later with a bundle of towels and a shirt. He's already changed into some new boxers and shorts. I grip on to the edge of the pool and lift myself out, grabbing the towel Trevor hands to me. I rush to dry off enough to pull on my jeans and T-shirt. Trevor puts his shirt on, with a picture of a mountain on it, and he looks like a Boy Scout. The cops stand there uncomfortably, trying not to look at us.

I stand up, taking Trevor's hand. He doesn't really let me hold his hand much anymore, but I'm not asking now. If we're tethered at the skin, they're gonna have to rip us apart at the cells.

"You need something?" I ask.

I'm still dripping, forehead down. Both cops come forward now and I can't look at anything but their lips. There's something about the way they hold them together, something about the way they're cracked that makes me think these people have mastered how to dry out a phrase, give some bad news with a straight line carved into their mouths. The man has lips bordering on red and I don't know if they look bloodied or like he drew lipstick on this morning.

The woman is clearly in charge here, walks stomach first, everything secondary to the pit of her, target in her belly button. "We're looking for a Kia Holt. Guessing that's you, miss?"

I know one of *them* sent her 'cause that's the name I gave Camila, gave everyone that ever saw me on the street. They must have found me out. Maybe this is the day they take me in, enter my fingerprint into their computers, and leave Trevor alone. "Maybe. You need something?"

The man takes his turn now, after lady cop tilts her head. She doesn't even look at him, just gives this little head tilt and they must have rehearsed this before because his mouth opens a beat later. "We're undergoing an internal investigation and we're going to need to speak with you. I'm Detective Harrison and this is Detective Jones."

I rub my free hand across my face, wipe up the water still running from my hairline. "Trevor, why don't you go upstairs and start on that cake? I'll be up soon." I squeeze his hand, look down at him. His face maps fear like a direct route to a panic attack, but I don't got time to comfort him when they're still standing here, staring at me straight out the shit pool. I release Trevor's hand, and give his shoulder a nudge toward the stairs, watch him go all the way up, and wait for the door to slam.

The woman, Detective Jones, scrunches her lips up toward her nose so they wrinkle. "Actually, we think it would be best for you to come into the station with us. We're going to need to complete a recorded interview and some paperwork and it would be best to do it all at once. Don't you think that'd be a whole lot easier?" She tries to make her voice higher than it is. I can tell because the pitch squeaks at the end of each sentence and the corners of her eyes squeeze, trying real hard to keep herself soft. I bet she's the good cop in their role-playing. Bet she don't like it that much.

I should have known it would end in this. The station. Cuffs must come next. "How long this gonna take?" I cross my arms to cover the way my bra shows through the shirt, sticky and wet.

Detective Harrison puts on his bad-cop face, knits his nose upward, chin tilt. "You'll be home before dark for sure. Unless you wanna make this harder on yourself and then it might take longer."

I don't know what he means, but it's clear they're not about to tell me, so I nod, pull my sneakers on. Jones motions her arm for me to follow Harrison out the gate. I trail behind him, sandwiched between them, trying to get one last flash of Trevor on the landing. He isn't there.

Lived here my whole life and never been in OPD headquarters. The building is larger than any other one in the area, plopped between Jack London Square, Chinatown, and Old Oakland. It hovers in the center of the city like a camera hidden in plain sight. All the cop cars emerge out of the headquarters, swarm the area.

I've never paid any attention to the building, though. Hoped there'd never be any reason to walk inside these doors. Inside, everything feels metallic even though it's not. Even the windows feel like they're made of metal, a thin kind that disguises itself as glass. I want to tap on it to see if it feels like metal too: cold and impenetrable.

They made me ride in the back of the car on the way here and I've been in the back of a cop car more times than I'd like, but this time I felt more like criminal than victim or woman. Jones kept her body turned halfway toward me in the passenger seat the whole time, stared at me through the metal bars that make up the partition. No way out.

My shoes squeak through the lobby, past uniforms and more uniforms, following Harrison to the elevator. I always take the stairs because you can't guarantee the doors are ever gonna open again when you step into an elevator and my legs are more reliable than any machine ever could be. But Harrison steps in first, puts his arm through the doorway to keep it open, and waits for me and Jones. The moment the doors shut and he presses the button, I think my eyes might split themselves open.

"I ain't done nothing."

I haven't spoken since we got in the car and they both look surprised that I got words, stare at my lips.

"We'll talk about it when we get in the office." Detective Harrison is trying not to look at me. Probably part of the bad-cop act.

Jones stares straight into my eyes, but I don't even think she's looking at me. I swear her eyes have blurred and I am just fuzz or the kind of portrait that has no distinct lines. Girl with her mouth open.

I make my hands into fists just so I can feel my nails digging into the palms, know I still got claws. "You arresting me?"

"If we were going to arrest you, we would have started with that." Jones is already bored with me.

We step off the elevator into a hallway indistinguishable from any other office building, except there are security cameras lining the ceiling and it is too quiet. Phones ring but there are no voices. Harrison leads us down the hall, past doors and more doors, all the way to one with INTERVIEW written in heavy type on the front.

This room looks just like every other interrogation room they ever showed on *CSI* or *Law & Order*. After Daddy got out, he'd sometimes talk about how the cops brought him in these rooms, tried to bury him, chip at his bones, how back in the '70s the Panthers brought pistols into the streets.

Jones tells me to please have a seat and somewhere at the base of my spine a shock crawls up my body, through my skin, makes me want to punch her. Haven't been in a fight since middle school, but if I had a chance to watch her peeling lip bleed, I would. I sit down in the chair on one side of the metal table and Harrison takes a seat across from me.

Jones turns around and wanders toward the desk, where she grabs cups from a stack and fills them with water from a pitcher. She brings two cups to the table and sets one down in front of each of us. Her hand tenses giving me the cup and I curl my lips into a small smile at how uncomfortable it makes her to serve me. Harrison licks his lips, takes a sip of water, clearly the one who will be asking the questions here.

Jones slides a notepad across the table toward Harrison and he grabs a pen out of his pocket. "Can you provide me with your name, age, and occupation?"

My eyes wander the room, make quick dashes to each corner. I thought they'd turn on a recorder or something, but I've been on camera since the moment I walked into this building and the "interview" room is no exception. My knee starts to shake. I ignore every urge to flip the table and run out of here.

Harrison raises his voice. "Answer the question."

"My name's Kia." I pause, trying to think about how to answer his questions. Truth doesn't exist in this jumble. "Just turned eighteen, but I'm guessing you know that."

Harrison's pen scribbles across the page, stops. He stares at me for the first time and his eyes are simple and inviting. He looks curious, studying me.

"And occupation?"

"Unemployed." By federal standards, anyway.

Harrison leans forward and his chest is on the edge of his water cup, about to tip it over. "Unemployed?"

"Ain't filing no taxes, am I?"

He leans back, picks up his water. I can see his leg has started to bob and I think part of him enjoys the fight I'm putting up.

Jones isn't too happy, grabs the desk chair, and drags it over to us. "Look, we both know what you do and I really think it would be best if you told us the entire story."

I lean forward, getting as close to their faces as I can. Watching

Uncle Ty over the years has taught me a lot about how to rip some-one apart with only your eyes. Don't need to be in control to make them feel powerless. I switch my eyes between them, keep my lips nice and curled up, don't let the remaining shiver from wet braids and those metal windows show anywhere but my hands, which are hidden beneath the table, forming claw marks all over my skin.

"And what story would that be?"

Jones and Harrison look at each other for the first time. His lips open. Hers seem to press even tighter together. He turns away first, lets his tongue roll just like I thought he would. He really isn't too good at this bad-cop thing.

"We have reports of a possible incident involving you and some of our force." I watch his tongue move up and down as he speaks, play-ing tag with the roof of his mouth.

I lean even closer to him so my face eclipses his vision. "Incident?"

"Involving possible sexual exploitation."

Jones's chair screeches backward and breaks the severity of the air between Harrison and me.

It all makes sense then. They brought the woman cop in to keep appearances up when they interviewed the girl they would later need to bury in some report.

Jones is pacing now, looking for a window in a windowless room. She spins back to me and her lips have gone wild, squirming in every direction. "All we need is you to tell us about how you sell yourself to men. One day maybe a man ran into you, you told him you were a couple years older, had sex, he found out later about your profession, your age. Maybe he didn't know because you lied to him, like you always do, isn't that right?"

"I don't know what you're talking about, but this some bullshit." I claw so deep into my wrist, blood seeps out.

She keeps on talking, her voice receding into its natural groove. The way she speaks is rhythmic, penetrating every cavity of my body, and I almost feel like she won't ever stop. Harrison's face has faded into stone and I don't know if he's listening or not, but she is the one who fills up the room.

"Tell me." She stops to breathe for a moment.

I don't know what is worse: telling her what she wants to hear, even though I know it's a crime, that they could lock me up if they wanted; or denying, which could make them even angrier, risk things I don't even know I'm risking.

My upper lip is twitching now, like it can't decide how to speak. "Won't tell you shit."

It begins again, a stampede of her voice and story after story and her words erupt in my head seconds later like they have been there for decades and pretty soon my water cup is empty and Harrison has left the room and Jones's lips have cracked open but they don't stop writhing and it has been hours since this metal building swallowed me.

She sits down on the edge of the table this time and I bring my hands out from under it to rest them on the cool metal. They are adorned in blood and crescent marks from where my nails have reminded me I'm still breathing.

"I hear you've got a cake at home. Bet you're hungry." Her tongue whips out her mouth so quick I almost miss it. "Tell me and I'll walk you out."

I can't feel my mouth anymore. It's gone numb with the rest of me and maybe my body has dried and maybe I'm still swimming and maybe I drowned in that shit pool. The only thing I'm sure of is that this woman's smell has suffocated every inch of the air and I gotta get out of here. I speak. Don't hear none of it, but I say what she says, repeat it, let it flood out like they say the truth does. Truth like water. Truth looks a whole lot different once the metal closes in.

Part of me is surprised when Jones opens the door for me and Harrison is standing outside the room, when she leaves and he takes me back to the elevator. We get off in the lobby and a woman in a purple suit is waiting. She stares at me longer than she should and then looks at Harrison. He mumbles a hello and glides past her. I follow him, her eyes still lingering on us all the way out the building.

On the short walk from the exit to the waiting police car, I hear the sound of megaphones, drums, and chants. A few blocks down the road, hundreds if not thousands of people march toward the building, their voices a thick chorus, a call-and-response with Freddie Gray's name sharp in the center, and I watch Harrison's head lower as we reach the car. I climb in the back and look out the window. I wonder if they'll ever chant about the women too, and not just the ones murdered, but the particular brutality of a gun barrel to a head. The women with no edges laid, with matted hair and drooping eyes and no one filming to say it happened, only a mouth and some scars.

Harrison pulls the car away and I wonder if he's thinking the same thing, how maybe they didn't need to force a confession out of me, because who would have cared anyway? But he is probably thinking about getting away from the protesters, about how wrong they are to hate him, about the sacrifices he makes to protect the people of this city. He's probably thinking that the cost of one life or one thousand is a price he's willing to pay. That the ravaging of a sad girl with frizzy three-month-old braids is a price he would happily pay for this car, this gun, this power.

I don't remember much about the rest of the ride home, except Harrison wouldn't look at me and I think he turned the sirens on because we sped like we were on a car chase. He dropped me off in front of the Regal-Hi and it looked bigger than it did this morning. He didn't say goodbye, but he looked at me and bit his lip and something told me it wasn't over.

I open the door to the apartment and expect to see Trevor on the couch or bouncing his ball and pacing, but he is lying on the mattress, snores up and running like an engine. My cake sits on the counter. Uneaten.

H IS CONTACT NAME identifies him only by his badge number, 190, and I pick up reluctantly, the first person I've talked to except Trevor since my birthday a couple days ago.

"We had another girl bail on us and we need you tonight. Birthday present for my colleague," he says. His voice reads cold over the phone.

"I can't," I tell him, thinking of Jones and Harrison. I want out of this mess.

"No really isn't an option tonight. We need a girl, he likes 'em young, and we don't have time to find another one." He pauses. "I didn't wanna have to do this, but you're looking at an arrest if you aren't here by nine. I'll pay you, five hundred up front."

I wonder if he's really sorry, if he really doesn't want to threaten me, or if it's all for show like the rest of what they do: the uniforms, the smirks, the good-cop-bad-cop routine. I'm starting to think there is no such thing as a good cop, that the uniform erases the person inside it.

I'm ready to give up, to let them arrest me just for the possibility of never having to feel another one of them inside me, but then the image of Trevor's mouth covered in stale syrup cake springs into my mind. I can't leave him and we need this money. What's one more night?

"Okay," I say.

He sighs and his voice sounds a little more like I remember it: soft. "I'll text you the address."

The phone beeps off and I am left thinking back to all the moments I might have been able to avoid ending up here, then I go to the bathroom to prepare myself, leaving my selfhood in my apartment with Trevor, untethered.

When I arrive at the door of the house, which is really more of a mansion, I'm welcomed in by men dressed in undone button-downs and slacks, no uniforms, but their badges fastened tight to their pants pockets. Everyone has a different badge: Richmond to Berkeley to San Francisco to Oakland. I recognize a handful of them from smaller gatherings over the months.

190 pays me and then leads me through the door, holding my hand, and everyone within sight explodes into applause and beer-fueled roars that remind me of Marcus and Cole when they think they got a platinum song on their hands. 190's hand is colder than mine, but they're the same color and it almost looks like our skin has been knitted together. From what I remember from the last time I saw 190 at the Whore Hotel, he likes to talk. Takes me to the parking lot and gets me in the backseat of his car, fondles a little, but mostly he just divulges everything he's been sealing into the lining of his throat. Told me about how his daddy's not happy he joined the force, said he done raised his daddy like he was the parent and not the child, let the crevices of his body flood. Men don't mind crying as much if they pay for it, knowing they won't have to see me again if they don't want to.

Not surprised he's cold, though. The house is clearly air-conditioned, walls lined in paintings I'm sure no one knows the names of, and I'm guessing the price tag's more important than the art because I could paint something better in the dark and nobody's hanging it in their house.

"Boys, this is Ms. Kia Holt." 190 holds both our hands up like we just won a championship, my lifted arm pulling my skirt farther up and none of their eyes look at me, just at my thighs.

They make a chorus of greetings, all seated on leather couches watching some baseball game, drinking beers, and glancing at me. There are others up the stairs to my left—I can hear them howling—and more walk in and out of the room, coming back with plates of food and drinks they down in single gulps. 190 leads me toward the room with the couches and two men make room for us, let me sit. I cross my legs and eyes shift.

Beside us sits the cop who drove the car the first time, in that alley on Thirty-Fourth. He snickers. "Don't go hogging her all night, Thompson."

190 coughs, removes his arm from around me, stands. "Getting a beer. You want something?" he asks me.

I shake my head. I want a drink more than anything, but part of me is still afraid they'll drug me, lay me out in the living room, and feast.

"She doesn't talk?" a Richmond officer asks 190.

190 squints at him, says, "Apparently not to assholes," and walks out the room.

I think 190 might have a moon in place of his heart: waxing and waning, trying to decide if it is whole. Don't understand men like that—like Tony, like Marcus—but I can't seem to shake them. Wanna rest my head close to their moons and see if they beat too. Tonight there's a room upstairs they blocked off just for me and a rotating door of men with belts they're too eager to remove. 190 comes up every once in a while and checks on me. He knocks on the door and I slip my skirt back on before he enters.

"How about you come downstairs and have a drink? Something to eat?"

I consider it again, but decide against it. Too easy to put something into it, have me out cold and they won't even pay me for what-ever they do when my body has slipped into dark. 190 looks like he wants to sit on the bed, but he keeps his hand on the doorknob and I'm too exhausted to hold him while he sobs right now.

I smooth my hand over the edges of my hairline, try to fix the baby hairs. "Just need some air," I tell him.

He nods, motions his hand for me to walk out the door. He closes it behind me. I hesitate at first, then reach out to him and take his hand. It's nice to touch without being told you have to. He smiles, walks a little straighter.

The moment I am back in the swarm of them, another obnoxious eruption of their hollers begins. 190 shoots some of them looks that they don't even seem to process, just tip their drinks back down their throats. 190 leads me through a couple hallways and I swear this house is as large and endless as the Alameda County Fair corn maze. There are a lot more people here than I originally thought, gathered in different rooms or lounging in doorways. I see a few women with eyes like mine, probably on their way back to their designated rooms, each of them fulfilling some kind of fetish. I see some women in suits and uniforms too, and I wonder if they know what I'm here for, but none of them lock eyes with me and I can't tell if that's because they don't notice me or they're trying not to look.

Finally, 190 pushes open a sliding-glass door and we are standing on the largest patio I've ever seen, stretching out with heated lamps, more couches, and a barbecue. Probably about twenty more people are scattered across the deck. I breathe in, look up at the sky. We're in Berkeley and I think the stars might just be a little more visible across the city limit because after a couple minutes I spot the Big Dipper.

190 stands with me while I watch the sky for a couple minutes, then nudges me. "Is it cool if I leave you here? Head back in when you're ready."

I nod.

He leaves me on my own and it's such a relief to be alone, the way my arms feel free and this patio doesn't feel so alien because the sky's been my friend for as long as I can remember. Spread out big. I think whatever is upward is only comforting when it is dark enough to imagine that there is a beyond.

Most days I say I don't believe in nothing, except something about the way the night colors everything makes me want to. Not in an afterlife, heaven, or any of that shit. That just makes us feel better about dying and I don't really got nothing to fear about dying in the first place. I just think that the stars might line up and trail into an otherworld.

Doesn't have to be a better world because that probably doesn't exist, but I think it is something else. Somewhere where the people walk a little different. Maybe they speak in hums. Maybe they all got the same face or maybe they don't have faces at all. When I have enough time to stare at the sky, I imagine I might be lucky enough to catch glimpses of the something. Always get pulled back to this planet, though.

I don't like when people touch me when I'm not expecting it, and the woman behind me does more than that, grabs my hand and pulls without a word. The sky dissolves into this woman's face and I raise my other hand up to slap her. If I didn't recognize her, I probably would have.

Purple Suit's face is stained into my mind like my fingerprint is permanently tethered to Marcus's neck. She won't never leave it. Now, standing in front of me, Purple Suit wears jeans and a blazer and she looks younger than she did outside the HQ elevator. Don't know if it's just that I can't see her that well in the dark or something, but she looks about the same age as my mama, maybe fifty.

She isn't wearing makeup like she was at the headquarters, and I have to strain really hard to look at her eyes and not at the group of scars on her cheek. They trickle down like a snapshot of rainfall, this brownish color that is only a shade or so darker than her skin, so it almost blends in.

"What are you doing?" I pull her fingers from my wrist, step back from her.

She reaches her hand out, begging me to return. "Don't go back into the light. Can only talk to you if you come back behind the lamp. Please." She's frantic, standing in the corner of the patio, shadowed by the lamp towering behind her.

"Don't understand what you want to talk to me about. You know I already talked to your people at the station. Thought we were finished with this." I step back toward her so I'm standing in the same shadow. I get a better look at her scars here anyway.

"You know why they called you in to talk?"

I nod. "Wanted to question me about some investigation."

"It's a suicide."

I pivot to the side. "Don't know nothing about no suicide."

"Suicide isn't the point. He left a note. An officer killed himself and left a note and he talked about you in that note. He talked about you and more men on this police force than I can name and when they found that note, they opened an internal investigation. My department does all the internal affairs investigations and all we got back was a transcript of your interview where you said the equivalent of 'it's my fault' and left within the hour. Thing is, I saw you walk out of that office six hours after our cameras say you walked in and I'm going to guess you told less than the truth."

A suicide. In the dark of the patio, it's hard to even process what she's saying, but that sticks. The word. How short and simple it seems, innocent, even though it's really the bloodiest image I have ever seen. Not that Mama succeeded. I imagine some man squeezing his eyes shut and waiting for the world to close on him, all because of me. I wonder how he did it, if he was smarter and richer than Mama and took some pills instead of trying to bleed his way to death. It's hard to even believe any of them felt remorse for how tight they'd grip the back of my neck or how they'd buckle their belts and open the car doors, shove me out, and say I'm lucky they don't arrest me. Hard to believe they'd bleed because of me.

Purple Suit is still standing and looking at me, waiting for me to tell her about that day in the station, when they kept me at that table, crescent marks on my wrists.

"Told them what I had to. Don't matter to me what they know or don't know. I ain't getting nothing from telling them the truth." I fold my arms across my chest, lean into my hip. I want her to walk away, to take the blood scene and the suicide with her.

She nods. "That's the thing. The rest of this police department might not have a moral code, but I do. And I'm betting they're doing more taking advantage of you than you even realize. Why you think they waited to interview you until you turned eighteen? Now you aren't a minor and these men will do whatever they have to in order to cover up your age, but it's unethical and unfair and I have too much respect for you to let them file this and forget about it. A man died and in his last hours he wrote about you."

I can picture some faceless cop scribbling, panicked, spelling a name he thinks is mine. Purple Suit needs to stop before he is all I can see, before I want to bleed too just so I don't have to carry another death.

"I don't know nothing about that. Don't matter anyway, this my job. They pay me or they give me information that might as well be payment."

"Bullshit." Her tongue is quick.

I step back again, halfway in the light. "Why you even here telling me this?"

She looks at the ground and back up at me. Her eyes wobble in their sockets and she speaks softly. "Only way any justice is going to come around is if this goes public. Kiara, right? They call you Kia, but it's Kiara?" I don't respond. "Kiara, I'm going to leak this."

The space between my lungs and stomach clenches and I feel almost seasick, like the bay has entered my chest when I wasn't looking. I step closer to her again and speak between my teeth. "If you do that, you fucking my whole life over."

"If I don't, I'm still fucking you over and whatever other girls they'll play with after they're done with you. We both know they've probably already got their hands on a handful of other girls younger than you are that no one knows about. This is a chance at saving them." Her eyes are pooling, but not with tears. Might be pity or guilt, but they've glassed over completely. "I'm telling you because I can take out your name. I think it's best for everyone to know, so you can speak for yourself, but it's your call."

She waits. The heat from the lamp has turned my forehead into a sweat, my teeth grinding so hard they might just chip. I don't look at her. I know she thinks she's doing right by me, but she's just another suit with a God complex and she's sure as hell not saving me. The men in this house would kill me before they let me ruin them.

"What's in it for me?" I ask.

Purple Suit shrugs. "A sense of justice? I don't know what I can offer you at this point, but I'm here to help if you need it. Here's my number," she says, handing me a business card. "Honestly, Kiara, I'm going to have to leak this whether you want me to or not. It's for the best, so I'm here to give you a choice: Do you want your name out there or not?"

I shake my head, can't believe I'm being pressed back into a corner and told I have a choice. "Don't you dare say my name," I spit. I walk away, not bothering to say goodbye.

I retreat back inside, through the maze of hallways, up to the room that is mine for these few hours, and begin again. Head to pillow, my face pressed into the cloth, I let the tears stain my cheeks. No one's looking at my face anyway.

THE PAST FEW DAYS a series of tingles have coursed across my forehead like that feeling when you're blindfolded, but your body feels the eyes. Trevor and I go to the basketball court for Thursday evening pickup games and they are lurking. Couldn't tell you where, but my forehead says they're watching.

We lose the first game and Trevor's face is patches of knots. He doesn't say more than a couple words to me. We win the second game and the latch on his tongue undoes itself.

My forehead prickles in spirals and the grass fades to a stale green. I survey every corner: street to courts to grass and those eyes must hide good because they have completely bypassed my vision. I grab Trevor's shoulder to maneuver him back toward home.

"Can't we stay a little?" Trevor asks, and he don't even know how the eyes are carving into his back. "Ramona say they getting popsicles."

I glance around, lean down to him so I only gotta whisper for him to hear. "We gotta get home, Trev. Somebody following and you not safe where they can see you."

I start pushing him into a full sprint and he's turning around to whisper-yell at me, "You done lost your mind? Acting like Mama." I don't got time to let Dee's face do more than flash through my head. Dee never tried to protect her baby like I do.

We are running again, like usual, but it isn't no play sprint this time. There are moments along the race where I don't feel the tingle, short spurts of street that we are free again. Then they come back. Chasing. The entire way home, Trevor groans and complains about how I'm ruining everything and I stay silent, but the moment we are inside the Regal-Hi gates, I grab the string of his sweatshirt, pull him toward me so he can taste my breath. "Boy, don't you go calling me yo mama when I'm out here protecting you. Better get your ass upstairs and read a book before I really go acting like yo mama and bring out the belt."

Trevor races up the stairs, bony behind sticking out in those shorts. I follow him up, go into my apartment, shut the door, close all the blinds until we are standing in darkness.

"How am I supposed to read if you gonna make it all dark?" his voice whines from maybe five feet in front of me.

"Use your head and cut on a light."

. .

It took less than twenty-four hours for the suicide note to be plastered all over the local news, article after article popping up in the Google search. As promised, Purple Suit blacked out the line that says my name in it. Still, it's been less than two days and I've had eyes tracking me every moment I step outside, following me. I should've known the cops would figure it was me, that they wouldn't just let me off. Only gonna be so long before they make themselves seen. Daddy always said fuck the cops, but don't fuck with them, unless you got a reason. Guess I fucked some cops, fucked with some cops, and now I've been reduced to a paranoid buzz.

I've been too scared to go out at night and I don't got much more money than Mama must. I called Lacy, asked if she could hook me up with a job, but she said she couldn't, not after what Marcus did.

Dee's still leaving twenty bucks on the counter every week or so and Trevor and I have started buying cereal and ramen, exclusively. My stomach feels like a straight-up sponge, sitting in the dark. Trevor fell asleep as soon as he started reading and I'm on my own, slowly gaining night vision.

I don't want to get too close to the windows in case they're there, watching, but I'm hungry. Eat every part of the chicken hungry.

I stare at my phone for a while before I finally dial Alé's number. She picks up, says, "Hey."

"Hey." I know she doesn't talk much, but the silence makes my stomach bubble. "Glad you picked up." I try to sound nonchalant, except there's nothing chill about me right now and my voice cracks.

She coughs. "Yeah. What you need, Kiara?"

I pause. Maybe I shouldn't run to Alé when everything else starts shattering. She done picked up enough pieces. "I'm hungry." I whisper it into the phone, sort of hoping she won't hear.

Alé's laugh is a familiar jingle. It recedes into her voice. "You hungry. Damn, aight, come in and I'll cook you something."

I suck in my breath. "Can't leave the apartment."

"What you mean?"

"Listen, I'm being followed and I can't leave and I need you to come here because I don't got no money and I gotta feed Trev and I'm so hungry, Alé. Please." My words are so tangled I don't know if she heard right.

"Give me twenty." She hangs up and I don't have the guts to say *I love you* first.

Twenty minutes turn into an hour real quick and my vision is now sharper in the dark than it is in the light. I sit by the door, knees to chest, watching Trevor across the room curled into a ball sleeping.

The knock rocks my diaphragm and I raise my hand up so quick it hits the wall. I cuss, wave it around until the initial shock of the collision reduces to an ache, then stand.

"Who is it?" I call, ear to door.

"Alejandra, who else?" Her voice fades to a mumble she probably doesn't think I can hear. "No seas cabeza hueca, ay."

I open the door enough that she can slip through. She's carrying a bag that smells like her mama's kitchen and all I wanna do is snatch it out of her hand and begin devouring, but then I take a second to stare at her. Alé is a picturesque image of herself, the whites of her eyes the brightest thing in the room. She is scared.

"Damn, you not even gonna turn on a light for me?" She walks slowly, arms out, like she's walking a tightrope, and I bet she thinks she's clouded in dark, but for me she is just as clear as ever. Almost too easy to see. The paper bag is clutched tight in her hand and it's wrinkled. "Can't get your food if you don't gimme some light." She isn't even turned toward me, facing Trevor across the room, and she's real close to running straight into the counter. I turn on the closest lamp to me and a dim orange illuminates half of the apartment.

Alé straightens her body and turns to face me. This must be the first time she's really seeing me because the lines in her face turn downward and her skin becomes this tender softness, rippled and babyish.

"Good to see you," I say, still standing by the lamp in the corner. Corners are safer, I think. Two walls instead of one.

"Yeah." Alé sighs. "Said you were hungry?"

I nod and she puts the bag on the counter and opens it, lets out this whirlwind of steam and the scent of fish and carnitas and food I've been dreaming of since the day "normal" suddenly faded to this. She lifts out three plastic boxes. "Snuck it past Mama like I was doing a delivery and she didn't say shit." She laughs, small bubbles of sound escaping.

"La Casa don't even deliver." I laugh with her.

Alé reaches into the bag again and takes out a purple spray paint can. "Happy birthday, by the way."

I smile. "Thank you."

"You coming?" She's still standing in the kitchen, her eyebrows lifted.

"Maybe you could bring it here?" I stare at the cracks in the lampshade, slivers of sharp light that break the subtle warmth of it.

Alé sighs. "You scaring me now, Ki." She piles the boxes and paint into her arms and walks over to me. "At least sit down." The usual light in her voice—the witty note at the end of each of her words—is gone and she just sounds exhausted.

I sit on the floor and Alé follows my lead. I want to just snatch the food and begin gobbling, but she's gripping tight and I know she won't let me eat until I talk. Quietest girl I know wants to talk. I nod my head to Trevor, place my finger to my lips to tell her we gotta stay quiet so he don't wake up. She nods.

"You gonna get right up and leave again if I tell you." The only thing left for me to stare at is my hands. All the lines in my palm Alé used to read are cut; some of them bleeding, some of them scabbing, some of them too deep to decide how to heal. I've been clawing at them, after I finished gnawing on the nails.

Alé puts the boxes beside her and leans toward me, legs crossed, coming closer until her knees are touching mine. She angles her head so that it is directly in front of my hands, looking up into my face. Makes sure she has my eyes. She does.

"I shouldn't have left in the first place. You tell me to stay and I stay. Say whatever you gotta say and I'll stay. Siempre." She doesn't blink.

I cough. "You heard about the story? Cop who killed himself?"

Alé's eyebrows do a quick wave and her eyes glaze a little. "Oh shit."

I can tell she wants to look away from me, can see the way her eyelids flutter like the last thing she wants to do is stare into my eyes, and I can't blame her because this is everything she ever told me not to do and I bet I'm splintering her bones like Mama splintered mine. If only some Sunday Shoes and a funeral could mourn all this shit, bandage us up.

"Didn't mean for it to happen. They found me and it was prison or that and you know what Mama been through, I wasn't about to get locked up." Alé's eyes close and I shut my mouth. "I'm sorry," I whisper.

"Why you sorry?" She's still got her eyes closed.

"I know you didn't want me in this mess and—"

"So you're sorry 'cause you think you disappointed me?" There's something scratching in her throat and I can't tell if she's angry or sad or if she thinks that's the funniest thing she heard in a damn long time.

I fumble. "I guess."

She looks at me and smiles, the brown in those eyes magnetic. "I just wanted to keep you safe, Kiara." She shrugs, and I wonder if she's thinking about Clara. "And the only reason I ever been disappointed is 'cause we never in the same place at the same time." She coughs, maybe to get rid of the nakedness in her voice and maybe just to fill the room with sound. "Except maybe when we eating."

Alé opens the lids, three tacos in each box, and slides them toward me. She scoots back so we aren't touching anymore and I lift a shrimp taco from the box and consume it in three bites. I reach for the next one. She could be eating, but instead she watches me, sly smile. I look at the newest tattoo on her neck. It's a beehive, except I don't think it's full of bees. I lean in, sauce dripping from the corner of my mouth. The swarm is actually a bunch of butterflies mid-flight. I want to touch them and see if the wings flutter because it looks like they would, but there's food to be eating and it's too dangerous to make contact with Alé's skin when it's this dark.

"Any for me?" My stomach leaps at the sound of Trevor's voice. Both Alé and I whip our heads to look at him sitting up in bed. We must not have been quiet enough.

Alé waves him over and he practically runs to us. I don't remember him taking off his shirt, but he isn't wearing it no more and his bare torso makes me want to scoop him up and cradle him, lengthening body and all. That boy is a wonder. He's my autumn rain. My last picture of the sun before it sets. Daytime is not possible without Trevor. Not even sure the sun comes out without Trevor.

He sits beside us and picks up his own taco. I pause to watch him bite into it and chew with his mouth open, like I know he will. He's staring at me and waiting for me to tell him to shut his mouth while he's eating, but tonight I stay quiet. If the boy wants to eat with his tongue out, don't he deserve that joy? Too dark for anyone else to ever know.

Trevor pauses before his next bite and looks around in the black. "Think there's ghosts up in here?"

Alé glances up at the ceiling like that's where she might find them. "Nah, just spiders."

ALÉ SLEEPS like a mix between a corpse and a starfish. She never said she was gonna stay the night, but we both knew she would the moment she laid her head in my lap. Never seen somebody sleep on a hardwood floor like that: extremities spread out and not moving a single inch. Mouth open just enough that you can see she got teeth, but not a tongue.

I watched her all night, waiting for my own body to swirl me into a slumber. Never did. After we finished the tacos, Trevor went back to the mattress and fell asleep. I told Alé everything else about the cops and Purple Suit and the tingle and she said I needed to have Tony or Marcus with me, just in case the tingle turns to a full quake and not even the blinds can keep me safe. I argued with Alé, told her about Marcus, but she wasn't having none of it, so we made a deal that I would go to Cole's in the morning and she would take Trevor to the taquería and make sure he's fed.

Now I'm just waiting for her body to show some sign of life again. It's bright out. I can tell because our blinds let in cracks of light that make patterns across the floor. The light spreads to Alé's sleeping body so she is a weaving of light and dark.

It starts with her jaw. It opens a little at first and then shakes side to side, goes in a full circle, and ends in a yawn. When she blinks, I want to touch her face. It's almost like my entire body wants to climb over her and touch the slope of her cheek.

"Morning." Her voice changes pitch a couple times and comes out a groan.

I laugh. "Morning."

"Trevor still sleeping?" she asks.

I glance over at Trevor's body still curled up and turned to the other wall.

"Yeah," I say.

Alé's hair has completely escaped from her usual bun and I grab on to it, smooth it into my hands, and swirl it back into its neatness, leaving a single black strand. I watch the way it feathers her face and I'd like to think sometimes it tickles and sometimes she laughs out of nowhere and her butterflies start singing.

She sits up and looks at me for a moment before crawling across the floor, big bulk of her looking like a child, all the way to Trevor. She shakes him.

"Buenos días," she sings, and her voice is a flat groan again, but I'm so happy to hear some sound in this apartment after all the hours of silent that I want her to just keep talking and singing all day.

Trevor rolls over with his arms covering his eyes. Alé moves them and leans down to him and yells buenos días into his face again, and he jumps up to his feet like he's a ninja and runs over to tackle me. I'm down on the floor laughing and his newly awake eyes are bright and wide.

Eventually, I shove him from me. "Get on off me, boy."

He climbs off and stands. "I'm hungry," he says.

"You always hungry." I laugh.

Alé is already putting her shoes on. "Go on and get ready, Trev. We're going to La Casa."

Trevor runs to the pile of clothes in the corner and changes faster than I've ever imagined anyone could change clothes. He pulls on his sneakers and stands by the door while I'm still on the floor by the lamp. Alé comes over to me and crouches down so she can talk to me without Trevor hearing.

"You good?" she whispers.

I nod. "Just make sure he's safe, yeah?" I tilt my head toward Trevor.

Alé smiles, touches my knee. The warmth spreads.

I watch them leave and I really hope the eyes are waiting for me and not him, that they follow me and not him. When they shut the door, images of Marcus and his fists and the last time I saw him imprint into my memory and the last thing I want to do is leave this apartment to go fix something this fragmented. Don't got a choice, though. Alé's right: if they find me alone, I'm fucked.

I grab my phone and dial. Shauna picks up on the first ring.

"What you want, Kiara?" Her voice is just as pissed as I expected it would be.

"You still got that car?" Cole's mama gave Shauna her old car when the baby was born. She's the only one I know who might just pick me up.

Shauna pauses. "Yeah. Why?"

"I'm in trouble and I need to see Marcus, but I can't be out on the streets alone right now. I need a ride." I insert a couple pleases and offer to take care of her baby for her sometime. She doesn't speak for a while.

"I can be there in ten, but don't go asking me for no favors after this. Lord knows you didn't do shit last time I asked for one." She hangs up, and even though it stings, Shauna's never been more right.

She arrives in less than ten minutes and calls me, says she's outside. My shoes are on but I haven't opened the blinds yet. When I step out the door, the light hits like the first sip of vodka on an empty stomach and I can't tell if it hurts or if the sun has never felt better. Feels like my skin absorbs it. There's no tingle while I walk down the stairs and past the shit pool, but the moment I step out the gate, it begins. Spreads top of the head down. I run to Shauna's car, an old Saturn station wagon, get in, and slam the passenger door shut.

A cry erupts from the backseat and I twist around to see the baby in her car seat.

"Shit. You done woke her up." Shauna reaches back and pats the baby's belly until she stops shrieking and returns to her sleep.

I cough a couple times. "We really can't be just sitting here like this." I try not to say it too loud, like the volume might lessen Shauna's eye roll, the heat flaring up in her cavities. I know she doesn't like being told what to do, but she returns her attention to revving the car anyway and we're off to Cole's house.

I let us sit in silence for a couple minutes and the guilt gnaws at my stomach, feels like it's reaching into me and squeezing. I can't handle it paired with the tingle that continues to trail me. I keep looking out the window, behind us, but I can't figure out where the eyes are, just that they're there. At least it means they aren't with Trevor and Alé.

"Look, I'm real sorry about last time. Shoulda listened to you, but you gotta understand that shit been rough for me too, and I ain't been in the best place to help nobody. Not fair to you though, so I'm sorry. And I really appreciate you doing this for me."

There's a click that continues somewhere under the hood of the Saturn and I tap my finger on my thigh in time to it.

Shauna glances at me at a red light. "Wouldn't have done it if I didn't need to talk to you anyway."

Her eyes are hungry again, the same way they were too many months ago when she was moaning and cleaning and her nipples were cracked. They aren't a predatory hungry, more like a sick bird waiting to be fed before nighttime, before it's too late.

"Talk about what?"

We're getting close to Cole's now, but Shauna slows down, pulls over to the side of the road. She parks the car and looks at me. I switch my gaze from her to her child, who is awake and staring at us with eyes that glitter almost like one of those windows with a one-sided mirror. You know there is a whole world behind them, but all you can see is your own face.

"They ain't just dealing soft drugs anymore." I can hear the Tennessee drawl in Shauna's voice, scared and squeaky. "And they running with some scary niggas who don't give a shit about them or they families. Kiara, I got a child. I got a child."

And Shauna begins to moan. This time her moans are more of a wail, ripping out inside the car. I swear they're gliding right out her mouth and down my throat because I feel like I've swallowed all the salt in Lake Merritt and I can't separate the tingles from the punctures from the nausea.

Shauna is sobbing and the baby is staring, both her hands held out to us, not moving, but waiting. I grab on first, put a finger in her small palm. Shauna sees me do this, still keening with everything in her, and turns to put a finger in the other palm. I use my right hand to touch the back of Shauna's neck, lightly rubbing it like Mama used to do for me when I had a nightmare that cycled into teeth chattering. We form a whole circle of internal moaning. Shauna lets it out large and bellowing. The child whimpers so softly I can barely hear it over Shauna's moans. I'm not sure what comes out my mouth, only that it kind of sounds like a hum or a song or an inverted lullaby.

Shauna's child releases her grip when the sounds fade to soft murmurs, and Shauna looks at me, tilts her head like she's trying to solve something but she isn't quite sure where the pieces are.

My forehead starts to pulse, really pulse, like my heartbeat begins in the head.

"Shit." I look out the rearview mirror and there's no movement on the street besides the swish of a basketball net in the wind outside an apartment building.

Shauna shifts her body back to the steering wheel, but doesn't start the car. "What the hell is wrong with you?"

I've heard her say this same thing a million times and it's never warranted a response before, but this time she looks like she wants me to answer.

"I got in some shit and I think I'm being followed."

There's no sign of shock or fear or any other expression I would have expected on Shauna's face. Instead, she just asks, "By who?"

"Cops, I think."

At that, Shauna leans her torso forward onto the steering wheel and puts her head down.

"How the fuck we end up here, Ki?" I've never heard Shauna talk like that, all barriers down defenseless, and it makes me think of when we were younger, how cold and confident she was.

The day I first met Shauna, Alé was teaching me how to skateboard and we were out off Eighty-First Avenue in Deep East. Shauna was sitting on her auntie's porch steps twisting her little sister's hair, and Alé got on the board and raced past them, me running after her like I could ever actually keep up. Shauna, thirteen and woman already, called out to us. She said, "Y'all keep doing that and you gon' make a breeze, mess up her hair," and we slowed down to stare at her because we'd never heard no girl talk like that or look like that or put her hand in the crease of her waist like she meant it. Really meant it.

My smart ass wasn't gonna have none of that, so I said, "Whatchu gonna do about it?" And Shauna came down those steps like a dog on the hunt, right up to me with a snarl. I was still skinny in every way, didn't have any meat on my bones to pound Shauna, who was all soft belly and hips that cradled it like they already knew she'd be with child in a matter of years.

Alé was circling back around to stand by me. Even her square shoulders could not compete with Shauna. It isn't that Shauna was that tall or nothing; she simply had outgrown the bodies we were still shedding. She was on to the next one, titties that spilled out her tank top and bounced when she walked—strutted—in beat-up sneakers that everyone told her she best replace. Shauna always said she'd rather be barefoot, but her auntie wouldn't let her leave the house like that. Eventually, she gave up and let one of the boys swooning over her buy her some crisp new shoes you could tell she never liked.

The day we met, Shauna was ready to fight. I didn't even know how to throw a real punch and Alé didn't believe in fighting nobody, just standing by and loving me. Shauna was starting to talk shit when the boys arrived on their bikes. We thought they were just passing through, about ten of them, older than us by a couple years maybe. Then one of them grabbed my ass and Shauna saw it coming, pushed past me real quick, lifted her leg, thigh shaking, muscle bulging, and kicked. Knocked the boy who grabbed my ass right off his bike.

The other ones had started circling, but Shauna's blow made them flee, tires squealing. The prelude to our fistfight dissipated into her huffing and me in complete awe, telling her, "Thanks."

"Don't worry about it." She turned around and walked back to her porch, where her little sister sat watching like nothing happened. Shauna sat behind her sister again and resumed the twists. Alé and I kept skating, went around the block a couple times, always returning to the porch, where we'd slow down and stare. Third or fourth time around and Shauna called out to us, "If y'all wanna watch, might as well sit down and have a Coke."

We watched Shauna twist every hair on her sister's head, sipping sodas and mesmerized. By the time Shauna got pregnant at seventeen and dropped out, she didn't seem like such a wonder anymore. Just another one of us trying to make it out here. Her auntie married some guy, moved to West Oakland, and didn't want her to come, baby and all. She moved in with Cole and his mama and every fantasy she ever had turned into moans and now we're sitting in a car running from things you can't run from and trying to forget that we were just babies who wanted to skate and walk around without no shoes.

"I don't know," I say, even though I do. Even though it all seems so clear, like one long road that was always gonna end up here. "Sometimes we all do what we gotta do for the people we gotta do it for."

I lean over to look back at the car seat, mirror eyes. "Like you said, you got a child."

Shauna wipes her last tear and starts the car again. She doesn't respond and she don't need to. We both know. It's another two minutes and we're pulling up at Cole's, my head still pulsing. I tell Shauna we gotta hurry in, can't be out here too long, and she grabs her daughter from the backseat and slides her onto her hip. We head into the house quickly, right down to the basement. It looks like Shauna has stopped trying to clean it because toys and Cole's dirty clothes are all thrown on the floor. Part of me wants to pick them up, but it also feels so fitting, like it would be wrong for the room to be crisp and spotless when nothing else is.

You can hear the beat from outside the studio door. "Cole's out but he'll be back soon. Won't stop you if you feel like kicking both they asses," Shauna calls to me. She's on the couch bouncing her baby in her lap and smiling. Not with her teeth, but with the slope of her shoulders. I keep walking, swing the door open. Marcus isn't standing in the recording booth like usual, but the music is blasting out. He's the only one in the room, sitting on the floor with his eyes closed, wringing his hands.

"Marcus?"

I step over him to shut the music off on the soundboard and the room goes silent. I crouch beside him. He shakes his head and opens his eyes, bloodshot and flooding.

"What's going on?" I ask.

"Like you give a shit," he spits, and I wonder if I should leave, let him be the same selfish person he's been since he gave up on me.

Then he sighs and whispers, "Sorry."

He looks at me. I breathe in. "I'll tell you my shit if you tell me yours."

"We ain't in middle school, Ki." He shakes his head again. "Ain't a game."

I ignore him. "I don't know if you seen the news, but I been having sex with cops for money for months and I guess one of them killed himself and named me in his suicide note and now there's some kind of investigation. I got cops out here following me."

The look that washes over Marcus is a new one for me, never seen it like that before. I expected him to be a little pissed or ashamed, not wanna deal with my shit. Maybe his left eyebrow would twitch like it does sometimes or his neck would show its veins. Maybe my fingerprint would dance. Instead, Marcus's face breaks open in the center, eyes looking up.

"Shit." There's a moment when neither of us says anything and then he starts looking around the studio like he's never seen it before. He chokes on his voice as he whispers, "It ain't gonna happen for me."

"What you mean?"

He looks so small.

"You were right. None of this shit is real, no record label wants to sign me, I can't get no gigs, and the only reason I got somewhere to sleep is 'cause Cole and I been hustling. And I didn't even do what I said I'd do, protecting you and shit. I should've been there to keep you safe."

Marcus looks like he's drowning in his face and for as long as I hoped he'd say this to me, I wish he didn't have to. I wish these words could fix it all. I lean in and kiss the top of his head. He wraps his arms around me and I can feel him shaking.

"We still family, Mars."

He keeps sobbing into my chest and I look over his shoulder to see Tony leaning in the doorway. He turns his grimace into a smile.

"I need you to do something for me now," I whisper to Marcus. He pulls away from my chest just enough to look at me and nods. "You too, Tony." Tony nods too, doesn't even bother pretending he wasn't listening.

Tony joins us, sitting on the couch, Marcus and I still on the golden rug. The whole studio looks different, everything flashy: new couch, gold carpet with a giant C in the center. Completely new equipment: speakers, soundboard. The low table is now occupied by a keyboard even though none of them can play, so I'm not quite sure why it's here, resting on the table like someone might sit down and bust out a tune.

I take a breath. "I need your help. Both of you. I told Marcus but I'm in some deep shit and cops are following me. Ain't safe for me to walk around on my own no more and I don't got nobody else to ask."

"Of course," Marcus says.

I look to Tony.

"You in trouble?" Tony asks.

I didn't want to tell him about it, have both of them look at me like I'm even more tainted than I already was, but now I don't have a choice. "The cops investigating me, they ain't arrested me yet and they say they ain't gonna, but they brought me in and questioned me and now I got cops following me."

"Why they investigating you?" Tony asks.

I avert my eyes. "I been helping some of them out. At motels and shit."

Tony doesn't say anything, but I know he's looking at me, imagining what it is I've done, trying to forgive me for it.

Marcus sets a hand on my knee and shakes it.

"We still family, Ki." And I think he means it, beyond words, beyond this moment, beyond the things our parents did to leave us broken.

I nod and, for the first time, I think about what I did, about the panic that sets in when anyone else touches me the way Marcus just did, how many guns have been pressed to my skull, fingers scraping my skin, fists in my hair. In this room, with these golden boys, all the things I've done feel vulgar, devastating, like I do not deserve to be loved good again.

"I'll text Cole and he'll come pick us up so we can get you home, aight?" Marcus is already collecting himself, pulling his face back in and removing his phone from his pocket.

"I think Cole got a bat or some shit in his garage. I'll go get it and meet you out front," Tony says, standing again, and disappearing out of the studio.

Marcus gets up too and pulls me from the floor, hangs an arm around my shoulders. We head back out to the basement, where Shauna is cradling the baby, and walk past her up the stairs and out onto the porch. It takes a couple moments for me to process that I'm back outside, that it's muggy and hot and someone is still following me.

Cole is pulling up to the house in his flashy Jaguar when Marcus and I step onto the sidewalk. He rolls his windows down and shouts, "Kia, baby, you back," before stepping out of the car, engine still running. He jogs around to take Marcus in, slap his back, and then turns to hug me.

That's when the car pulls up, sleek and black, flashing lights from the inside, when the men in the car leap out, reaching into their waistbands and pulling out badges and guns. I catch their numbers, 220 and 17, both of them from the Whore Hotel, both of them staring straight at me as they pull Marcus's hands taut behind him, then Cole's, slapping on handcuffs and mumbling something about their rights, something about searching the car. 220 leaving 17 to place them in the backseat of the undercover car while 220 pops the trunk in Cole's Jaguar, pulls out sacks of powder and automatic rifles.

I look through the tinted window to Marcus, who is crying, fear-crying like he did when Daddy got taken away, and I'm screaming for him, at him, pleading with 220, who smirks at me, comes up close enough that I can feel his breath, grabs my arm. He growls, "Don't you dare say my name or I'll make sure everyone knows yours. We're watching." He releases me, walks back toward the car, and gets into the passenger seat.

Marcus's face isn't visible anymore and suddenly Shauna is running at the car, pounding on the glass, sobbing. The car is screeching away, she's turning to look at me, raging, and Tony is behind me, appearing right when the danger is gone, pulling me into a hug. I don't think Tony's ever wrapped his arms around me before, not like this, not like he is capturing me and cannot let go. Part of me wants him to squeeze me until one of my ribs cracks, until I don't feel like I'm floating, wants him to squeeze me so hard the tingle fades and his arms are the only things worth feeling.

But the other part of me can't bear that he stood at the door and watched my brother get taken, didn't do shit, and my chest starts getting heavy. I start to push on him, shoving, my fingernails digging into his shirt, until he releases.

"Sorry," he says. I'm out of breath. I stare at him and my stomach heaves like this is the ultimate betrayal, but what did he really do to me? Men done so much worse than hug me for a minute too long.

"Why didn't you do nothing?" I scream, shoving him again, tears flying out with my spit.

Tony stumbles backward like my hands have the force to knock him down and he looks like he's about to argue, starts to stutter something too choppy for me to make out, then shakes his head, doesn't even look at me as he says, "I didn't wanna go down too." Tony steps forward, tries to grab my hand. "I'm sorry." He just keeps saying he's sorry, over and over again, but it doesn't change anything, so I tell him I don't want to see him right now and turn on my heels, suddenly unafraid of the tingle and the cops and the men who might find me because my brother just got taken and it's starting to feel like I don't have anything left to lose.

I get on the bus and there's no seats, so every time we hit a pothole I fall into the person next to me, my body doing internal flips. Everything a blur. At least I don't feel the tingle here, on the bus, behind these windows. Even when I get off at my stop, the tingle stays gone, but the image of Marcus's face mid-panic remains, feels like it will never leave me.

La Casa Taquería is small and comforting, the blue awning and the sounds of constant construction. Alé is at the cash register, Trevor sitting on a barstool in front of her, folding paper airplanes, and the two of them are something, some miracle I was gifted in all this shit. When Alé glances up, I can tell she sees my panic right as she locks eyes with me, tells Trevor to go help in the kitchen.

I walk up to her and she grabs both my hands. "What's wrong? You don't look right."

"They arrested Marcus."

Alé pulls me into her chest and whispers, "I'm so sorry. Lunch rush is almost over and I think the rest of 'em got it. Come upstairs with me?"

I don't remember Alé ever inviting me into her apartment like this before. Always thought she was afraid I'd judge or think she was some kind of a mess. I nod and wait for Alé to go into the kitchen and let her family and Trevor know where we going. She returns and gestures for me to follow her through the other door and up the staircase.

She tries to push the apartment door open, but it doesn't budge. "Gets stuck sometimes," she says, and proceeds to slam her entire body weight into the door until it swings open.

The place is adorned in color, kindergarten classroom amounts of color: ocean of reds and blues and every shade of earth. I've never seen so many blankets and drapes and knickknacks. They've got tablecloths and hand-stitched embroideries on the walls. There's a bed in each corner of the room and then a doorway that leads to another room with two more beds in it, plus a refrigerator. The bathroom connects to that room and I can smell the scent of soap that I'm almost sure they made because it smells just like some of the things Alé infuses her weed with.

The beds ain't even really beds: more like couches they converted into these magical dreamlands. The pillows scream to be touched, but more than that, they scream to be stared at: images of people mid-story. Family fables caught in stitching. It's something I wish I knew how to do, turn art into something I lay my head on.

"It's beautiful," I say.

Alé mumbles a *thank-you* like she's embarrassed to occupy something this perfect, but all her focus is on me.

"What happened?" she asks.

"They been following me and when Marcus and Cole were there, I guess they jumped at the chance to fuck with me. Busted them with pounds of shit and guns and God knows what else."

Alé walks fully into the room and over to one of the beds. This one is blue all over, has pillows with pictures of children on them. She calls me over to her and I sit. This must be Alé's bed, the cushions she lays her head on. She sweats into these sheets every night, picks at loose threads on these pillows. Of course this is hers: baby of the family, blue.

"You okay?" She looks at me, takes all of me in.

"No." I lean into her, let her have a little of my weight. "It's all my fault and I can't change none of it." I wonder if Mama felt this too.

"We gonna get you out of this. And Marcus too, we gonna figure it out."

"Okay." There's nothing else to say, no promises to make, no solutions to find.

"He probably ain't been processed yet, but when he is, he'll call. Or we will." She pulls me closer to her. "For now, I got something to show you."

Alé leans down and reaches under the bed, pulling out jars. Weed jars. I laugh at how hard it has become to remember when this would be normal, another day for us. She opens two of the jars and starts grinding, then rolling.

"Here?" I ask, looking at the door like her mama might walk in at any moment.

She chuckles at me. "Don't worry, ain't nobody coming. Anyway, Mama smoked a wood with me last week."

I think of her mama, try to imagine her high and hysterical, but all I can picture is her delicate fingers braiding Alé's hair and the creases that built in her forehead after Clara disappeared.

Alé opens the window beside her bed and it jingles the bell on her dream catcher. I want to reach out, hold it, hold all Alé's dreams in my palms.

She lights the first joint, passes it to me.

"I call this one Chava," she says.

I take it between my fingers and rest it in my lips, breathe in. It tastes like honey and mint, like consuming a stroll on the water. The smoke comes out in a perfect stream and I cough myself into a high. She's already lit the other joint and we switch. I breathe this one in and I'm immediately struck with its familiarity: Sunday Shoes. Lavender. Funeral day and clothes with holes we mourn like they are the body.

When the high hits, every guard I've kept raised these past months falls and I feel the creases of my neck filling in tears, Alé watching me as I cry in front of her for the first time in years.

"I'm so sorry, Ki," she whispers.

I try to swallow the urge to fully sob, but it escapes me anyway and I feel like an aching woman, like I'm old and wrinkling and my back hurts and there is no room in life for me to feel anything and yet here I am, overcome. Unraveling. Alé rubbing my back, between my shoulder blades.

"I just wanted a family. I just wanted something to work, something that was mine."

"I know, Kiara. I know."

I lean back into Alé's chest, fully in the bed now. We lie there until my sobs slow and both joints are gone and we're in a daze, arms and legs intertwining, forgetting that our skin is meant to be lonely. Every inch of the bed is solace, smooth, and smells like every dream I wish I had the space to have. Smells like Alé, like weed and never having to worry about the eyes. Feels like the warmth, the one that sends my entire body into a frenzy. And maybe the story we remember will be our sleep and maybe it will be her mouth on mine and maybe it will be her leaving, me waking up alone and not quite sure what was real.

When I get the call, the high has mostly faded and I'm still lying in Alé's bed trying to figure out how the ceiling got so cracked. I've decided it's probably the earthquake, that big one that turned San Francisco into a desert and made everyone take cover inside their nightmares. Bet Alé's mama and all her aunties watched it shake and fracture their ceiling into a labyrinth of cracks.

Maybe the high is still lingering in there because I don't register the meaning of the automated warning when I answer the phone, just press the number the robot lady tells me to press. It takes his voice to really shock me awake.

"Kiara." My brother's voice sounds like it exists in another dimension. This time, it's distorted and weak. The same pain from earlier is still in there, masked in fatigue, but over it all, he just sounds afraid. I can imagine his face now, everything pooling in fear like the day we found Mama in the tub. Like Daddy's funeral or the first time we visited Mama behind bars.

"Where are you, Mars?"

"They got us at county jail, Santa Rita." He's sobbing so hard my fingerprint's probably swimming in his tears.

I want to tell him I'm gonna fix it, tell him I'll melt down the bars to whatever cell they got him in, and take him away in the getaway car I don't own.

"I'm sorry."

He clears his throat. "Maybe they was there 'cause of you, but it was my shit they found. Listen, I don't want you to worry about me, aight? I need you to make sure you safe and then I need you to do something for me. Can you do that, Ki?"

"Of course."

"I need you to go find Uncle Ty, okay? He's gonna know what to do, he been through this and he owes me. Bring him here, I don't care what you gotta do to get him, aight?"

"I don't know, Marcus, I already tried—"

"I don't wanna die in here. Please."

Even after everything he's put me through, that's all it takes for me to want to help him. If he's ready to ask something of me instead of just taking it, then I will walk to the ends of the earth for him.

"Okay." Maybe it's the weed, the bed, Sunday Shoes, guilt. Didn't plan on ever seeing Uncle Ty again. Still, I say okay and Marcus hangs up and my limbs are attached at the hinges.

MARCUS IS SCARED. I could tell from the quake in his voice, the tremor. But, more than that, just him saying Uncle Ty's name told me all I needed to know about how his insides are rearranging. The metal heat will do that to you. So will a siren. I don't know how to find Uncle Ty any more than Marcus does, not after Mama didn't have his number. I called Shauna after Marcus's voice stopped reverberating through my jaw and she told me to fuck off, said I'm the reason Cole got picked up and she didn't want no more part in my shit. Her baby's glass eyes blew up big in my head, looking back at me. My face a sheet of gray.

If Marcus is saying Uncle Ty's the cure, I don't have anything left to tell me he ain't right. Nobody believes in God 'cause they got proof, only 'cause they know there's not any proof to say they're wrong.

Alé told me she'd keep Trevor for a couple days while I figure this out and now I'm kissing Trevor's forehead even as he squirms away from me.

"Aight. I'll see you in a couple days," I say, placing a smile just curved enough to be comforting on my face. Trevor nods and Alé reaches out to rest a hand on my cheek, brushing it with her thumb before letting me go.

I walk out the door, lingering in shadows on the long walk back to the Regal-Hi. Same walk Marcus and I took the last day he came with me to Alé's, when we started separating like my old bracelet beads when the elastic string stretched out. When I arrive at the gate to the Regal-Hi, I don't let the pool halt me with its blue, even though it tries to pull me in, that scent, that so-fresh-it-almost-seems-real smell. Then I catch a whiff of sulfur behind the chlorine and I remember you can't trust nothing that saturated.

Marcus and I used to fight about who got to choose the morning cartoon. We'd play war over the remote, scream, cry, plead, whatever we had to do to get control of those buttons. Eventually, one of us would take the remote and whack the other's head with it out of impulse. Whoever got hit would start bleeding or swelling and Mama would scold whoever done the hitting and give the other one the remote. When I was the perpetrator, I would go sit in a corner and sob. Not 'cause I wanted the remote or even 'cause I felt bad. I just wanted to be able to reverse time and never let that plastic collide with his bone. I just wanted to go back.

That's sort of what this feels like: the helplessness of it. Like standing on the road that leads to here and noticing a path you didn't know existed and not being able to take it. Like the road that leads to here was never the only road and time made me forget that until these sobbing moments when I remember, when the fog clears and I'm looking back and there's a fork on the ground, another way.

I enter my apartment, empty without Trevor, and sit on the edge of the couch, dialing the number Purple Suit gave me and biting off every last bit of white fingernail until each one bleeds. She answers on the second ring.

"They got my brother."

"Hello? Who is this?"

"Kiara Johnson. Some cops pulled up on my brother and he's in Santa Rita and I didn't know who else to ask."

Purple Suit is silent for a moment. When she speaks next, she sounds tense. "I'm sorry to hear that, Kiara. I actually need to tell you something, if you haven't already heard."

"What?"

"Your name was given to the press yesterday. Only your alias, at the moment, but it won't take long before they have your real name and address. It's all over the news, especially in the bay, but it made it to the *L.A. Times* this morning. I'm sorry."

I think about what 220 threatened, that he'd say my name if I said his, and I didn't tell anyone anything, but I should've known one of them would out me, that I wouldn't be able to make it through all of this with my anonymity too.

Purple Suit coughs. "I want to help you and your brother, but I don't have any jurisdiction over arrests, Kiara."

"That's not what I'm asking for. I need to contact my uncle, but I don't got his number and I thought maybe you would know how to find him, investigate or something."

I can almost feel Purple Suit nodding in her HQ office. "I have access to a driver's license database, if he's licensed in California, that would give me his contact information. I'd be willing to look, but I need you to do something for me too."

"Haven't I suffered enough 'cause of you? You really asking for more?"

"I'm just trying to help, Kiara."

I'm weary of people asking me to do shit, but if Purple Suit is going to give me the thing I need most, I don't really have a choice. "Fine."

"I have a friend. Her name is Marsha Fields, she's an attorney, and she can help you out with everything that's about to happen with the investigation. I want you to call her, okay?" She sounds like she's trying to talk someone out of jumping from a roof.

"Okay."

She reads me the number and I write it down on a slip of paper.

"As for your uncle, could you provide his full name and date of birth?"

I've rarely called Uncle Ty by anything but his nickname, so I need to pause to even remember what Ty stands for.

"Tyrell Johnson. He was born August 8, 1973."

I remember Marcus used to make him cards on every birthday, walk them down to the mailbox himself. I wait while Purple Suit types something into a computer, the click of the keyboard floating through the phone.

"I have three results in California."

Purple Suit gives me each phone number, which I scribble beneath the lawyer's.

"Thanks," I say.

"Of course. Don't forget to call Miss Fields."

I hang up and look around the room. At the same walls that we've lived in since both Marcus and I were born, since our parents found each other and thought they were creating a miracle of a family before we spiraled into a disaster. Into kin more dead and caged than free.

I call each number for Tyrell Johnson, in order. The first one I get voicemail, but I can tell it's not him from the voice on the answering machine. I dial the next one. Calling these numbers feels like making some kind of fundraising call, knowing the stranger on the other end doesn't want to buy none of your shit. I'm surprised when I get an answer and it's his voice, sounding the same as it always did, a lower echo of Daddy's. Uncle Ty is younger than Daddy, even younger than Mama, and I think he tries to make his voice younger too, how he swings each word into the next.

"Uncle Ty?"

Silence.

"How you get my number?" He doesn't sound happy to hear from me, but he doesn't hang up either.

"Don't worry, I ain't calling 'cause I want your money or for you to come take care of us or nothing. Marcus and I in some shit and didn't know who else to call." I pause, hoping he'll interject, say that he's happy to help, that he regrets leaving in the first place, but he doesn't. "Marcus says you owe him."

"So why he not the one calling me?" Uncle Ty's voice is softer, the mention of Marcus cushioning him.

"He's in Santa Rita."

"This family got some kind of death wish? I told your mama I didn't want no part after the trial."

I remember the day Uncle Ty left, how he didn't even bother telling us he was leaving and instead just stopped picking up his phone, got a new number, told Mama to tell us the next time we visited her, but Mama was so far gone at that point that she didn't even remember the conversation. At first, Marcus was convinced that Uncle Ty had been killed or kidnapped, but I knew better. Uncle Ty's voice showed up in that club and then I listened to it on the radio later and it was unmistakably him, with a beat drowning out half his words. We looked him up and he suddenly had a Wikipedia page and was signed with a record label when before he was a blank page, untraceable.

Marcus kept looking him up for months, watching as new articles came out about him, photos of him on red carpets. I didn't expect to feel so angry, but hearing Uncle Ty on the other end of the phone, so righteous, makes me want to rage, want to tell him he doesn't get to judge a family he's not a part of anymore.

"I don't really give a shit why you left, I just know Marcus needs you and he said you gotta come back out here and visit him at Santa Rita. This ain't me asking, you know I never wanted nothing from you, but he needs this."

Uncle Ty doesn't say anything, but he breathes loud, like he's swishing his breath around in his mouth before letting it out. "Okay. I'll fly up there tomorrow, but I ain't staying, I got a life out here to come back to. You still at the Regal-Hi?"

"Still here."

Uncle Ty says he'll get a car and meet me at the Regal-Hi in the morning, take us to visit Marcus because he doesn't want to see him alone. He sounds like he wants to hang up, but I don't let him.

"I don't get it. Why don't you wanna see him? Thought he was the only one you liked."

Uncle Ty clears his throat. "I told you, I made something of myself out here."

"So? You ain't care about him?" I don't even know why I give him the time of day to explain, but I need to hear it.

"Course I do, I just don't wanna see him like that, aight?"

His voice is still too cold and for some reason I don't believe him. It ain't about watching Marcus locked up or hurt, it's about him, about how he doesn't want to feel remorse for his life or hold on to his regrets. After we hang up, and my anger evaporates into empty air, I can't help but wonder if Uncle Ty might do the thing we stopped hoping he'd do and save us. Take us back with him to L.A. or even just start calling every week, buy Marcus his very own microphone and a soundboard worth dreaming about so he wouldn't need Cole, help us live out a life we never chose. But I'm not stupid and I don't trust Uncle Ty enough to let myself hope for him to change who he is.

. .

I'm pacing inside the gate to the Regal-Hi, watching the shit pool glimmer in the morning light. Uncle Ty is on his way, texted me a half hour ago that he had landed and would pick me up out front. He doesn't even get out of the car, just honks the horn of the black sedan and I unlatch the gate, step off the curb, and pull open the door to another face I never expected to reappear in my life.

Uncle Ty's grown his hair out into these short locs that hang down like a crown and I can tell his white T-shirt cost more than his shoes because it's got pre-ripped holes in it. Uncle Ty smiles with his teeth, like they're the most important part of the grin, pats the passenger seat, and then, when I'm fully in the car, touches my shoulder. This might even be the first time I remember Uncle Ty touching me at all and I can tell he's only doing it to dissipate the awkwardness of this car ride, this world he's stepping back into for only a moment.

"You all grown up." He pulls back out onto the road, speeds up the ramp and into the stream of freeway cars.

"Been a while," I say.

Uncle Ty still doesn't look like he's aged a day, but I can tell that something in him has. He's got his phone plugged into the stereo system and he's blasting a song he features on, a flurry of ego filling up the car. His face can't trick me, though, not with how his eyes dart across the road, his lips squeezing together.

Uncle Ty clears his throat. "I just want you to know that I read the articles about the cops and put it all together and I know it's you." He coughs again. "I think someone's gotta tell you this, so I guess it's gonna have to be me. Your daddy would've been real disappointed."

I whip my head to look at his face. "You don't get to say shit about my daddy when you left his kids alone. You don't know nothing about me or my life or what my daddy would've thought."

The day of Daddy's arrest, Mama was doing our hair. It was the first time she gave me real box braids, ones that went past my shoulders. Marcus was nine and she still did his hair too, mostly twists or cornrows at that point, if it wasn't buzzed short. It was an all-day activity and Mama sat us down on the floor in front of the couch, letting us watch cartoons on the old TV.

Halfway through the day, two of Daddy's Panther friends came over to watch the football game, so he turned off our cartoons and I threw a fit until Daddy promised he'd put me to bed that night. I always begged for Daddy to tuck me in because Mama wouldn't do nothing but kiss my forehead, but Daddy would stay until I fell asleep, tell me all kinds of stories about times before I existed, when it was just him and Uncle Ty.

That day, Daddy's friends sat next to Mama on the couch and one of them leaned down to me, his beard long and crooked, and told me that my hair looked just fine. We had no reason to think that day was any different from our other hair days until the door pounded and Daddy opened it and next thing we knew guns were being pointed and Daddy was handcuffed along with his friends, charged with accessory to drug trafficking even though Daddy claimed he never even knew what drugs they were talking about. Mama begged for them to let Daddy go while Marcus and I hid behind the couch with our hair only halfway done and waited for the door to finally shut, for Mama to rush us into the bathroom just in case the cops came back, and get on the phone with every person she knew, trying to find a way to get to Daddy. That night, I waited for him to come home and fulfill his promise, tuck me under my covers, but he never did.

Daddy knew what it meant to disappoint and be disappointed and I never once thought he'd look at me and say I had failed him, say anything but that he loved me.

"I had to say it." Uncle Ty shakes his head.

"You don't have to say shit to me. This about Marcus." I keep my head straight on the road and try to drown out Uncle Ty's presence in music that sounds far too similar to the kind Marcus tried to make.

Uncle Ty tries to tell me about L.A., but I don't listen, not as we near the jail, the long driveway lined in cop cars and a looming building of cement, a trap just smaller than the one Daddy spent three years inside. He pulls into the parking lot and I get out of the car, leaving my phone on the seat. Uncle Ty does the same and then follows me up the ramp and into the building where we check in and wait for our appointment with Marcus.

They call us in and Uncle Ty stands first, jittering, looking like he's about to start heaving as we follow a guard through the corridor and into the large room lined in tables, different men dressed in gray across from their visitors, and Marcus sitting there with his eyes scanning until he sees us, his whole face lifting upward as he takes in Uncle Ty and then me, then back to Uncle Ty.

We sit down across from him and he reaches for one of my hands, squeezes. None of us say anything, the hand holding mine shaking. Uncle Ty looks down at the table and then back to Marcus, finally speaks.

"Flew all the way up here to see you."

I shake my head, thinking how these men never learn, how Uncle Ty only needed to show up and care and instead he starts with this.

I glare at Uncle Ty before turning back to Marcus. "Say whatever you need to say to him, but know I got a lawyer and I'm gonna help get you outta here."

Marcus nods and I wish he looked more angry but instead he looks resigned or wounded, his eyes floating around the room and landing on Uncle Ty.

"You the reason I'm in here." Marcus says it calmly, like he's telling Uncle Ty what he ate for breakfast.

Uncle Ty looks taken aback. "I didn't do nothing but help you out, bring you with me when you asked, help you learn how to spit better. Don't go blaming this shit on me, this all your mama's fault." He pounds a fist on the table.

"I ain't trusted Mama to do nothing for me. It was you, you was the only one raising me and then you turned on me and I didn't have nothing left of you but music, so I got myself in a mess so I could keep on living like you would, but I ain't you." His eyelids are crinkling the way they do right before he starts crying. "I left Ki alone for you and now we here and I need you to see it. Look around, Ty, look."

Uncle Ty's eyes jerk around for a second, but Marcus waits until he twists his torso, takes in the knees in sweatpants shaking under tables, two toddlers chasing each other up to the metal detector and back, two pipes in the ceiling taking turns dripping. He looks back at me, sitting in this chair grasping on to the only family I got left, Marcus holding right back, both of us staring at Uncle Ty, at this man who don't belong to us no more.

Uncle Ty's neck loses its ability to hold up his head and he droops, a man sunken in shame. He looks up. I watch as Marcus and him stare each other right in the face and Uncle Ty's hand shoots forward to try to hold on to Marcus's other palm, but Marcus moves it back into his lap. It feels wrong for me to be sitting here, to be witnessing this ultimate break between them.

"You gotta understand I been taking care of your family so long that when your sister died, I realized I didn't have nothing of my own. That you wasn't my child and your mama wasn't my wife and I didn't have no place here. So when a friend of mine offered to let me live with him down in L.A., it felt like my chance, like I could have something bigger and you was eighteen so I thought I would just let you live your life. How was I supposed to watch after y'all and have my own shit at the same time?" Uncle Ty's arms are resting on the table, supporting his head, and he's looking up at us with these big eyes with red all up in the whites of them. "Both of y'all just started to remind me of your mama and I couldn't stand looking at you the same, not after what she did, who she became, so I did one last thing and paid her bail and then I had to go. I had to."

Marcus is shaking his head, his tears flowing, squeezing my hand so tight the fingers are turning yellow. "It don't matter no more what you meant to do, this what you did." Marcus slams his free hand down on the table, the vibrations shooting Uncle Ty back into an upright position.

"I'm sorry." He glances toward me, then back to Marcus. "What I gotta do to make it better?"

I still don't trust him or his apology, but I can sense the desperation in him, the desire to be forgiven.

"You can't." Marcus's voice shatters.

The guard standing closest to us gives a five-minute warning and Uncle Ty leans farther across the table, toward Marcus. "I'll do anything."

Marcus nods slowly. "Take Ki back to L.A. with you."

Uncle Ty looks at me fully, like he's assessing whether or not Marcus is worth it.

"You know I can't do that, Marcus. I got a family out there, can't take neither of you back."

Marcus's lips tilt into a smile that is actually more of a wince, more like the face Trevor makes when he loses a game. "Then I guess we done here."

Marcus starts to stand, letting go of my hand.

"Wait." Uncle Ty stands too, almost Marcus's height. "At least let me pay your bail. They set it at a hundred thousand, yeah? I can pay the ten percent."

I watch as Marcus shakes his head, looks back down at me, and returns his gaze to Uncle Ty. "Pay Cole McKay's bail, not mine. I spent too long not doing right by no one. Least I can do is give his baby her daddy back."

Cole's child's eyes come back to me again and this time I see Cole in them, when he bursts into laughter and they glitter. I don't know if Marcus does this for me or for Cole or for his daughter, but I don't think I've ever been that proud of him, ever looked at him and thought, *That is a good man.* He's still got a lot to make up for and I don't know if I'll ever really forgive him for what he's done this past year, but seeing a glimmer of the person I know my brother to be gives me hope where I thought I didn't have any.

The guard approaches Marcus to take him back to his cell, back inside the tunnels of this place, and, for the first time, he doesn't look at Uncle Ty or any of the other faces in this room but mine, leaves me with a last glimpse of a smile I recognize from back when we didn't know how lonely we would be, before he is pulled beyond the table, a flash of my fingerprint disappearing down the hallway.

* *

Uncle Ty pulls into a parking spot right in front of the Regal-Hi and stops the car, turning to look at me for the first time since we were at that table with Marcus. He didn't play his music on the drive back, didn't talk either, but now he opens his mouth to speak again.

"I know I made my choice years ago, when I got in that car and didn't even leave y'all my number. I know that." His eyes are still red, no tears, not that I expect them. "And y'all made your choices too, but I want you to know that I'm still living with the consequences."

"You got more than one car and a fucking mansion, Uncle Ty. You don't know nothing about no consequences."

"I got one car and a house big enough for my wife and kids, aight? I don't know where y'all got the idea I was rich, but I'm about to spend money I would've spent on a vacation on your friend's bail, so don't go talking to me about money. Biggest consequences ain't about no money anyway." He looks past me to the Regal-Hi. "Last time I saw your mama she was locked up and it was like she was a whole different person than the woman I knew. The kind of shit she went through, the kind of shit we all did, changes a person and I couldn't handle that, aight? I still don't know how to handle that. Instead of hating your mama for not being who she used to be, I should've just figured out who she turned into, but I decided to leave and now I don't know none of you, not really. That's my consequence."

"So now you just gonna get on a plane and leave? Never see us again? You out here talking about Daddy being disappointed when you're the only one who really would've disappointed him."

Uncle Ty turns back to the steering wheel. "I made my choice. You made yours."

He doesn't even glance back at me or say goodbye or nothing, just waits for me to get out of his car before gliding away, back down to where the sand is warm and he doesn't have to think about Marcus, about all the things we should've done different, about what it means to have a life you can't drive away from.

I OPEN THE DOOR to my apartment and Trevor is there, standing on the mattress in only his boxers, dancing to some Backstreet Boys song on the radio. He glances at me and does that nod, a little boy masquerading as a man.

"What you doin' here?" I ask. "Where Alé at?"

"She brought me back here 'bout an hour ago. Said she'd call you."

I pull my phone out of my pocket and a missed call from Alé flashes. She must have called while we were with Marcus.

"Lemme call her back," I tell Trevor, retreating into the kitchen and raising the phone to my ear. Alé answers on the second ring and I can hear it in her voice: how her heart is pulled taut.

"Hey. You okay?"

"They thought they found Clara's body." Alé's voice shakes. "Called us down to identify her, but it wasn't even her face. Just some other twenty-year-old woman all beat up and dead." Alé doesn't sound like she's going to cry, she just sounds like she's ready to sleep, like she needs to block it all out before she breaks. "Mama's a mess and I gotta take care of her, run the restaurant and everything. Can't be keeping Trevor no more." She says it harsh, not like she doesn't care, just like she doesn't know how to right now.

I don't know what to say. "I'm so sorry, Alé. If it ain't her, that means Clara could still be out there, though. There's still hope. You need help? I could pick up a shift at the restaurant or—"

"No. I just don't know how to be around you right now, not when you chose this. She didn't get a choice, Kiara, and now she might as well be dead. I just need a minute, okay? It's too much, you and Mama and Trevor. I can't do it right now." Alé hangs up before I have a chance to say goodbye and Trevor is standing there, staring right at me, so I can't even begin to think about how her face must be streaked and wet. How she can't even stand to hear my voice right now.

I gather myself. "Just me and you, boy," I say, slipping my sneakers off and going over to where he's still balancing on the mattress, lump of a belly and the rest bones. I try to forget Alé's voice, push it behind all the other shit we gotta think about.

He beams. "Can we make some pancakes?"

Like always, the only word I got for Trevor is yes. Ten minutes later and we're covered in flour, his hand dipped in a bag of M&M's. He scoops them out 'cause we don't have any chocolate chips and adds them to the bowl of batter. The pan is sizzling on the stove and he's now tall enough to pour the batter in. When he does, he pours so much it fills up the whole thing, makes a perfect circle.

"That's enough." I grab the bowl before all the batter is added to the massive pancake now sizzling, except at the center. "You know it's gonna take a long time for that to cook."

Trevor shrugs and I smile, shaking my head. The song on the radio is this new techno bop and I don't think it's got much beat, but he starts to jump, twisting and jerking across the room, throwing himself on the bed. He turns the boom box volume up and the apartment is blasted in techno wheezing, so loud I don't hear the knock on the door. It's the light that floods in when it swings open that makes me turn.

Vernon stands there, looking just like I remember him: a boxy 'fro, cargo pants splattered in what could be grease or paint or water.

For such a short man, he seems much taller than he is, his step a heavy thud on the floor. I watch him take in the image of us. The pancake, the stereo, me with flour still covering my palms. Trevor mid-shimmy.

"Is Dee around?" He turns to me, voice a gravel scrape against the techno.

I shoot a look at Trevor and he turns the volume down.

"No, she ain't," I say, crossing my arms so I can hide my hands against my chest. "Why don't you check her apartment?"

He nods slowly, surveying the room again. "Already did. I don't s'pose you know when she'll be back?"

"I'm babysitting. Why you asking me?" I fight the urge to charge headfirst at him, push Vernon right out the door, and slam it in his face.

"Thought maybe you'd know. I'm collecting the rent." He pauses. "Now that I'm here, though, I should tell you it's in my job protocol to alert the authorities to any neglect of a minor. You understand me?" He speaks slowly, like what he really means is hidden in the space between each word.

"Don't see why you'd have to do that. I'm sure Dee'll be back soon and I'll let her know you need the rent." I'm still leaning against the counter, waiting for him to leave. He looks me in the eyes for a moment and then nods once more before stepping back out and shutting the door. I turn and Trevor is facing me, still standing on the mattress, and I'm not even sure he's blinking.

The smell snaps my head back to the stove, where the liquid center of the pancake is now hard and the sides are burning black. "Shit," I say, scavenging for the spatula. I turn the flame off, but the pan itself is hot enough to keep it cooking. I dig the spatula under the pancake and attempt to lift. Only part of it comes up, lopsided.

Trevor is beside me a moment later, fork in hand. "I got one side if you got the other," he says, slipping the end of the fork under the mass of pancake. I lever the spatula under the other side of the pancake, counting down, and on "one" we each raise our arms up and flip.

The pancake splits in two, its charred side facing upward now, so black. I look to Trevor and his face has filled up with grief, bottom lip sucked in.

"Hey, it's okay. We gonna cover it in syrup and it gonna taste just as good." He doesn't have any tears yet, but I can see them getting ready to streak down his face. "You sit on down and I'll fix it."

"Like you fixing things with Mama?" he shoots back.

"What you say?"

"You always saying you gonna handle it but we still here."

Trevor shakes his head and slinks away, goes to sit on the floor in front of the mattress. I try to gather a response as I search the cupboards for syrup, finding Aunt Jemima in the top cabinet where we replaced the empty bottle from my birthday. I remove each half of the pancake from the pan and fit them back together again on a plate. It may be burnt and split down the middle, but it's still a perfect circle.

I pour a thick layer of syrup on and it comes out slow, viscous. This is the magic of Aunt Jemima: always releases the same sickly scent. Perfect mix of sugar and something way too cutting to be natural. Can't taste no wood, no maple. Just the crunch of toaster waffles smothered in sweet.

I bring the plate and two forks to where Trevor is seated on the floor and set them down. I hand him a fork and sit across from him. His eyes are cast down and I can't tell if he's looking at the pancake or the inside of his own eyelids.

Before I get a chance to say anything, he starts talking. His speech is mumbled and I've never heard him speak like this: with no clarity, just a trace of a voice.

"What you say?" I lean in so I'm closer.

"Is my mama coming back?"

"I don't know," I tell him.

I know there's more to say, more questions harbored under his tongue, but I don't know how to give a child answers that will fracture him. How can you tell a child he's alone? There's no way to explain the type of loneliness that finds its pit in your stomach, makes you think there must be something hidden inside your flesh, something to make this world turn on you. Like when Daddy died and Mama told me how they were gonna turn his body to ash after the funeral. Daddy's body a pancake kind of burnt. I didn't look Mama in the eyes for a week. How could I? Everything falling apart and she wanted me to think she'd stay, be the exception.

"Where's Marcus?" Trevor still hasn't taken a bite, still hasn't looked up at me.

"He's not around no more," I say, mostly because I am too scared to say anything else.

"Why?" Trevor glances up at me and his eyes flash a rage I don't think I've ever seen before.

" 'Cause he's in jail."

"That where my mama is?"

"No."

It's almost worse to tell him this. To watch his face wrinkle trying to understand how someone could leave him without a cell or a grave to keep them away.

"She coming back?" he asks again, and this time he keeps his eyes on me.

"I don't think so," I say, and he rests his head back on the mattress so he can see only ceiling.

An hour later and Trevor is snoring, full of pancake. I dial the phone number I promised Purple Suit I would dial because there really isn't any alternative when these two breaking boys need me and I don't have enough of a body to give them both what they need and keep on breathing. Marsha Fields answers with a chirp and I start talking; nothing left to do but let the words out.

MARSHA IS BLOND. Not only blond, but she's got the bluest eyes I've ever seen and she stands petite but tall in stilettos and a pencil skirt, just like every TV show predicted she would. Yet, here she is, standing right next to the shit pool, trying to pretend that it doesn't bother her: the traces of scent, sulfur still locked into every molecule despite the chemicals Vernon drops in once a month.

When I called Marsha, I didn't expect her to say she'd be here first thing in the morning and for that first thing to be nine a.m. and her face to be this angelic, not a splotch on it. She's got hair so thin I bet I could rip it all out with one pull, and the shirt beneath her blazer has tiny cats on it, a casual Sunday look tucked into her pencil skirt.

Marsha steps forward so she's close enough to hold her hand out to me, and I stare at it for a moment, the length of her fingers, before shaking it. Marsha starts her nice-to-meet-you speech. She's all bright, a dusty foundation covering her face, and she seems like she's having the time of her life while I am shoved into rooms with men and suits and uniforms, getting calls from cells. I want to be grateful, want to think Marsha a god, but so much of me resents her, resents her heels and the way she gets to walk in and out of a room without asking nobody for permission. Bet she makes six figures too.

She talks faster than I've ever heard anybody talk before, like her tongue is in some kind of relay race with her words. I catch snippets of it, digest only the words I really understand. Marsha throws in a whole bunch of legal bullshit that she knows only somebody who went to law school could understand.

As she talks, her hands move, acting out her words. Whenever she says "them," she lifts one of her hands up and flings it over her shoulder, does a half eye roll. I don't know if she's talking about the cops or the detectives or the police department or, shit, maybe she's talking about all them white people in those little rooms, playing dress-up with handguns. Probably not, though, because that would put Marsha with "them" and she seems to think she's part of the "us," as if she'd walk into my apartment and feel right at home in its emptiness, bare walls, no bed frame.

When she's done with her speech, Marsha turns right back around toward the gate, eager to get away from the Regal-Hi, like it's gonna come clawing after her. Her car is all the way down the street and Marsha walks fast, takes these giant steps that shouldn't even be possible with how short her legs are. I attempt to mimic her gestures, releasing my fists and making my arms swing wider. I wonder why she does that, makes her legs extend farther than they could possibly need to go.

Marsha keeps walking the same way and I think this must just be the way she moves. I'm out of breath from it, let my body dip back into its usual stroll, stomach rolls, and slouch. Marsha stops outside a black car that must be hers and gets her keys out. She presses a button and the car blinks on.

Marsha doesn't know how to sit still and immediately starts driving, continuing to talk. "Today's normally my day off, but Sandra and I talked last week and she said you'd be giving me a call, explained your situation." At first I don't know who Marsha's talking about, until I realize Sandra must be Purple Suit's name. "I don't typically perform pro bono work, however, you are a special case, my dear. I'm guessing it's going to be rather difficult for you to get proper representation. Next time, always ask for a lawyer if some strange detectives want to sit you down alone and question you. Good thing you called me when you did."

"I don't think you understand, I'm not the one who needs representation. It's my brother, Marcus, he needs a lawyer," I say.

Marsha smiles. "No, sweetheart, you're the one who needs a lawyer. Didn't Sandra explain this? Pretty soon you'll be in court and having a good attorney is half the battle."

"But my brother's the one locked up. You tryna tell me they gonna arrest me too?"

Marsha's smile drops and she looks tired of me. "No, I don't think so, but that doesn't mean you're safe. We can talk about your brother too, maybe I can help, but we need to start with you."

Marsha continues to talk and her ramble leaves me time to stare out the window, enjoy the speed of the freeway and the bay spread out endless, cut up only by the bridge as we make our way toward downtown, closer to the water than any route I normally take. I think back to the interrogation room, the metal, what might have come out of my mouth after all those hours, when I just wanted to go home to Trevor.

Every time I look over at Marsha, I want to move farther away from her, climb out the car window, and dive right into the water. Never really been this close to a white lady before and been expected to believe what she's telling me. It's not that she doesn't look trustworthy; she's got nice eyes, they move a little too much and she's kind of erratic, but more like how Trevor gets giddy after we win a couple games in a row and the bets add up, enough to pay a bill or two. Marsha probably never thinks about her bills, just wants to feel like she's winning, leveling up, buy herself a second car.

She flips on her turn signal to exit the freeway. "When we get back to the office, you'll need to sign some things so we have attorney-client privileges, contractual agreements. Then we can discuss the details of your case. Generally, I work as a defense attorney, however, at this point, you aren't looking like the defendant. I can guarantee you're going to need a damn good lawyer, though, with the crap they're already pulling, you can expect this might get messy. It's high-profile, or will be, and we'll need to be extremely careful about appearances. From now on, everything you do, you discuss with me."

At that, I press my body against the window. "I didn't ask for none of that," I say, breath fogging against the window. "Just tryna help my brother."

Marsha continues to use her hands while she talks, letting the steering wheel drift for a moment or two before she catches it again. "Nobody ever does. If you don't want my help, I can't promise you won't be the defendant in a couple months, weeks, days. Like I said, I can try to help with your brother too, but nothing I say is going to do anything if you don't listen to me."

I don't get nothing out of being in opposition to Marsha, so I keep on looking out the window and wait for her to pull into the parking lot of a giant office building. We're in Jack London Square, the coldest part of the city, right on the water. She opens her car door and I open mine, follow the click of her heels through the maze of cars to the building's entrance.

She takes a key out from her purse and unlocks the door, holds it open for me. There's a security guard sitting at a desk, chewing on a toothpick. He gives Marsha a wave and she says, "Good to see you, Hank." Hank blushes on the spot and spins side to side in his chair.

Marsha makes a beeline for the elevator.

"We gotta take this thing?" I ask, flurry exploding in my chest at the thought of being trapped in another metal box.

Marsha looks back at me, blond hair flip. "You'd rather walk up six flights of stairs?"

I know she thinks it's a rhetorical question, but I don't mind a little sweat if it means the freedom of my own two feet.

"You the one wearing heels," I say. She stares at me like she's confused, like she's trying to decipher my face. Then, she removes her shoes, leaving only her stockings covering her feet, and carries them toward a door beside the elevator. It opens into these concrete stairs that don't look like they belong in such a corporate building.

Marsha lets me proceed in front of her, mostly 'cause I think she expects me to give up by the second flight. I don't. By the time we hit the sixth floor, Martha's thin hair is damp and her foundation is dripping. I'm huffing, but not any more than I would after a scrimmage with Trevor. Marsha says she needs to stop on the landing and I watch her collect herself, pull a tissue out of her bag, and dab every inch of moisture she can capture.

Marsha's not only short but she's tightly packaged, got these muscular shoulders that hide beneath her blazer until she removes it in her sweat. If you didn't know better, you might think Marsha works out, some kind of casual gymnast, but the muscle is really just her natural frame and I doubt she's seen a gym since college.

I crouch down, just so my knees can have a break, rest my arms on them and look up at her. "I really gotta be home soon, we gonna get this over with?"

Marsha leans to put her heels back on and then rolls her body up like we're in a yoga class. She doesn't speak, probably still too out of breath, but continues down the hall. These halls look exactly like the OPD ones, except they've got carpeted floors. I have the urge to remove my own shoes and slip my feet into the carpet, feel something soft on my skin.

Marsha unlocks her door and invites me to sit down on an orange chair, the only bright color in the whole room. Marsha's office looks like I imagine a therapist's office might: framed posters with quotes on the walls, all a mild blue-white tone, like she copied and pasted it straight from Pinterest. She has paintings of flowers on the walls and her desk is glossy. Behind her desk, she has sliding-glass doors that open up onto a patio overlooking the bay.

Marsha looks around like it's her first time in here too, sighs, says, "Wanted it to be peaceful, you know? Everything in the world's too heavy."

Marsha done looked up "how to be your best self" and found some *Cosmo* article about actualization. Bet it's working for her, too.

The orange chair actually feels like a cloud, like I'm sitting inside dandelion fluff.

Marsha hasn't sat down yet. "Would you like some tea? Coffee?"

"How 'bout a burger?"

She laughs harder than she should. "It's barely ten in the morning."

"For real, I'm hungry as shit." And I really am, haven't eaten since Trevor and I had the pancake, and he ate most of it anyway.

"Oh." Marsha scrambles, glances around like she can pull a burger out her desk. "I could order you some food."

"You gonna pay for that?"

"Of course." She smiles, happy to see me agree to something. "I don't know what's open right now, maybe this Italian place down the street."

"Italian?"

Marsha says she doesn't know many other delivery places, so I tell her to just order a pizza and she asks what I want on my pizza and I tell her whatever got the most meat. She laughs like she's uncomfortable and trying to figure me out. I say she should get a large so we can share and she says she's cutting back on carbs and I call bullshit on that because Lord knows Marsha could use some good food.

Twenty minutes later and Hank knocks on the door holding the pizza.

Marsha finally sits down in the chair beside me. I put a couple pieces on my paper plate and a couple on hers. Marsha tries to refuse it, but I tell her I ain't talking if she ain't eating and she rests the plate on her lap and begins picking off all the cheese, careful not to eat the crust.

I watch her, how meticulously she removes it.

While we waited for the pizza, Marsha had me sign the contract she told me about. It was pages and pages of fine print, but Marsha made me read it all, said you should never sign anything you don't read first. Then, she brought out the pictures. Don't know how she got them so quick, but she has each of the cops' faces printed out clear as day, uniforms and badges with their numbers. All she's missing is their voices, would have had me knowing each of them in half a second. Still, I remember them all, remember their skin, the way their fingers curled, every dimple, every bald spot.

It makes sense. That's all I could think when I saw him: makes sense. 612's splotches were redder in this picture, like a blush was mixed in with his usual discoloring, and he was smiling with his teeth. It looked forced. Everything with him was forced. Jeremy Carlisle stared at me through the photo the way he didn't stare at me that morning I woke up in his bed.

612 is the one who wrote my name in his suicide note. He is the one who has set my world spinning.

I haven't told Marsha any of this because she told me not to start talking until she said to.

After she prepares each slice to be eaten, she returns her attention to me. "I'm going to record this conversation, so I can type it up as part of your file. Completely between us, so feel free to say whatever you would like." She places a recorder on the table and presses the red button. "Alright. First off, I need you to explain to me your relationship with any and all members of the Oakland Police Department, particularly Officers Carlisle, Parker, and Reed."

It's funny hearing their names, names I can't place to a person because they were never that to me. They were never branches in a family tree or men who gave those surnames to their brides. They were numbers and badges and jaws. I tell Marsha I don't know exactly who Parker and Reed are, that all I know is how the first cops found me that night off Thirty-Fourth, got me in their car. All the times they refused to pay me, said protection was my payment. I tell her about the day the detectives showed up by the pool, that room that closed in on me, the eyes, the tingle. I tell her about 612—Carlisle—and how he touched me, how his house was fit for five and seemed to house only him and his gun. I tell her how they came for Marcus and Cole.

Marsha asks for dates, times, names, like I remember. All I know is the detectives showed up on my birthday, that the heat followed us.

When I tell her that, she pauses, tells me to go back. "Did you have contact with the officers prior to your eighteenth birthday?"

I feel like I'm on the verge of saying something that's gonna land me in some shit, hesitate.

"It's all confidential, Kiara," she reminds me.

I take a bite of my pizza just to stall. Swallowing, I say, "Yeah."

"And did they know of your age?"

I stop to think about that, take another bite. "Not sure. Some of them asked and I usually just say I'm old enough, but I don't think most of 'em wanna know. Can imagine whatever the fuck they want that way, you know, little-girl fetish without the consequences."

Marsha asks more questions that I wouldn't have even thought had to be asked and it's slowly getting clearer that this isn't some sort of quick blip that's gonna end in me and Trevor back on the courts in a week. I'm scared to ask Marsha, but our plates are empty, and we're getting closer to the point when she tells me what I don't wanna hear.

"What exactly's gonna happen next?"

Marsha crosses her legs, wipes the last couple crumbs off her skirt, and tilts her head. "With all the publicity, probably a criminal investigation."

I snicker. "They gonna arrest half the police force?"

Marsha raises her eyebrows, shakes her head more times than she needs to. "Oh, no, that's not how this works. Not with law enforcement. If things go as I expect they will, we aren't talking about any arrests, not at first. Instead, there'll be a grand jury."

I don't know exactly what that entails, but I've seen enough news to know the only time a grand jury ever comes up, it's because some blue-suit shot a black man and the government wanted to pretend they actually gave a shit. Never ended in nothing but black boy on the news, hood up, some report about how he smoked some flower in seventh grade. I've done so much worse.

"So I'm on trial?" I ask.

Marsha breathes in, talks out with her breath. "You have to understand that a grand jury isn't a trial. It's what comes before one. If the jury decides to indict, then they're basically saying they think there's enough of a reason to have a trial. So, there'll be no arrest and, even if there was, you shouldn't be the one being arrested. You're the key witness, so you'll be the framing testimony. Like I said, this is high-profile, even though technically grand juries aren't supposed to be public."

"And in my case?"

Marsha bounces one of her heeled feet. "In your case, the media will make it so there is nothing private about this, except for what occurs in the courtroom. That is entirely private." Marsha pauses. "Trafficking is a very serious offense, Kiara."

"I ain't been trafficked," I spit back.

"Whatever you want to call it. You were a minor and they are full-grown men with authority."

The blue in the room is getting louder with every word coming out Marsha's mouth. I shut my eyes for a couple seconds, hoping that when I open them the room will be a pink or a yellow or anything less sunken than the strange blue walls and the KEEP CALM AND CARRY ON framed poster.

I open my eyes, the blue still blasting, and now the nausea is returning heavy, pizza threatening to show itself again. My face must be giving me away because Marsha asks if I'm okay and I ask her if the door to the patio opens and I think she says yes, don't really care either way, I stumble toward the door and pull on it until it releases and I'm out over the ledge of the patio, looking down to the bay below.

If there's an opposite of seasick, I think that's what the bay does to me: everything stills the moment the scent of salt hits me, ocean breeze wrapped around my exposed waist, wind exacerbating the knots in my hair. It ain't that I feel free, but I feel home. Probably more home than I do anywhere else, which is ironic 'cause it's blue too, and I know I'd drown the moment the waves took me in.

Marsha follows me out, asks if I'm okay a couple more times, but I don't have the energy to respond to her yet. I open my mouth enough that the bay-infused air can touch my tongue. I want to taste it, know the bay exists beyond any of this. Don't matter if everything else caves in tomorrow, the bay will still be here, will still taste like salt and dirt and wood from boats that carried too many bodies.

I look for the ships down there, spot one passing beneath the Bay Bridge. I imagine somewhere in there a girl just like Clara with hair blacker than Alé's or Lexi from Demond's party, small and shaking, is pressed between stacks of cargo. The sound of water, waves, thrashing; the only constant.

And here I am, above water. I think about what Alé said to me, how I chose this and Clara didn't and somehow I'm here and she's gone and the world just ain't fair. Death is always a possibility in the streets, but it didn't feel real until now, knowing Alé could've been planning her sister's funeral and I am simply a reminder of what might have happened to her.

The least I can do is be grateful to still be breathing. If I'm lucky enough to not be submerged, then maybe Marcus can be lucky enough, too. I turn back to Marsha, who is awkwardly standing and watching me.

"What about my brother?" I ask. None of it matters if I can't have Marcus back and, without Uncle Ty, I have no other strings to pull. I need to get him back, so that he can do things different, be better.

Marsha takes a minute to look out at the water, joins me by the ledge. "This looks worse for the department than they're going to let you know. If we play our cards right, we can use your brother as leverage, like a deal."

"What kind of deal?" I've entered too many negotiations that ended in my pockets empty, chest a tight knot, exposed.

Marsha smiles. "That's the fun part. We have the power here. They're going to try to make you feel like they do, but you aren't the one with everything at stake."

Feels like I am.

"And what if I decide not to testify?"

"They're going to subpoena you whether you like it or not, so you won't have a choice about being there. The only thing you have control over is what you say."

"What if I lie?"

Marsha sighs, slips her bottom lip under her top one. "You will be under oath and I will never advise you to break that. However, if you do decide to lie, then most likely your brother would go to prison for a considerable period of time and the grand jury wouldn't indict, meaning all the officers who were involved can continue to do whatever they would like without consequence."

"And if I tell the truth?" The sun's finally found its way into the peak of the sky and Trevor's probably starting to stir from his Sunday sleep.

Marsha's whole body relaxes, letting her shoulders drop for the first time. "If you tell the truth, then we have a chance at an indictment and changing the way this kind of thing works. After that, we can sue the police department and get you enough money you won't have to do this anymore." She sighs. "For now, we prepare. They're going to throw everything at you. As soon as the district attorney's office alerts us of a subpoena, we'll need to be ready for every question, every little thing they might ask. Only the district attorney, the jurors, and a court reporter will be present for your testimony, since the grand jury is closed. That means we need to get you ready, so you won't even need me in the courtroom. For now, you stay under the radar. I don't want you on the streets and I don't want you near any officer under any circumstances. Understand?"

I nod and I know that by trusting Marsha, I'm giving up these streets, giving up so much of what has become my world, at least for now. I thought it would feel like a celebration, and it does, but it also feels like a grieving, still trying to make sense of the months and the men and what I have given up in the name of feeling like I am in control, like I belong to myself even for a moment before it fractures and I remember. When I am tired and cold and just want to curl into a bed that isn't a couch or eat something that isn't microwaved. Marsha is telling me I'm free, but I'm still living with the repercussions of the streets, of the job that was supposed to just be a job until it became much more.

Marsha looks satisfied enough, says she'll take me home. There's still half the pizza left over and Marsha says I can take it with me. Trevor's gonna devour the rest of it, stuff his belly until I can't see his ribs no more. The thought of it has me really smiling for the first time all week.

Before she lets me out of the car, Marsha reaches over and squeezes my hand. Hers is so small I bet two of her fists would equal the size of my one. "If you act like you know what the fuck you're doing, people will trust that you do. That's it, that's how you win." Hearing Marsha cuss is like hearing a dog talk and I know she meant it like that, no way for me to ignore it. I nod, step out the car, and walk up to my gate.

The shit pool greets me and this is the last time I walk past it without the scream of reporters, cameras flashing, security guards Marsha hired telling me they're here to escort me. This is the last time I look into its murk, the subtle swish, whirlpool of water right outside my door. The subpoena arrives the next morning and I almost forget what it was like to wake up to Dee laughing, to Marcus on the couch, and a whole day blurring into streetlights.

TREVOR WANTS TO BE ON CAMERA. Every time we leave the house, he gets mad 'cause I take us out the back, the route none of the reporters know about. He whines and says that if I get to be famous, he should too. He doesn't know what he's asking for, but the way he clutches his ball in his hand reminds me of the way I want to grab his wrist, keep him right next to me.

We're stuck inside today because Marsha called and told me not to leave, not to open the gate for nobody. She sounded panicked, talking quick, and I thought maybe it was finally happening: they getting the handcuffs ready for me, adding me to a family line of prison cells. Marcus has been calling every day, sounding more gloomy than ever, and I can tell losing Uncle Ty is sending him spiraling. I keep telling him I'm working on it, but Marsha won't say nothing about him and most days I think it'd be better to stop picking up when she calls. Except then I'd have to tell Marcus the truth: that most likely he don't got a way out of this. Then I'd have to tell myself the truth: that I'm as alone as Trevor.

Trevor's sitting on the bed with a whole deck of cards spread out in front of him, happy he doesn't have to go to school today. I don't know what game he thinks he's playing, but it looks more like the way I used to shuffle before Alé taught me how. I keep trying to call her, but she hasn't answered in days and I've got too much pride to call again just to hear her voicemail on the other end.

Marsha told me to meet her at the back gate at eleven. It's 11:03 and I tell Trevor I'll be right back, circling down the stairs, and to the back gate. I can hear the mumble of reporters from High Street, the other side of the pool. When I open the back gate, Marsha stands with her hand on her hip, head tilted to the side, eyebrows raised like she does when she's irritated by me.

"You're late," she says.

I don't bother responding because it won't change anything and Marsha should know better than to expect me on time. I lead her back up the stairs to the apartment door. I told Trevor this morning that a white lady was gonna come by and talk to me, so he's sitting there with his head resting on one of his palms, not looking at his cards, and waiting for her. His eyes light up just from the look of her, like she's a new toy, and I can't blame him.

I watch her enter. Marsha steps ball of foot first in her heels while we step heavy and barefoot and, in our apartment, she looks misplaced, afraid the floor will crack beneath her.

"You wanna sit?" I ask her, pointing to the rocking chair.

I lift myself up onto the counter, so I can see both Marsha as she sits in the chair and Trevor, staring at her from the mattress. Marsha releases her body weight into the chair and flinches when the rocker starts to move. Back and forth. Back and forth. She settles into the sway, crossing one leg over the other.

"There's been movement over the weeks," Marsha says, and I feel like she's a news anchor about to give me a tragic report. "The police department has turned over three chiefs in the past week and we've been asked to come and speak with the acting chief, Sherry Talbot."

"Okay." I don't know exactly why Marsha seems so antsy, her shoulders tensed halfway up to her ears. She starts to tell the whole story, from start to finish, building it up like she always does. I glance toward Trevor and he is fixated on her, not blinking.

Apparently there are photos of one of the chiefs at the same party I worked at, the one where Purple Suit—Sandra—first found me, and so he'd been linked to the cover-up. That's what they're calling it: the cover-up. Not sure if that refers to me or them, whether they covering up the fact that it happened or the fact that they all known about it. Marsha says it's unclear, all tabloid talk.

"The point is, the newest chief has invited us in to speak with her today and I advise that we take the meeting."

"Why?" I swing my legs back and forth on the counter. "If you don't like her and we ain't obligated to or nothing, why go?"

"She knows people. Whatever she's going to say could impact the investigation or your testimony." Marsha tells me she's not too sure they'll indict at all, even though she says most grand juries end in indictment. Most grand juries aren't looking to nail the very people who are constructing them in the first place. The worry is peeling at her. She speaks again. "Or it could help Marcus."

My head snaps up at that and I jump down from the counter. "I'll go. When?"

"Meeting starts at noon. My car's parked outside."

I nod, already sliding my shoes on.

I walk over to Trevor. "I'll be back in a couple hours. There's food in the fridge, okay? Don't be going out or nothing." I kiss the top of his head and he squirms.

Marsha is struggling to pull herself out of the rocking chair. She regains her footing, smooths out her skirt, opens the door, and light floods the apartment. I follow her out, all the way down those stairs, which takes forever because Marsha has to pause on every step to make sure her heel is fully secure.

We exit the back gate, heads down, but right before we reach the car, the flock of reporters catches us, asking me what I thought about Chief Clemen's resignation mere days after Chief Walden resigned, if I had spoken with both of them, was the mayor involved in the cover-up, had I met the new chief.

Marsha ushers me into the passenger seat and runs as fast as she can in her pencil skirt around to the driver's side, climbing in and starting the car.

The past two weeks have been a whirlwind of me thanking every god that might exist that I got Marsha and wishing she'd shove her heel down her throat. Marsha arranged to get some nonprofit to pay me emergency fund money so I can pay the bills and buy us groceries. I stopped trying to pay Dee's rent and a few days ago I heard the pounding on her door, the newest eviction notice taped to the paint. Vernon's serious this time, won't hold off kicking them out any longer. All their things will be out in a week. Nobody's come for Trevor yet, but some nights when I watch him curled up on the mattress, I worry they will.

When Marsha showed up with the emergency fund check, this whole-body guilt stirred me up and I had the urge to scream at her even though all she was doing was keeping us alive. Side effects of relying on nothing but my own feet and the swish of my hips for so long: can't release none of it, let the bay flow.

Marsha has a list of charges she said we're gonna need to file against the police department and city the moment the grand jury is over. I tried again to tell her I didn't wanna do none of this, wanted to just return to life before sirens. Marsha said it's where I get the money, and I've never seen a petite white lady sound so much like my brother.

She brought Sandra in after that to convince me that it's about justice, about telling them they can't do none of this shit without consequences. Even though I know a woman can be just as dangerous as the men, like Detective Jones, you find the ones who have scars painted into their skin like constellations, and you've got something better than the moon, better than anything. Someone who knows what it's like to hold on to what has happened to them, whether they want to or not. I doubt she knows the streets like I do, but there is something about Sandra that makes me feel known.

On the freeway now, I plead with Marsha to let me drive, like I always do when we're in the car together. It's a ritual.

"Do you have a license?" she asks.

"Not yet, but I'm telling you, I'm a real good driver. Please, Marsh. Come on."

She shakes her head. "I'm not letting you drive my car without a license."

Whenever she tells me no, I start rifling through her glove compartment. She lets me do it for a couple seconds before she starts twitching, then asks me to "please leave that alone," which of course I don't. She's got sticky notes scattered around in there with strange messages on them like "potatoes" and "call him back."

Huffing, Marsha says, "I can't believe I voluntarily subject myself to this." She ties her blond hair up into a ponytail while attempting to drive straight.

"Why do you?" I've never actually asked Marsha why she devotes half her time to me and my case, even though she's got a whole lineup of people who'd happily spill their pockets for her.

"Justice, right?" She laughs it off, but I can tell from her pitch that's not it. Plus, I don't think Marsha really gives a shit about justice. It's not that she don't care about it, I guess, she just lives for the short term. And woman loves her money, her things.

"Bullshit."

Marsha glances over at me, sees something in the glove compartment, and grabs it. They're sunglasses, the designer kind. She uses the hand not on the steering wheel to place them on her eyes, then speaks. "I told you when we first met. This is high-profile, meaning my name will be out there and I'll get more clients." She's unconvincing.

"And?"

"And most of my other clients are only willing to pay me so much because they want a woman to defend them in domestic violence cases."

"I see. You tired of representing assholes."

She raises a hand up. "I never said you weren't an asshole."

I nudge her playfully. "Fuck you." And for the first time since we met, Marsha doesn't correct me, doesn't tell me to stop cussing. She smiles, reaches past me again to rummage around the glove compartment, pulling out another pair of glasses. She hands them to me and I place them on my head. The world goes this auburn color that makes everything hushed.

We pull up to OPD headquarters and, this time, the metal doesn't seem so daunting. It almost welcomes us in; maybe it's the auburn, the way it fades everything into a familiar brown. Or it could be Marsha. I've learned how to keep up with her strides now, so we walk side by side, her heels clicking, my sneakers squeaking, the linoleum not prepared for our kind of women.

Marsha doesn't stop at the front desk like I expect her to, beelines straight for the personnel elevator. Nobody stops a woman who looks like she runs the place. Don't matter that she don't got a badge, that she's got this black girl in ripped jeans following her. Most white women default to thinking they own every room they walk into, and Marsha is no different.

I hesitate, but follow Marsha into the elevator, which is empty except for us. The elevator lets us off at the top floor and it's like taking a stroll down memory lane, to the first time I entered this building. They already replaced the name on the chief's door, a piece of tape with "Talbot" written in Sharpie. The door is cracked open.

Marsha announces us by knocking on the door and we're told to come in, take a seat. The room is covered in gray, accented by the peeling yellow cushion on the empty chair.

Talbot stands up as we enter and we complete every cross of handshaking. She's short, racially ambiguous in that way that makes me sure people asked her what she was growing up and she probably just responded with "human" because when you blur every line it's easier to become rigid and frank like Talbot. She sticks her hand out and I shake it, fight every notion my skin has of right and wrong. Marsha says impressions are everything and we're expected to keep them up.

Marsha pulls a folding chair from the corner of the room to the desk, where Talbot has sat down again. I take the yellow seat and look out the window. It's early May and spring is in full bloom, our sky bluer than ever, bridge not even clouded by fog. A flock of seagulls flies straight across the bay, skimming the water, producing a shadow mirror.

I swallow and sit like Marsha, back straight, legs crossed. There's a rip in the knee of my jeans that I instinctually start to fiddle with. Whenever I do something I'm not supposed to, Marsha sucks in her breath, like the noise that precedes a lecture, and doesn't say anything. Waits for me to figure it out. I move my hands under my legs and give Marsha the eye roll she hates so much.

Talbot doesn't even take a beat before she starts making offers to pay me off, something about "making this easier on everyone involved." Marsha interjects, says if there is a settlement, it will be done legally.

Talbot begins to talk about Marcus. I ain't never heard such nasty words come out somebody's mouth without one ounce of feeling. She's monotone, like she is simply talking about her dinner plans while bashing my family, saying she knows some judges who love a good long sentence for the druggies. Says she knows some parole officers too, if my mother is looking to make a trip back to her cell. The way Talbot speaks makes me twitch like Marsha in the car, her teeth clicking between words, bony chin sticking out, smile that never seems to fade.

Marsha's spine straightens and it's clear she doesn't want to be here no more. "While I don't believe we've met before, Chief, I happen to know some people a little higher up in the department than you. If you would like me to contact them about unethical blackmailing and intervention in an investigation, I would be more than happy to." Marsha matches Talbot's smile and adds some teeth.

Talbot coughs. "That won't be necessary."

"I'm glad." Marsha picks her purse back up from the ground. "If there isn't anything else, we'll be on our way." She stands, gesturing to me to do the same.

Talbot stands as well, looking right at me. "I was actually hoping to notify Ms. Johnson of our protocol on knowledge of neglected minors and the harboring of minors. We are legally obligated to notify Child Protective Services." Talbot closes her mouth and I can hear her teeth meet in the middle. "Just thought you should know before you testify."

Sickly smile. Same shade as that yellow cushion.

Marsha's hand is on my back, pushing me forward and out the door, shutting it hard behind her. Before we start toward the elevator, Marsha reaches up to the door and rips off the tape with Talbot's name on it.

Back in the car, I realize my whole body is shaking, a light but constant tremor, and this is my worst fear made real. Trevor is my reason for so much of these past few months and now he's at risk, another casualty of a choice I didn't know I was making when I climbed into Davon's car that first night. Marsha is the one who's supposed to fix things, but when she starts the car, she breathes out all the breath in her body and starts cussing. I ain't seen Marsha cuss so much since her heel broke when we were walking through her office lobby last week.

She's still going at it, punching at the wheel of that sleek car, as she lets me out in front of the Regal-Hi, the cameras out of sight. We started staggering my drop-off time so the reporters wouldn't know when we'd arrive, and most of them would have already left. There's two sitting on the curb, staring at their phones.

Before I can ask what we're gonna do, Marsha tells me she'll call me later and waits for me to shut the door to her shrill voice repeating *fuck*.

W HAT THE FUCK HAPPENED TO YOU?" The moment I
open the door, I see the drippings of dried blood trailing
to the mattress, to Trevor curled up and spitting into a pile
of bloody saliva on the sheet where his playing cards are still spread.
I can't even see his teeth with his mouth open, the red coating the
white.

I kneel down to him, place a hand beneath his head and lift, so he
doesn't have to support the weight of his own skull. He groans and
tilts his head a little more until he's puking into my hand, full vomit
out the mouth: his favorite cereal colored deep burgundy.

"Oh baby." I use my other hand to grab a dirty T-shirt from the
floor and wipe up his mess. It smears together into a swirl of oranges
and reds, chunky and watery all at once. I pull up Trevor's body,
which is limp and unmoving, so he's fully on the bed, and rest his
head on a pillow. "That it? You got more in there?" I ask. He doesn't
answer, but he shakes his head just enough that I think it's safe to
leave him on his back while I grab a rag and wet it at the sink, bring
it back to him.

Trevor's face is caked in so much blood, swollen into a blur of
features, you can't even tell he's got the most gorgeous eyes, wouldn't
even guess he can move from land to water and still be this graceful
length of boy.

Even with his new muscles and height, Trevor is skinny. I lift his shirt up and his left side is slowly turning blue. I can physically see it morphing colors, deepening and spreading down to his hip. I repeat, "Oh baby," and he groans again. I tell him I'm gonna touch him now, that it's gonna hurt.

I start dabbing his face with the rag, but it doesn't do much for the blood that's already dried. I start wiping it and Trevor opens his mouth as wide as it will go and roars out into this gurgling scream. I've never seen a baby lion in real life but I imagine that they would sound just like that when they are young and scared.

The blood isn't fading from his face, really only migrating from eyes to mouth. "I gotta get you in the shower, Trev. It'll be cold, help with the swelling 'fore your eyes swell shut."

He shakes his head, small shifts side to side at first, getting bigger as I start to move him.

"I got to, baby. I'm sorry." I lift him into both my arms and even though he's taller now, his bony frame is light enough that I can curl his body into my chest and cradle him, his legs swinging as I stand and shuffle toward the bathroom.

I set him down in the shower so his head is leaned into the corner. He slumps the moment I let him go to turn the water on. It runs pink.

I tell Trevor I will fuck up whoever done this to him, that he best tell me everything the second that mouth learns how to talk again. I don't know what else to say, but he's groaning again, gurgling, vomiting.

I get into the shower with him to make sure he doesn't swallow none of the vomit or the water, wipe his eyes off. His noises get louder and all I can think to do is sing to him. I ask if he wants a song and he doesn't respond but he also doesn't shake his head, stops groaning for a moment.

Every song I ever heard runs through my head, except mostly only the instrumentals, only the trumpet or the bass. The only one with lyrics is the one Daddy used to sing me, only song Daddy ever sang me. I think it's by some dude from the '50s about how he wanna beat his girl, but the way Daddy sang it would've made you think it was a love song.

> *no kiddin'*
> *I'm ready to fight*
> *been lookin' for my Trevor all day and all night*

I change it for Trevor and when I say his name, his face twitches a little and I can't tell if it's a smile or a frown, but he isn't roaring no more and the blood is almost completely washed from his face. I turn the water off and strip his clothes from his body before picking him up again, naked now. I rest him on the toilet and stand back up to take my own dripping clothes off, leaving me in a sports bra and a pair of Marcus's old boxers. I reach up to the bathroom cupboard and grab the tub of shea butter. I sit down on the floor in front of the toilet and pull Trevor's body down into my lap, cradling him again.

"Alright now, worst of it over." I hum. "This gonna help too."

I scoop out a handful and begin to rub it over his torso, tracing each rib until his brown shines. I move up to his collarbone, the left side large and puffy. He winces, but doesn't fully growl. When I get to his neck and face, I move my hands in circles. He starts to moan again, this time the kind of moan that comes out when you finally scratch an itch. I trace the letters of his name across his forehead, trying to be gentle, but still get the blood moving.

After he's smooth and glowing, I carry him back to the bed and set him on the floor, grab some new clothes out of the drawer, and start dressing him. I make a bed out of pillows beside the mattress, so I can wash the sheets, and put my hand on his cheek. Even with the shower, his eyes are swollen shut.

"You can sleep now, baby, just let yourself sleep."

He's snoring that familiar snore in minutes and I start wrapping the sheets up to stuff in the hamper. Every time I turn away, I get so lost in the rhythm of his snores that I expect to look back and see his face: lips so perfect, tranquil, childlike. The image ain't none of that, though. He is beaten and puffed up and his lips are a mix of colors that I wish did not exist inside his world and he looks like he could be a man inhabiting the body of a boy.

I start singing again. Not because I think he can hear me but because I'm getting dizzy and all I want is Daddy to come up from the grave in ghost form or moon form and sing to me.

I wake up to a knock, stumble to the lamp. Peek through the peephole first. It's bright out and I'm not really sure if it hasn't gotten dark yet or if it's Saturday morning. Tony stands right where the sun must be, so his face is dark, but his outline is drawn in light.

I open the door and slip out to the landing, shutting it quietly behind me. The sun is visible now and it must be morning because the sun rises in the east, right over the shit pool.

"Hey." I lift my hand up above my eyes to shield them where Tony's body does not.

His hands are in the pockets of his old jean jacket and he's smiling like I done lit up his world with one word.

The thing about Tony is he thinks he's gonna fix me, thinks he's gonna fix everybody. He won't do nothing for himself, would rather follow me around hoping he can love me into a different life. There are days when I look at Tony and just wanna touch his cheek to make sure he's still warm, that he keeps a little heat for himself. Then there are days when Tony's mass robs me of my own shadow. How am I supposed to do nothing when he's watching, ready to jump in and save me?

After Marcus got arrested, Tony gave me a break. Answered when I called, but didn't show up unless I asked. Then, a couple days after the subpoena, I called him sobbing after one of the cops grabbed me outside the liquor store and stuck his fingers down my pants, up into me, and pulled, scraped his nails along my insides and came up with blood dripping down his fist. He put those fingers down my throat, said I gotta remember the taste. Said this what's gonna happen if I say his name. Thing is, I don't even know his name, don't even remember his number. Vaguely recognized his mustache, the voice from some party. Now I can't remove him from my tongue.

Once I called Tony, he met me where I was huddled beside the pool, avoiding the apartment where Trevor would be waiting for me to cook him dinner. He kneeled down to me and he didn't ask me what happened, except I'm sure he could smell it. I let him hold me because I didn't know what I wanted and the default is always touch, always skin, and Tony was eager to provide.

Ever since then, Tony's been by my side. Shows up at the Regal-Hi by the time I'm getting Trevor ready for school just to escort us out to Marsha's car or onto the bus. Comes by for dinner sometimes. There are days I come home and he's standing outside, waiting. I don't even know why Tony insists on getting messed up in my bullshit when he doesn't have to. I called him while Trevor was sleeping last night, asked him to bring a first aid kit.

"Said you were gonna call me last night when you wanted me to come by. Got you the kit," he says, holding out the metal box.

I nod toward the door to the apartment. "Fell asleep." I take the box. "Thanks. Trevor ain't talking yet but I'm guessing he got jumped."

"Shit."

I thought seeing Tony here, having him come in to help pull Trev's limp body up, spoon-feed him would make it all better. But seeing Tony standing here, ready to stitch up anything I say is broken, only makes it worse.

I love him, I really do, but I don't know him. Don't know him any better than I know Cole or Camila: they been there, but never close enough for me to know their mamas' first names or how old they were when they started taking the bus by themselves.

"Can I help?" His face is this hopeful blend of nervous and sad. It can't be later than nine in the morning and he's here when he could be finding a life. He's here, sunshine probably blistering the back of his neck, staring at me, hoping for anything different than what I've always given him. He doesn't deserve fractions and that's all I got, all I'm willing to give.

"Tony." I say it slowly enough that I think it might be enough for him to grasp. He looks down at his big feet, back up at me. He wouldn't cry in front of me, but this is the closest he's gotten. "You don't gotta do this no more." My hands are stained from Trevor's blood and all I can think is how much I wanna get out of the sun and I bet all Tony can think of is me.

He opens his mouth just enough that sound can come out. "You know I don't mind."

And that's the worst part; that he would do this for decades, do this until funeral day came to my doorstep and left him grieving and visiting the grave of somebody who never gave him nothing but ash. I think in the otherworld that midnight reveals, that place where everybody walks a little different, there is a version of us where I am okay with Tony being everything, holding everything. Not a better world but one where we are content with this, where there is no chase and I let him grieve me after so many years of my back spinning, repeatedly walking away from him and wishing he wouldn't follow.

I always expected it to end like this: me finally getting the balls to plead with him, talk him into leaving me. "Get outta this. You don't need me." Been avoiding that drop on his face since the day Marcus introduced him to me.

Tony will never argue with me. That's part of the problem, I think. Anytime I call him back, he's gonna answer, gonna run to me the way I wish Alé would right now, when everything seems to be dissolving. Can't sit by the pool and let Tony hold me just because I don't like the breeze, don't like night without him shadowing me.

He takes my hand, lifts it all the way up to his lips, opens up my palm, and kisses it.

I watch Tony exit the complex, probably back into a swarm of cameras, and I know I gotta decide sooner than later how I'm gonna make my life mine. How I'm gonna get to that moment when Trevor and I make this city ours again, win every bet until we've got an empire of our bodies restored. Maybe it all starts in that courtroom in two weeks. Or these streets. Or us dipping our toes in the pool. One way or the other, I know I don't have much time left to choose, find a way out of this trap.

I CAN'T STOP CHECKING the peephole. I'm not even sure who I'm expecting to see peeking out from the landing, eyes bulging. Maybe the cops, maybe some woman in a suit asking for Trevor, maybe Mama. Definitely Mama. She called me less than an hour after Tony left, from a new phone, saying she was released a couple days ago from Blooming Hope, that the parole officer really liked my letter. I almost forgot I had sent it, all the way back after I visited Mama in February.

When she called, she told me she was staying with an old friend in Deep East, and she gave me the address. I hung up before she could say anything else.

Mama didn't say she was gonna show up at the Regal-Hi, but I can't shake the feeling that she's about to appear at the window, tap-tapping on the door. That I'll peek outside and see her face reflected in the pool.

The sun already set and Trevor's sleeping again.

Trevor and I have spent the last three days with the shades pulled because he says his skull feels like it's got a drum instead of a brain, and Marcus's football days taught me that a concussion calls for two things: dark and quiet.

Problem is, a nine-year-old boy gets bored pretty quick and don't like the sound of silence when he's not sleeping. So, I read him the entirety of the second Harry Potter book and I've been humming him the instrumentals to every song I know. When I get tired, I put on one of Daddy's old CDs and hope Trevor will fall asleep to it. He usually does.

I'm hoping he's fully recovered in the next week or so because we've got some twelve-year-olds to give a beatdown. He started making full sentences again on Sunday, two days after the incident, and explained what happened. Apparently, Trevor decided to sneak out while I was with Marsha and headed to the courts to bet the seventh grade's best basketball player that he could beat him in a one-on-one. Boy said yes and a whole group of them gathered at the courts for the show.

When it began to look like Trevor was gonna win, the other boy got a little antsy, so he shoved Trevor and traveled with the ball all in one swoop. Trevor called foul and boy got upset, got his friends in on it. Trevor says it was all an excuse to end the game before he lost, but the boys were bigger and had numbers on their side and when it's a quiet spring day and everyone gets bored, kids love a good fight. Wasn't really a fight, though, because Trevor was on the floor getting kicked around without even throwing one punch. They left Trevor on the ground when some older boys came over and said they best get home. The older boys helped Trevor up, took him back to the apartment.

The whole time Trevor was reciting the story, my eyes filled with flashes of bright light, like what Daddy used to describe as cataracts, except these ones were painful and searing, full of rage. I told him that we were gonna find these boys, don't care if I'm six years older, we gonna beat they asses the moment the grand jury is over and he's all healed.

Trevor's been asking what the grand jury is and why we got reporters outside all the time. I've been telling him that it's about Marcus and getting him out of jail, which isn't a lie, but it's not true either. I know I don't have any reason to be ashamed, it's not like Trevor didn't know I was out in the streets doing something I shouldn't be just like he known his mama was high all the time even if he didn't know what she was high on. Still, he doesn't need another reason to be scared, another reason to not trust nobody. He's got enough.

Trevor said he wanted to go out this morning, tried to stand up, but he was walking all lopsided and I put on my mama voice and told him he best lie down. I've been telling Trevor I got cameras set up around the apartment so I'll know if he tries to move or watch a movie or something while I'm gone. I don't know if he believes me or not, but it's better he get used to being tracked with the amount of people we've got following us around for an interview. I can't let the reporters see him looking like this anyway, so swollen that CPS would be here before dinner.

The apartment is darker than it's ever been before and Trevor's face lying in his own blood plays on repeat in my head, along with Chief Talbot and that smile. She's right, though. Maybe I am making it all worse for him: taking away his only opportunity for bliss. This apartment doesn't know how to hold a child like Trevor. I don't know how to hold a child like Trevor.

Marsha won't stop calling. I haven't answered in days because what am I supposed to say? That I'm ready to testify and tell the truth, sign myself away to a cell, let them raid the apartment, grab Trevor up, and put him in some house where nobody gives a shit about how fast he dribbles or which songs make him shake like he ain't never had a fear in his life? But, if I don't tell the truth next week, Marcus isn't getting out of Santa Rita. They'll probably send him right to San Quentin and by the time I get to touch him again, my fingerprint will be wrinkled and sagging on his neck.

I'm sitting on the floor by the mattress when the noise comes, faint but persistent. It's unmistakably Dee. The cackle, the way it trails out and then drifts into the next wave, next burst of air and laughter that is so distinctly her. I get up and slip out the door as quietly as I can, down the row of apartments.

Dee's apartment door is flung open and she's sitting in the center of the room, feet pressed together in the butterfly position, her head closer to her feet than to the ceiling. Her head stays where it is as I enter the room, but her eyes roll up to look at me, her hair matted onto the top of her head, shoulders jutting upward. Like she's climbing outside of herself, or her skeleton is.

"You got my boy?" she asks through the bubbles, involuntary giggles coming from her mouth.

"He's safe," I tell her. "Look, Vern's been looking for you, so are you gonna be back and paying the rent or not? I ain't paid this month and he getting ready to evict you."

She lets her eyes drop again, her giggles fading into an offbeat hum. Her head drifts lower, closer to her feet. I hear Dee say something unintelligible from where her mouth meets her body.

"What?"

Her neck snaps up. "Why you asking me, girl? I ain't owe you shit."

I almost forgot how Dee could do that. How she could oscillate so quickly from that giggly mania to this: the sharp.

I step closer to her, crouch down until my head is just slightly above hers and I'm staring down into her eyes, looking into her. She is fierce.

"You owe me everything," I tell her, saliva flinging out, my lips parted just enough for her to see the edges of my teeth. "Owe me a whole goddamn life." I spread my arms out and she looks around like she's really seeing the place for the first time: empty, mattress sitting fully made, blankets folded, no traces of living.

Dee doesn't look at me, looks at her feet, but something in her shifts. Some bundle of the woman who lay on that mattress midbirth comes back.

"I wanna see him," she says.

I shake my head and even if she don't see me, I know she can feel it. "You don't get to come back in here and have him whenever you want. What kind of mother leaves her baby alone for weeks? He could be dead if he didn't have me, you understand?"

Her head rolls back up to look at me with that snarl, which then relaxes into a strange sort of pout.

"I tried." Dee says it soft, like somebody might say *I love you*.

"This you trying?"

"I love my baby, but love don't fix the other shit. It don't make it all go away. Your mama knew that and I bet your daddy did too. That boy in there? He loves me." She isn't blinking. "He loves me just the way I am, but pretty soon he'll decide that I should've been better. You ain't know what it feels like to have yo baby know you fucked up and not be able to change none of it."

Dee stands up and I see her fully, even thinner than Trevor. She walks past me and out the door. When we make it outside, she spits down off the railing and I hear it land somewhere below, somewhere beside the pool. She whips back around to look at me.

"I'm leaving, so you can have my boy all to yoself, aight? Just don't forget that even he ain't gonna forgive you for everything and you ain't gonna be able to do nothing to change it." Dee spits over the railing one more time and then shoves past me into her apartment, slamming the door shut so I'm left in the evening dark, unsure what's real, what kind of mother can raise a child like Trevor and succeed.

I head back into my apartment and leave Trevor a note saying I'm going out before I even know what I'm doing, signing it with a K because I don't even know which name is mine anymore. I pull on shoes and the black blazer from funeral day, checking the peephole one last time to make sure nobody's there. Just streetlights and pool.

This is my first time out of the house since Trevor got beat up. I go out the back gate and walk around the block onto High Street, bypassing the cameras. High Street looks the same and when the only constant feels like change, it's both comforting and chilling to hear the same whistles from the same old creeps on the same corner as I have since I was twelve. The 80 bus pulls up to the corner and I hop on, put in all the change from my pocket to pay for the bus fare, and sit next to this old woman who's mumbling something about buying herself a sandwich.

Daddy used to take Marcus and me on random buses just to kill time until Mama got home from work on the weekends. We'd hop on and he'd start talking with the driver, trying to get them to not make him pay for Marcus and me. We were cute enough and Daddy was charming enough that they'd normally say yes and Daddy would sit me on his lap and whisper, "That's how you get what you want, baby. Anybody who says words don't mean nothing is lying." Then he'd start shaking his legs so it would compound the turmoil of the bus and I'd go wobbling in all directions, laughing so hard that Marcus would catch it like a cold.

The best and worst part about the bus is the people. The woman beside me is listing all the things she wants on her sandwich. I'm gonna be on this one for a while, so I settle in and look past the woman and out the window. We pass a bunch of taquerías, none of which could compete with La Casa, then we enter the strip of churches, liquor stores, funeral homes, a couple apartment buildings and houses sprinkled in. International Boulevard is a weave through every kind of East Oakland living. We're going deeper into East and I'm hoping my memory serves me well enough that I know when to get off.

Spent my whole life waiting to fall into something that would make my body wanna turn into its own instrument just so I could be a part of every song that jump-started a pop and lock, make everybody dance. Like when Daddy joined the Party and hid his biggest joy under his beret, tilted just right. Like when Mama stumbled into

Daddy's smile and knew all she had to do was lock it into her fist. Like Marcus and his microphone. Sometimes, when I paint, I think I feel that, but the painting is never enough, never erases all the other moments I can't seem to find no peace.

The bus window reveals so many people living inside their music. A group of boys biking in circles, stereo balanced on one of their shoulders, heads nodding. At a red light close to the library, two kids—maybe twelve or thirteen—walk together. The boy has his arm around the girl's shoulder and her hips are too wide for them to be pressed that close together and still move comfortably. She leans into him and he kisses her forehead, and it looks halfway like a choke hold too, but they're so young and so happy, street-dazed, bag full of books on her arm.

I think I must have missed that moment when you stumble into the tug-of-war with your happy. A couple weeks before Demond's party, I ran into Camila again before dark and she bought me dinner at the taco truck off High Street, where we sat on the curb eating together. I asked her how she was always so content with this life, why she even started walking these streets in the first place.

Camila's face twisted into a tense stitch before flushing in calm.

"Don't help me to fight a life I'm stuck in." In that moment, I saw just a glimpse of the truth I didn't want to see. Camila is not a glowing woman walking free, walking godly. She is a woman who survives, even if that survival means tricking herself into believing this world is something it is not, that her life is all glory.

I don't know why, but that night by the taco truck, Camila kept on talking, told me about parts of her life I'm not sure she's talked about since she lived them. So much of her started to make sense. All she ever wanted was to live in her body however she damn pleased, twist her hips, and strut around in neon.

Camila started out answering ads on Craigslist when the site was still new, the internet sparse.

"My specialty was answering to 'Man Looking to Dominate Young

Tranny." All them fuckers was nasty, but I was young and I was just happy someone wanted to fuck me and pay for my rent at the same time. Ended up getting all the shit I wanted from that money, got my face done, paid for hormones. Eventually got hired as an escort at a real agency, but they took a good cut of my money and I wasn't even getting no good gigs. That's when Demond found me.

"I couldn't have dreamed of any of the shit I got now when I was your age." Camila tapped her green acrylics on the curb. "It ain't perfect, but it's better than what I used to have."

There was something about the way she talked about it that night that was different. It was like she was jealous of me, like she wished she could reverse time. She told me about how she used to get beaten up a lot more, had men bring knives to their meetups and start trying to mutilate her.

"Demond makes sure I don't get hurt as long as I keep bringing in new girls. I only got johns who won't fuck me up now and Demond makes sure most people don't even know about me."

After that, Camila finished her taco and stood up, brushing my cheek with her finger, and returning to the next car ready to pick her up.

Camila found a way to survive and Marcus found something to live for even if it failed and, hell, Trevor even found his own thing, always galloping toward the nearest hoop. And I am still waiting to be hit by some universe-halting love that will turn me inside out and remove all the rotting parts of me. Or at least something to make life bearable that isn't another person who will leave.

The bus is nearing Eastmont and I pull the wire to let me off at the next stop. The streets are flat here, but the potholes only get deeper. The sandwich woman still sits beside me, murmuring, and I wonder if the sandwich is real because there ain't no more restaurants the way this bus is going and she doesn't look like she's getting off anytime soon, head bent down nearly touching her lap.

I stand and think about waving goodbye to her, but I don't think she ever registered that we were sitting beside each other in the first place, so I exit without glancing back, without ever knowing whether or not she got that sandwich.

Just because I know where I'm going doesn't mean I wanna be heading in its direction, her direction. In my pre-streets lifetime, I would have said I'd never step foot in no trap house like this one. Today, I don't even knock on the front door, just go around to the side door and open it like it might as well be my second home. Scariest thing about this kind of place is how quiet it is. There's thumping from the bass of some music, but it sounds distant, muffled. Everything is dark and some whispers float through the room, some groans and teeth chattering.

Number one rule about entering somewhere you not supposed to enter is don't never question none of it. Don't ask nothing and don't act like you don't know what you doing because that'll land you right where you don't wanna be. It's all wood, floorboards splintering. When Mama gave me the address, I knew exactly where she was talking about, the place where one of her friends lived, from back when Mama wasn't sure what side of grieving to be on. I climb the stairs and knock on the door of the apartment with a large C on it.

Mama opens it.

I haven't thought about what it would be like to have Mama back here, back in the same city it all happened in, not in years. Once I turned sixteen, I was pretty sure I'd never see Mama again, had my own funeral day just for her.

Here she is, though, slipping her hands under the sleeves of her old *Purple Rain* sweatshirt. "Didn't think you'd come."

I nod. If Mama told me she was a shape-shifter, I'd believe her. Woman standing in front of me don't look nothing like the one from a few months ago, swallowed the one from a few years ago, chewed up the one from last decade.

"Why you here?" If I didn't know better, I would think Mama

didn't want to see me, her cheeks swishing side to side like her mouth is full.

"I don't know, I was talking to Dee and I just—I wanted to know if you'd tell me why you did it." I need an answer, need Mama to patch together the pieces of these lives we've made for ourselves, give me a reason that would make her feel like mine again, like someone I might know. I need her to tell me mamas can change, that there is hope for Trevor, for Marcus, for me.

"Alright, chile. Let's go on a walk. I gotta show you something anyway." She holds her sleeved hand out, like the emptiness is an offering. I take it and she steps out into the hallway, closing the door behind her, and leading me back down the creak of stairs, out of this warehouse coffin.

The chill from outside creeps into me. "You sure you wanna be out here? It's late, Mama."

"It won't take too long. Promise." She nods her head toward the street.

I don't know if this is a good idea, but the damage is done; I'm here now, holding Mama's hand like it's going to dissolve right into mine. I follow her, give Mama her last wish. We walk until I can smell ocean, somewhere just close enough to leave traces in the air, but too far to see.

"Before I answer you, baby, will you tell me something?"

I shrug.

"Why you start fucking with the cops, especially after what your daddy been through? I saw it on the news and I ain't mad at you, I just want to know."

I can't look at her. "I don't know, I didn't really have no choice. I just kind of ended up in it and then there wasn't no way out, you know?"

Mama pauses before a crosswalk, waits for a car to pass. "Then that's why, baby. That's why I did what I did. After your daddy died,

I felt like I didn't have no mind of my own, no body of my own, and that turned into something I couldn't get out of. Some part of me must have remembered the door didn't lock but I couldn't handle breathing another minute in that pit your daddy left, so I tried to stop it all without thinking about the lock or you or Soraya, but I didn't cut deep enough and then they told me Soraya had gotten out **and** drowned in that pool and I couldn't handle nothing no more. It was like something shut down in me that ain't never gonna come alive again and I still feel like I never made it past that day, like I haven't lived a minute since."

Mama's hand is warm in mine. For the first time, I see something about her that isn't familiar, but it's soft. It's the most honesty that's come out her mouth in a real long time.

She starts talking again, a wispy voice this time. "Soraya took her first step right down by the pool, remember?" Here we go again; Mama always comes back to her spiral. I let go of her hand, slip mine into my pocket. "We was out there listening to the radio 'cause the game was on and it was a nice day and Marcus was out with the boys and you was complaining about how all the other girls in yo class was going to some party and I wasn't about to let you go on a Wednesday. And I swear you was about to throw a fit and I was ready to give yo ass a beating and I turned around and she was standing, bubbles coming out her mouth, lifting one foot up and setting it in front. Then she moved the other and did it again and I just wanted to watch that child forever but she was walking straight toward the water, like she was tryna dive in, had this look in her eyes like all she wanted to do was taste it."

"And you picked her up and set her down further from the pool, but she dropped right down to her hands and knees, back to crawling," I add, image clear as the sky that day.

"Never got to see her walk again." Mama's tears are running again and we're on International Boulevard, but it looks different tonight:

Mama's face, my skin covered, not knowing where I'm walking. Following. She walks slightly in front of me, quiet. Don't know the last time I saw Mama this quiet, and even though she says she's showing me something, the pace is slow enough you'd think we were walking aimless.

At Foothill Boulevard, Mama reaches for my hand again. I wrench my arm away from her and then let it slowly trickle back down to my side. Mama tries again, this time looping her hand around my fist so hers is like my fist's shell. I don't bother trying to move it, let Mama shuffle us forward toward where the streetlights go hazy. It ain't no shock that Camila is standing there, that she is so easy to see in her silver flash, arm looped with a girl who I know is at least twenty years younger than her simply from the way she walks: zigzagged and tender.

The intersection runs wild with cars that are so beat-up they don't even have speedometers. Camila doesn't see me, probably because I blend into the night. I tell Mama to hold up and she releases her grip on my hand tentatively, like she's worried I'm gonna run.

Camila has her friend half jogging to keep up with the stride of her legs, their length amplified by heels I couldn't dream of walking in without tripping. She reaches up into the air in front of her and swats, closing her fist around some invisible fly or bit of fuzz that only she can see.

I run across the street, Mama quick-walking to keep up with me, and shout out Camila's name. She spins, her smile already telling me she knows exactly who's calling her. Her arm is unlooped and springing toward me in seconds, wrapping around my waist in the tightest hug.

"Mija." She's got silver hair to match, with bangs that flutter right toward her eyelashes, adorned in glitter flakes.

I ask her how she's been and she ignores the question. "Seen you all over the news. My baby ho didn't tell me she got a whole ring out here, shit." I don't know if she's proud or impressed or jealous, but I don't think it matters with Camila. She don't really give a shit if it ain't hurting her, gonna help you till she can't no more and she doesn't mind leaving after that. Never met someone who could love you that hard and leave you without a second thought.

I shrug. "Didn't mean to or nothing."

She looks me up and down, at my sweatpants and sneakers. "You really ain't about to get none tonight looking like that."

"Not doing that no more," I say, nodding my head toward Mama. "My mama and I just taking a walk."

"In that? Girl, I always knew you was crazy."

I glance toward the other girl, who is fidgeting with her necklace and bending her knees like an old woman trying to regain mobility. I scan the area for one of the cars always nearby Camila: tinted windows. I don't see anything even close to that nice out here, look back at Camila, and ask her again, "How you been?"

"Things been a little rough since Demond got taken in. Lot of the girls got put in group homes and some of us got locked up too. I spent two days in one of them cells, but they fined me and let me go, prob'ly 'cause I'm old as shit and it ain't no waste having me out here." She laughs, combs her fingers through her wig. "Lost most of the regulars so I'm back to escorting. I ain't mind but hard to keep 'em from getting too handsy, you know?" She tugs at her skirt. "Been a little rough."

I hadn't even noticed the bruising until she started pulling at her skirt, trying to cover up the blue that spots her thighs: the constellations of finger to finger pressed deep. I don't feel or think much of anything besides *oh*. Of course this is the way it plays out. Of course Camila is silver and bruised. Of course.

I nod and Camila smiles through her ache. I lean in to hug her again. "You be good, okay?"

She touches my cheek and nods. "See you soon."

This time, I am the one to give a pat on the back and walk in the other direction. And we both know there will be no soon, no running into each other on the streets in a week or a month or a year. Maybe there will be a sideways glance from a bus window, a *could that be her behind the wrinkles,* but there will never be another seeing, another embrace. When I walk back to Mama, I take her hand voluntarily and she lights up from the chest outward.

She takes us beyond Foothill, beyond International, down the hill toward the underpass.

"You lost?" I ask Mama.

She shakes her head once and keeps us moving down until we are encompassed in black, the only sound coming from the occasional *whoosh* of a car on the freeway in front of us. Mama pulls us to the right and I stop in my tracks. "This ain't a road, Mama."

She tugs a little harder and keeps me moving. "Trust me." And I don't, could never, but I want to, so bad, more than anything, so my feet move heel to toe, heel to toe. The ramp is an illusion of emptiness, a stream of black that looks like it only leads to more black until, suddenly, it doesn't and we're in the rush of cars, barely over the line that separates freeway from debris.

I tighten my hold on Mama, like grip is somehow a sanctity that will protect me from the tire screeching, the sheer speed of cars when we are most human. If I didn't think Mama was off her shit before, I know she is now: bringing me up here, onto the freeway like it's a sidewalk or a detour and not a chasm of speed.

At this time of night, the cars are relatively infrequent, but when they come, they are full throttle, running at least eighty or ninety miles per hour. When the trucks come, I can feel it on my back, the wind beneath my blazer.

I think this is the closest thing to being a live ghost. Disappearing into roadside trash and trees that somehow figure out how to grow in California's eternal drought. Existing as the most salient and invisible thing on the road, both sinking into the dark and so terribly misplaced.

"Mama, what the fuck are we doing out here?" I'm close to done swallowing her insanities. I don't know how much longer I'm willing to walk beside her on the freeway with her not even answering a simple question.

Mama takes a breath and holds it. I wait for her to blow out, release a flood into the air, but she doesn't. I'm starting to think she's trying to kill herself by way of self-inflicted suffocation when she opens her mouth and lets it out with an explosive howl. A scream that seems to continue past the time she closes her mouth, seems to travel upward, right into a waiting cloud, and spits back at us with a high-pitched echo.

I let go of Mama's hand when the noise bursts out her lips, jump to the side, and step on a castaway plastic bag with a crackle. I have half a mind to run back down the ramp, right into oncoming cars just to get away from Mama and that sound. She turns her head to look at me, where I have retreated farther into the brush, and gestures for me to come back to her. I stay put, hands up so Mama knows not to come near me.

She relaxes the smile slightly. "It's alright, baby." She has to yell to be heard over the car rush and persistent echo. "You need to scream."

I shake my head. "You done lost your mind." My voice is a low quake. Maybe she hears me and maybe she doesn't.

She repeats, "You gotta scream. It's all gonna get better, but you gotta scream."

"I'm going home," I tell her, but I don't move.

She lifts a hand to her chest, almost like she's checking for her own heartbeat. This time, she whispers. Could be me reading her lips or could be something my mind made up, but I'm pretty sure Mama says, "Let it out."

I open my mouth, shut it again. "Why?"

"Nobody learns to walk when they got weights inside they bellies. I want you to walk toward the water, baby. I want you to swim." Mama lifts her chin up so her head is pointed toward the sound of ocean, sound of the bay somewhere beyond sight. Mama don't make no sense and, at the same time, she has never said something my gut understands more clearly than that.

My mouth opens slowly, jaw creaks until there is just enough space for the sound to travel out my throat. Still, when I try to scream, nothing comes out.

Mama steps closer to me and I pivot away. She takes another step and she's within an arm's length from me, lifts the hand that was on her chest, and places it on mine. Not over my heart, but in the space where my ribs make way for esophagus and blood vessels. I can hear her voice crisp now, same voice that told Soraya to get away from the pool, same hand that scooped her up before she hit the water. Cars race by behind her, leave us in the aftermath of their wind, and Mama's hand is warm.

"Silence starves us, chile. Feed yoself." Mama's Louisiana comes out in a drawl that sounds like music and I try again but don't no sound come out, and if I am really my parents' child, how can I not turn my body to musical note?

Mama takes both of her hands and moves them up, toward my face, places them on both cheeks, then slides down to my jaw. Mama hooks her fingers in my mouth and spreads my jaw open like a door with hinges, until I make an oval with my lips, keeping her hands on my cheeks and telling me to scream. The screech comes out in bursts, spasms of sound morphing their way from an eruption of rage to an infant's cries, moans and whines and all the in-betweens of woman and child.

The sky takes each flurry and sends it right back with just a hint of music lingering in the echo, a belt from some invisible trombone, the lowest note on an organ drawn out. Sound after sound flooding from my body like war-zone fire on a cold day, Mama rubbing the tightness out my jaw, melting the tears back into my skin, until there is no more noise and my chest is heaving, out of breath and raw and Mama is holding me and the cars have not stopped, have not slowed, all of it, all the time racing past us while we are stuck between the sky and asphalt that does not know our names and Mama will walk me to the bus stop and leave me there and we will not speak of what the freeway does to us when it is nighttime and we are ghosts. But Mama taught me how to swim and I can see underwater. I can see.

•

I DON'T REMEMBER what time it was when I got home, I only remember the moment I woke up. The pounding on the door. The fists. Vernon's eyes through the peephole. The woman standing behind him. Her clipboard. The way her lips turned inward.

Trevor's healing body is still cocooned in sleep and I retreat to the back of the apartment, to the mattress, like distance from the hole they already saw me peek through will erase us. Maybe I should have seen it coming. All the warnings were there and I still thought we could escape them, make it out of this together. I still thought I had a choice.

"Open the door, Kiara. We will call the police." Vernon's familiar growl.

Trevor's stirring from his sleep and I want to will him back into it, so he won't have to be conscious for whatever comes next; for when they pull us apart, pry his fingers from around my neck like an infant. The pounds keep coming. Trevor's swollen eyes blinking open as much as they can, brown peeking through to stare up at me, frantically looking around for some kind of shield against the rupture. Trevor's face crinkles and his lips part, trying to ask me what's going on, but the cuts in his mouth sting him into silence.

I lean over and touch his head. I shaved it so I could patch up his wounds and now it's grown out enough that I can feel it instead of just the bare scalp. I whisper to him, "Trevor, baby, some people are here and they might be taking you someplace else for a while, okay? Don't you worry, though. I'm gonna open the door, you just rest there." I steady my pitch so my voice won't crack like it's threatening to: reveal all the wounds that make me up, all the fear I'm harboring in my gums.

I inch toward the door again and I'm scared of it, scared of what comes from this, what Mama opened up. Maybe she called Vern or the government or whoever owns the woman-in-the-suit's ass. Somebody always owning the woman, knocking on the door so all she has to do is stand there.

My hand on the knob, twisting, pulling, no longer any barrier between me and them. Vernon standing there with a snarl. The woman, waiting.

"Can I help you?" I ask.

"This is Mrs. Randall from Child Protective Services." For the amount of work Vernon put in to get me to open the door, he seems wildly uninterested. Bored, even. "I'll leave you to it." He directs this at the woman, Mrs. Randall, and retreats back down the stairs.

Mrs. Randall's got the kind of face that looks like one a child draws into the sun. Circular, sloping. With these locs that make her look like she should be a poet, like she should be wearing a shawl and not a suit.

She holds out her hand and I shake it. "Nice to meet you. May I come in?"

If I didn't know better, I would tell her, "No." Would tell her to get the fuck away from Trevor and that bed, to not enter the only space we have left to call ours. Instead, I say, "Of course," and she steps inside.

It's all over the moment she sees him. I can tell from the way her whole face arches as she takes in his scabbing. I can't blame her. Trevor's body is a visible testament to how this place has chewed him up. How I haven't been able to do nothing about it. Part of me is even relieved because what if it's me? What if I'm the one who has done this to him?

Mrs. Randall begins to walk toward the bed and I can see Trevor starting to shake, his body writhing, and I know if he wasn't so injured he would be pressed up in the corner, trying to get away from her. I bypass Mrs. Randall to go sit on the bed with Trevor, gather him into my arms. He presses his head into my chest so he's not looking at her or me or anything.

Mrs. Randall crouches down by the mattress. "Hi, Trevor. My name is Larissa. I was hoping I could speak with you."

Trevor pretends not to hear, doesn't say shit back.

Mrs. Randall redirects her attention to me, standing again. "How about we talk first? Outside?"

I nod, leaning into Trevor's ear. "Imma get up now, Trev. I'll be right back."

I have to physically remove him from his place on my chest. He flops back into a pillow and buries his head in it.

I follow Mrs. Randall back outside and close the door behind us. We lean against the railing facing the pool, half turned toward each other.

Her eyebrows tilt. "Look, I'm going to be frank with you, Ms. Johnson. You are not that child's legal guardian and clearly he is in some form of danger, which doesn't look good for him or for you. Social workers have visited Trevor and his mother three different times over the years and I understand that you may have just been trying to help, but that is not your responsibility and it would have been far more appropriate had you called us.

"Typically, I would report you to the police for possible kidnapping and child endangerment, but I don't believe that to be the case. He clearly trusts you and I will do my best to minimize the harm to either of you." She pauses, glances away from me and toward the pool, then back to meet my eyes. "However, I cannot leave him in your care, not after there is so much evidence of his immediate danger and neglect. I will need to take him and he will be placed in a temporary home while we figure out the most stable circumstances for him. I will be pursuing a warrant which will allow Trevor to remain in protective custody. You will not be permitted to have any contact, at least for the time being. Do you understand?"

I know she's telling me something that at any other moment would tear at my membrane, break me apart. The only thing I can focus on is how she must do this every day, how this woman stands in front of people like me and tells us the very thing that will most devastate us. How heartbreaking it must be to destroy that many spirits.

"Can I tell him?" The last thing I want to do is tell that boy he's gonna be even more alone than he already thinks he is, but I also know it would be wrong to do it any different. I would rather break his heart than let a stranger do it.

"Sure. He'll need a bag with all his necessary belongings. I'll wait out here." Mrs. Randall nods off at the pool, like it's all over. She done her job.

When I reenter the apartment, Trevor is huddled in the same position I left him in, except now he has the blanket pulled fully up over his head and I can see the curled ball he has formed out of his body, as compact as a lanky boy can be. The floor creaks when I walk over to him, and I can see him shaking, the blanket rippling.

"It's just me," I say, trying to keep my voice as steady as I can. Try to make it sound like this is not the death of our life together, of dribbling and parties in the kitchen. "I gotta talk to you."

I'm by the edge of the mattress now, kneeling on the floor. I lean my torso onto the bed and pinch the edge of the blanket, peeling it slowly from his head. His face is crumpling, everything scrunched up and puffy, tears trying to find their way out of his swollen eyes and getting trapped in creases above his cheeks. He's shaking his head, his mouth moving without sound.

The boy is collapsing right in front of me, Trevor coming undone. I touch his forehead and it is hot, burning even. Like his body is rejecting itself, turning to flame so he might be able to defend himself against what comes next. It is tearing me apart and I think this must be the hardest thing I've done: being the adult for him, the woman who can keep it together as he falls apart because we don't got another choice.

"I know, baby," I say, nodding. Maybe I can reverse the hurt, stop the destruction with a smile. "Listen to me."

His head is still shaking, pupils eclipsing his eyes.

I start humming again, lean so my mouth is right by his ear, loud enough that I know my hum is all he can hear, vibrations all he can feel. Gradually, he stops shaking his head, starts to sniffle. I stop humming.

"I need you to listen to me. Can you do that for me?"

This time, he nods once.

"That lady, she's the woman that's gonna bring you to a new house for a little while. She's real nice and I bet if you ask her to turn on the radio in her fancy car, she will. Your mama ain't coming home right now and I'm not allowed to keep you here no more, so you're gonna go somewhere else until I figure it out. Okay? It's not forever."

Even as I say it, I know it might be. This might be the last time I see his face and I want to curl up with him, hide away until I'm ready for the goodbye. But I will never be ready to let him go and Mrs. Randall is outside waiting. His already plump, bruised lip jutting farther out and I know he's trying real hard not to let this flood him.

I smile. "You might even go somewhere with some other kids. Then you can kick they asses in a pickup game, huh? Show them how you can dunk?" I put my hand beneath Trevor's head and push up, so he knows it's time to pull his body back into a seated position on the bed.

I grab his cheeks in my hands, just like Mama did for me last night, and stare at him like he's the only thing that exists in this world. He might as well be the only thing that exists in this world.

"You gonna be just fine."

I kiss the tip of his nose and pull him into my arms, where he burrows into the crease between my shoulder and neck. If I could stay just like this forever, I would. Holding him. Knowing he's still intact. That Trevor's gonna light up and dance again. I can almost feel Mrs. Randall's heel clicking outside, her patience waning.

I rub the back of Trevor's head, the only part of his body that hasn't entirely blown up in the wake of his beating. I reach behind my back where Trevor has locked his arms around my waist. I have to fight myself to not stay still, to untangle him from me like untying a knot even though it's the last thing I want to do, and he's heaving by the time I remove myself from him and begin stuffing his clothes into his blue-and-yellow backpack that I got him for his ninth birthday because I couldn't afford the actual Warriors backpack. I watched him scour it for a logo until he realized it was off-brand and there wasn't one and then try to mask the sinking feeling in a thank-you. Dee might have failed in most ways, but she taught her baby some manners.

I zip the backpack up and put it on the edge of the bed, returning to Trevor. He's back in the fetal position, so I grab his hands and pull him up, his head hanging backward and heavy. I have to hoist him off the bed and set him on his feet, but he's gone limp, won't lock his knees to hold up his body. I could threaten him or scold him or put on my mama voice, but I can't bear that being our last moment together. Instead, I crouch and place my other arm under his legs, lifting him up like you carry a small child to bed after they fall asleep on the bus. He's heavy with blood and tears and too much going on for him to figure out how to walk and breathe. I struggle to open the door, twisting the doorknob so it's open just enough that Mrs. Randall sees us and pushes it open the rest of the way.

"He won't walk. I can bring him to your car if you go on and get his backpack from the bed." I don't look her in the eyes, just stagger past her in an attempt to get us to the stairs. I take them one step at a time, Mrs. Randall following with Trevor's backpack in hand. Once we're down the stairs, she takes the lead, but I tell her she's gotta take the back door because of the reporters, so I lead her out past the pool and nod my head toward the exit gate. She opens it for Trevor and me and then marches down the street in front of us, toward a black car.

She takes a key out of her pocket and clicks a button. The car beeps and Mrs. Randall holds the back door open. Trevor's shaking again, my shirt soaking in his tears. I lift him up in one last exertion, laying him across the backseat. His arms are wrapped around my neck and, before I pry them off, I tilt down and kiss his forehead. "I love you," I whisper. As much as I want to climb into the driver's seat and take him somewhere I know he'll be safe, where he won't have to tremble, I know we don't have that luxury. The only option is this: him, breaking in the backseat of an unfamiliar car. Me, removing him from my chest and shutting the door so all I can hear are his sobs.

Mrs. Randall turns to me before she gets in the car, says, "Thank you, Ms. Johnson," but I'm already halfway down the street in the opposite direction, toward the bus, toward the cars. She can't say nothing to make this okay and I can't stand to watch her pull away from the curb with only his shrieks left to tell me he's still breathing.

I'm dialing Marsha before I even realize I've memorized her number and, when she picks up, all I say is "I'm ready." She tells me she'll pick me up in twenty minutes and I tell her to get me from the courts. I'm standing in front of them, empty now, and I walk up the hill to find a bench right behind one of the hoops, looking out to High Street. Everything is moving, quick and relentless, like the city don't know it should be stopping, should be kneeling, grieving for Trevor. These courts are a memorial, the only thing pausing for him. The only thing left of him in this whirlwind.

I T'S BEEN A WEEK since Trevor was taken and five days since the grand jury officially started and today is my turn to testify. When I walk out the gate to the Regal-Hi, the swarm of reporters is on me, throwing a flurry of questions that I can't decipher. I swing open the passenger door of Marsha's car and climb in. She immediately sets a ball of fabric in my lap and says, "Put that on." I hold it out in front of me. It's the plainest, most modest black dress I've ever seen. "I put some shoes in the back too, so you can change back there."

I glance toward the backseat to see my very own pair of black shoes, a slight heel on the bottom, but mostly flat. Marsha's feet are at least three sizes smaller than mine, so she had to have bought them just for me. She starts the car as I clamber back and begin undressing, pulling the dress over my head and replacing my Vans with the black shoes. I stare down at myself, my ashy knees, the scars up and down my shins.

Marsha's been prepping me every day for the testimony, giving me all the information she has about how the grand jury is going so far. Apparently the cops have already testified and today is the last full day in court before the jury deliberates. I've been trying to get ahold of Alé, but she hasn't answered her phone. Every time I start to leave a message, my throat closes up on me and I hang up. Last night, I figured out how to say three words, *"They took Trevor,"* before hanging up and proceeding to bury myself in the script Marsha told me to memorize. She says it's not about saying the lines, it's about knowing the story. As if I could forget it.

I poke my head up between the two front seats and stare at Marsha: the peak of her chin, the barely visible click of her jaw side to side.

"You remember the plan?" Marsha asks and I can tell she's jittery.

I take a rubber band off my wrist and pull my twists—new ones Marsha paid me to get done a few days ago in preparation for today—into a ponytail just to feel the weight on my neck.

"Calm. Secure. I'm the golden child that got swept up in this mess," I repeat. "They all gonna be watching me?"

"That's kind of the point," Marsha says.

I rest my cheek in my hand and stare at her stone face. "You really think I ain't done nothing wrong?"

She tears her eyes away from the road for a moment to glance at me. "If you did something wrong, then so did Harriet Tubman and Gloria Steinem and every other woman who did what she had to do even when it wasn't respected." She coughs. "I'm not saying you couldn't have made other choices, but I don't think you deserved any of this either."

In moments like these, I remember Marsha's just another white woman who's never gonna understand what I been through, who can't find anyone besides Harriet Tubman and Gloria Steinem to compare me to. I try to think of Daddy's face plastered on that poster instead. Maybe my thighs are just like Daddy's fists: lovely and soft until they are not; leading us closer and farther from the other limbs that make us up and call us holy.

The rest of the car ride is filled with the hushed hum of Marsha's car, her index finger tapping on the steering wheel, waiting for the light to change. Marsha knows what happened to Trevor, but we're both avoiding it. She tried to talk to me about it after she found out—from God knows who—but I shut her down with a quick side glance. She don't got a right to put his name in her mouth. I'm doing this now because there ain't no reason not to. Because if Trevor is gone, I gotta do everything I can to try to get Marcus back. If not, I'm more alone than I was that night in the alley, than I have ever been. I will testify and I will hope Marsha is right and it ends in Marcus's release and some kind of payment so we will have a chance to start over, and if it doesn't, I will have to return to some kind of hustle, find some other way to live or end up on the street. Freezing.

We pull into the courtroom parking lot and Marsha puts the brake on, pivoting her torso to face me. "We've had reporters on our tail all the way here. We're going to wait about two minutes and, by then, they'll be positioned by the front doors. You walk straight past, just follow me. Got it?" Her ice eyes bulge.

I nod.

She's about to turn and open the car door, but her head swings back to me. "They'll be in there. Men, I mean. Not the exact ones who . . . *you know,* but ones just like them. They might stare at you, try to intimidate you. Don't look."

"How am I not supposed to look if they staring at me?"

"Just don't."

Marsha clicks the doors open and puts her heeled feet on the ground. I open my own backseat door and place my feet on the asphalt, pulling myself up. I haven't walked in anything but sneakers in weeks and it's like my feet have forgotten how to step delicately, the shoes so slippery and new. At first, the only thing I hear is the occasional *whoosh* of cars behind us, the lake's salt winding its way up the county courthouse steps with us, now lined in people dressed in half-business, half-casual, cameras out. I hear my name like a chorus of bees with a few distinct words coming through.

"Ms. Johnson, do you have a moment?"

"Do you have hopes for the outcome of the grand jury?"

Their voices are high-pitched and squeaky, always saying something, but none of it really for me. They want it for the camera. They want it for the quick news segment that never extends past city limits. I focus every muscle on the walk up the steps, the back of Marsha's head, her ponytail swinging. She pulls the door to the courthouse open and I shiver in the breeze, slide inside, let it thud behind me. Marsha keeps walking, but I stop. I guess she hears my shoes stop tapping on the marble floor because she turns around and saunters back to me.

"What's wrong?" She looks at me, hip jutted.

"They not following us in here?"

"They know there will be legal ramifications if they try to enter and broadcast that footage. You're safe."

I roll my eyes, as if safety was ever enough of a possibility to be in question. The courthouse is too big to hold us. Wood and marble, paneling and carvings in ceilings that aren't even reachable with the tallest ladder.

Marsha follows my gaze up, sighs. "I need you to be ready for this. Are you?"

I rub my nails across my forearm, jagged and scratching. "I guess."

Marsha don't have time for my shit, twists back around on her heel, and starts strutting. Down the hallway. Marble and echoes following us, shivers up my legs, thighs rubbing in the slick frame of a dress that could never be mine. We're at least five feet apart at this point and she isn't slowing down for me anytime soon, instead quickens her pace.

We're at the door, a security guard standing in front of it. I know this must be the one, the walls that hide everything they been telling me to fear, because Marsha, steel-framed and glowing, pauses. She turns to look back at me and I catch her eyes for a moment, see the pupils give way to just the tiniest remnants of Marsha as a child, Marsha small like me.

"I wish I could go in with you, but you know I can't. If you need me, you can ask for me and they'll allow you to come out here for legal counsel."

I don't expect it, but my eyes swell with tears and I don't want to leave her.

"You're going to be just fine."

Marsha's hand is on my back, rubbing it, and then pushing me toward the door. I look back at her, but she's not moving. After so many hours practicing, I can't imagine looking out at the room and not seeing her face. I stare at the wooden arches, the guard stepping aside so I can lift my hand to the knob and pull it open.

I guess I expected some sort of chorus, a chaotic rumble or something. Instead, the doors give way to silence punctuated by a single cough. The room is close to empty, at least it looks empty since the back three rows are vacant. As I walk down the aisle, the faces in the front two rows become recognizable, if not for their owners, then for their familiarity. Man beside man, hollow cheeks, patchy noses, woman placed like a divider between them, legs crossed. All pasty and sun-deprived. Bet they've never felt the heat like I have.

At the end of the front row, two girls sit, huddled under sweatshirts that swallow them whole, leaving only their bare legs exposed. The girls are Lexi's type of skittish, a young that reveals itself without even a word. My eyes linger on them for a moment, how they sit on the left side of the aisle with all the uniforms and suits. We're always out of place. I'm not sure where to sit, but then I see the back of Sandra's head, and I'm relieved. I sit on the right side of the aisle, which is close to empty besides her and a couple men with their heads down. She doesn't have her purple suit today, but she is colorful and moon-lit in burgundy.

Beside her now, I don't know if I should cross my legs or not.

I swing one over the other, but it feels wrong, the way everything points straight to my knees, trails up my thighs where the dress gives way to skin. I uncross them. Ain't no right way to be in here, under lights that are more white than lights should be, like they overcompensated and now they're blinding.

Sandra hasn't looked at me yet but she reaches over and squeezes my hand.

"Who are they?" I whisper to her, nodding my head toward the girls across the aisle.

Still not looking in my direction, Sandra responds, "My guess is they're witnesses, like you."

"They done it to them too?"

"I don't know, but from the way they're dressed, they're probably here to discredit your story, put you in a box with them, say you don't know what you're talking about."

"Maybe they just don't got nothing else to wear."

"The lawyers who called them here do." Sandra stares down at her legal pad. "Probably hired by Talbot or someone working with Talbot to prep them."

My knee is shaking now. "I don't even know them. How they gonna say shit about me?"

"This city's not known for its ethics."

"So they paid them to talk shit about me?"

Sandra, who has continued to stare straight down, tilts her head just enough to lock eyes with me. In a low, measured voice, she says, "You worry about you. This is for you and your brother and girls who need to take that money because they don't know another way to survive. You hear me?"

She straightens her head again and I nod, though she probably can't see it. For a moment there, I really believed she was some incarnation of the mother I used to have, some piece of Mama revitalized.

There's a large clock on the wall directly above where the judge is seated and, just as it strikes nine, the whole room quiets. Feels like I've entered a *Judge Judy* scene, the judge slamming the gavel down with three bangs. I half expect her to call out *Order in the court* but she doesn't and next thing I know she's talking in legal speech and a man is standing, responding. The whole exchange is alien to me and I don't know what's going on until Sandra leans toward me and whispers.

"One of the witnesses failed to appear."

"Who?"

"An officer."

"Good," I scoff.

Sandra shakes her head. "I don't think so. It sounds like he was the only one corroborating your story."

"Why would any of them do that?"

"Decency, I guess." Sandra starts to crack a smile that never makes it to her mouth, leaves only the slightest dimple in her left cheek.

I don't think that's it, though. Not that none of them are decent, just that decency has never provided enough to unbury their egos. I think it's just how time works. A man's crescent will always catch up with him. The way I seen Marcus's moon chest recede so far I thought it was dark in there. The way I'm seeing it come out now, slowly, but I know it'll be full again. That's the only reason any of the cops would have tried to save me: they got their moon back.

A bald man seated at one of the tables in front of the judge stands up and turns, walking straight to our row. Sandra stands and they begin whispering. After a few moments, Sandra turns, smiles at me, and exits the courtroom, leaving the bald man to return to his desk. The silent courtroom is soon filled with murmurs, small chatter escalating. The back of my knees itch, sweat accumulating in the crease, and I wish Trevor was sitting next to me, holding my hand the way only a little boy can.

With not more than a swift motion of the judge's neck raising, the

whole room hushes. The judge speaks. "Due to unforeseen altera-
tions to the schedule, we will now begin. Jurors have been chosen
and sworn in and we will begin with Ms. Kiara Johnson. All those
who are not the DA, the court reporter, Ms. Johnson, or members
of the jury will exit the room, myself included."

Everyone shuffles out of the room, the judge following behind,
leaving the bald man, the jurors, the court reporter, and me.

I stare at my feet, first glancing at my breasts squeezed into the
black dress, then my belly's soft bulge, then my knees all gray, finally
to my feet stepping one foot in front of the other up toward the
stand. Halfway there, I hear the man cough behind me. I remember what Marsha would say, raise my head up, shove my shoulders
back so my spine aligns, and lift my eyes to meet the bald man—the
DA—standing beside the desk with his hands clasped in front of him.
I give him a curt smile, but he does not even make eye contact with
me, instead looking down at the papers in front of him. Everyone
trying not to look at me.

I step up to the stand, taking a seat in the round oak chair. It's so
different from when I testified at Mama's trial, when I felt like the
victim and not the defendant, even though I know I'm not really, not
legally at least. The stand is set up like a podium, except I don't have
anything to read from and I would never voluntarily put myself on a
stage, not in front of these people. I'm not Marcus. I look out at the
jury, but my vision won't focus long enough to let me see any of their
faces. Just his. The DA stands with a poise that makes me think he's
done this so many times, I'm just another face to him. Just another
out-of-place girl stuck in someone else's dress, speaking someone
else's words.

Now it feels like I'm the only thing he can focus on, eyebrows
strung together with a downward dip in the center like he's evalu-
ating me, assessing what's about to happen like it ain't entirely his
choice. I chew on the inside of my mouth just to keep my face soft

enough that it won't look like I'm staring him down. Marsha said I need to stay calm, sophisticated, but childlike. I push my lips out enough that it might mimic a smile and wait while he recites a list of proceedings Marsha's already explained more than enough times.

And, just like that, the DA begins, doesn't miss a beat. "Ms. Johnson, is it true that you go by an alias?"

"It's not an alias, it's a nickname. Some people I grew up with call me Kia."

"And the last name? Holt, yes?"

I blink. "I didn't want to give strangers my real name."

"Why not?" His forehead is a map of lines.

"It's dangerous?"

He nods, taking a few steps, head down as if he's pondering something, when we all know this is just for dramatic effect.

I dig my nails into my wrists to see the crescent marks, see anything but his face.

"What do you do for a living, Ms. Johnson?" He walks closer to me, staring up at where I'm seated. I know Marsha drilled me on this, but his face, the way his mouth gapes a little, makes all of it flush out of my head.

"I don't got a job."

"However, you do have a steady income?"

My knee starts to shake involuntarily. "No. Used to make a little but it wasn't no salary."

"Where did that money come from?"

"Men." The moment I say it I know I said the wrong thing. One of Marsha's rules is one-word answers are golden when the response is yes, no, or maybe. Not when that word can be twisted into a target on my head.

He looks surprised by my bluntness, coughing once and taking a moment. His demeanor shifts, from an interrogative scowl to a stare too intimate for our proximity, for these wooden walls. He comes closer. "Would you mind telling me about why these men were paying you?"

In my head I'm speaking, but no words come out. Then I think of Mama, of how we screamed together, the sky cradling us. Of Trevor's body tremors. Of Marcus sobbing in a cell. All that shit just to end up here without a tongue? I keep making marks with my nails until I find the words.

"They was paying me because I didn't have no money and I needed it so I could survive and so I did what I needed to do."

"What would that be, if you don't mind me asking?" Of course, it don't matter if I mind or not, but at least he's trying to be gentle, at least it's less of an attack than I expected.

"I kept them company."

"By company, do you mean sexual relations?"

"Not always." I think of Officer 190 and how he talked on and on for hours, how sometimes he turned into a puddle with his cries. "Wasn't always like that."

"And with Officer Jeremy Carlisle? What was it like with him?"

I pause for a minute, close my eyes so I can get a picture of him again, the splotches on his cheeks and that big gray house.

"I didn't know him by his name, only by his badge number. I saw him a couple times, mostly in groups. He picked me up one night and took me to his house." I glance at the jury. None of them have any expressions on their faces, like they're just waiting for me to finish so they can go piss. I wait, like Marsha would tell me to. She says if I leave enough silence, the DA might forget some of the things he wanted to ask me.

"What did you do at his house?"

One of the jurors, a black woman with her braids tied into a bun, makes eye contact with me.

"We had sex."

"How much did he pay you?"

"Nothing."

The DA stops and looks directly at me, like he's registering my personhood for the first time. His nose scrunches. "You're saying that Officer Carlisle never paid you for the time you spent together?"

"He said he would, but when I woke up, he refused. Said he'd already paid me."

"Had he?"

"He said telling me about an undercover operation was enough of a payment."

He nods, up and down, spinning to pace closer to the jury, then asks me to explain what I mean by an undercover operation. He faces me again. I tell him about the party, about how Carlisle picked me up in that Prius and took me to his place, how I didn't mean to stay the night, how it all spiraled. He continues to ask me questions about Carlisle I don't have the answers to and then pauses.

"During your interview by detectives, you said, 'I shouldn't have been there.' Is that correct?"

"I guess."

"And would you say you understood after that interview the seriousness of these allegations?"

I don't know what he's getting at, so I repeat, "I guess."

"Yet the next week you attended a party in which you had sex with several members of the Oakland Police Department and did not believe that to be morally questionable?"

"I never said that—"

"You didn't bring this to anybody. Nor did you refuse to attend said party. Is that correct?"

I stare at him, his eyes still and glaring. I try to think, but the way he says it, I don't know what the answer really is, how to respond.

"No, I didn't. But they threatened me, so I didn't have no choice." I move my nails up my arm, dig deeper.

He nods. "Who do you live with, Ms. Johnson?"

"Don't live with nobody."

"Let me rephrase. Who is your apartment leased to?"

"My brother," I say, raising my shoulders.

He nods like he was waiting for me to say this. "And where is your brother currently?"

I look around the room, hoping Marsha might appear, but the rows are still empty.

"He's at Santa Rita."

"The jail?"

"Yes."

"What is he there for?"

I close my eyes, squeezing them like it might transport me back outside to where the sky is large and nobody's eyes are on me.

"Drugs."

"Is that why you were involved in prostitution?"

"What you talking about?"

"Drugs." He gestures up into the air. "Did you enter prostitution to pay for drugs?"

I just about spring out my chair, then repeat to myself the mantra: *calm, calm*. "No, I ain't done no drugs."

He already has an idea, though, starts down the path of asking me about Marcus, Mama, Daddy. Says something about familial histories of erratic behavior or some shit and this is everything Marsha told me it might be, but I still want to crawl out my skin, shed it and return to only bones.

He takes a second to go to his table and take a sip of water. I look out at the jury again, hoping the faces might cement some sort of hope for me, but they're still just a mesh of blank stares.

"Ms. Johnson." I snap back into the room, the click of the court reporter on the keyboard. "Did you believe it to be wrong to have sexual relations with members of the police force?" The question is innocent enough, not even worth being asked.

"Of course it ain't right." I'm still thinking about Marcus, about getting him out the moment I exit this wooden trap.

"So why did you participate?"

"I told you, I didn't have no choice."

"You couldn't have gotten up and left that party? You couldn't have refused a ride from Officer Carlisle?"

The tremors start in my fingertips, right beneath the nails, and spread inward. Not up, not down, but inside. Vibrations to the rib cage. I wonder if this is what Trevor felt when they took him.

"I mean, I could've, but they didn't give me no choice—"

"So they forced you to stay? Did Officer Carlisle use handcuffs on you, put you in the back of the car and lock the doors?"

"No." I start tapping my hands on the podium, then scratching, like the wood might take all the tremors and make me hollow.

"Were you angry that you never received monetary payment for these acts?"

I stare at him. His glasses are slipping down his nose from the sweat.

"I guess."

"Did you believe accusing these men of violent acts would result in payment of some sort?"

"What?"

"Did you believe that these accusations would make you money?"

The whole room stills, no one dares to tap a foot or brush a piece of hair behind their ear, thinking they might disturb the fragility of it: the moment they all expect me to crumble.

"No." One word. One word. One word.

He takes a minute to turn around and survey the rest of the courtroom before coming back to look at me, a trick Marsha says they all use. I wonder if she's included in "they."

"You were underage at the time of the events in question, correct?"

"I was seventeen."

"You understand that would make this statutory rape, yes?"

Marsha's told me enough about it. "Yes."

"Did you notify these men of your age prior to intercourse?"

This is the question Marsha and I hoped he wouldn't ask, hoped he might skim over.

"They knew."

"So you told them?"

"Not exactly, but they knew. I'm telling you they knew."

He smiles, this soft smile that reminds me of these interviews I watched with Marsha when we were preparing where he talks about battered women, how he wants to keep us safe. He looks at me not like I'm the battered woman, though, but like I'm the little girl standing by watching. Like I'm confused. "How would they know, Ms. Johnson?"

The tremors have made their way outward now and every limb is shaking. I'm rocking in my chair, its legs squeaking on the platform.

"Because they saw me. I was lying there and they looked me in my eyes and they knew. They knew and they kept them eyes open the whole time, staring at me while they had sex with me, like that only made it better. Because they looked at me and they saw how small I was, I was a child."

Creak on the floor, splinter in my tap-tap fingernail, rigid shake, eyes blurred, Oakland sky so bright inside my throat. I might not have been Soraya, too small to stand up on the shallow end of the pool, but I was still small. I felt so small.

"But you never told them your age?" He knows this is it, the last question.

Fingernails deep inside my skin, blood trickle. "I was a child. I was a child."

And even though Trevor and Marcus and Alé and Mama are out there somewhere, even though there are so many reasons why I gotta say it all, why I gotta let it erupt from my lungs, I'm not thinking about none of them. All I can think about is the way my fingernails stay pressed into the skin even when it breaks, even when I start to bleed. When everything turns to chaos, when I'm sitting in a room full of faces I can't distinguish, when my body doesn't feel like mine no more, I still got these nails. Still got a reminder that I can exist broken, like Trevor facedown in his own crusted blood, still finding a way to get air into his body. That these nails are a miracle. Don't need nobody to make them pretty, to trim them, sharpen them. All they gotta be is what they are: mine.

"Thank you, Ms. Johnson."

He says something about how I can step down, a juror sneezes somewhere in the corner of my vision. Everything keeps on moving, colliding, a wood room where I set myself free like the sky that one night when stars showed themselves over the freeway, before I went back to the apartment that would never really be mine again.

I was a child.

EVERY MOMENT PASSES like water through a clogged drain, barely getting through. Marsha took me home straight from the courthouse, dropped me off without a single word the whole ride, not that I would have heard her if she had spoken.

Somehow, I exited that courtroom with a different body than the one I had when I walked under its ornate wood ceiling, sat on those benches so many before me sweated into. This new body has a chain of holes from the throat to the stomach, where I have tried to bury myself in carvings. This new body got scars more permanent than any tattoo and calls them glorious. This new body got too many memories to hold up inside.

I'm sitting in the center of an apartment that don't nobody really own and hollering. Like Dee finally infected me, like Mama crawled up inside me to massage my jaw open. And the sun has set—left me in the dark seeing only a glitter of pool out the window—and risen again. Over and over. Maybe three times before the knock. It comes when the sky is just starting to pastel. When my mouth has found its close.

I don't move, but she doesn't wait for me to. Alé opens the door like it's hers, marches in with a large bag that she swings onto the counter and then beelines right for me on the floor, kneeling, pooling me into her until we are a singular body and I can smell every scent she's ever carried. Every spice. Her mama's crochet blankets. The skate park.

She loosens her grip a little and I can see her skin, where I get a peek of what must be her newest tattoo, on the back of her neck: a pair of shoes, colored lavender with a K in the sole of one of them.

She fully lets go of me now, so I can finally look at her eyes, which are spilling. I don't know if I've ever seen Alé cry like this and I can't help but lean forward and kiss her cheek, taste the salt, trail up to the corner of her eye with my lips. She is the bottom of the ocean, where all the magic hides beneath too many layers of dark and water and salt. The warmth got hold of my chest, other side of what they say about the heart; when it's not breaking, you might just get lucky enough to have it feel full, blood pulsing.

Her hands find my waist and a series of thoughts flash across her face, an internal debate surfacing in mouth quivers. When Alé touches me this time, we are on the floor, we are without barriers. My mouth is already so close.

"Kiara." Her tears have stopped running, but I haven't moved, and my name is a question.

Hers is an answer and this is the first time I think that this all might have been worth it, that the only way back to Alé was wading right through the shit pool. She is kissing me. I am kissing her. She's softer than I ever thought she could be and I've never been more relieved to be touched, to have her lace her fingers through my hair. Her on top of me. Her pulling back just to stare into me like the stars found their way beneath my eyelids, and I think this might be my universe-halting love, the one that undoes me and keeps me whole all at once.

Alé comes back down to me slow, traces my stomach with her finger like she always does, except this time she doesn't pull away. This time, she tells me she is sorry, tells me she came the second she got my message. And even though she's saying all the right things, it is the look she gives me, the way her eyes pull open so big I know she's seeing me more than anybody has. That she sees me beyond the shit that got stirred up inside me. Sees me beyond this new body or that old body or any body I have ever existed in because she don't give a shit about how many layers of shea butter I rub into my skin. Alé just wants to hold me. Alé just wants to be mine.

We are tangled on the floor of this apartment, this living relic of all the lives I've lived. This girl who has held me through it all. We are gasping and laughing and crying and I don't know if I've ever told her I love her, but I can't stop saying it. Because it has never meant this much. It has never filled my mouth like this. Like the only flood I have ever wanted. She is saying it back, again and again, and there has never been a truth like this one.

Alé is feeding me and I am telling her about the women I have known. All Demond's girls from that party, Camila, Lexi, the two sitting on the wrong side of the aisle torn up. Mama. Me. I am telling her how these streets open us up and remove the part of us most worth keeping: the child left in us. The rounded jaw that can't even hold a scream no more because they take that too. They take everything.

Alé nods, doesn't look away, spoons soup into my mouth when I fade into mutters. Kisses my nose. Tells me about how it feels to look at her mama's face, numb, tells me about the bruises distorting the cold body of the girl who could've been Clara, about her fear, about how she wants more than this for me, for us. I tell her I want more for her too, want her to be a doctor or a doula or whatever will soothe the part of her that needs more than a kitchen.

She brought me all kinds of food, healing me the best way she knows, and we're sitting on the floor still, nothing but flesh, leaning against the edge of the mattress. The soup is hot and I can feel its path from tongue to stomach, feel every sip absorbed. I tell her about Trevor, his bruised eyes, how I had to pull his arms from my neck and set him in the backseat of a car because his mama don't know how to love him the way he needs to be loved and I am not enough.

Alé stops me there, says, "Just because you ain't his mama don't mean you ain't given him something can't nobody take away." And if it didn't sound like a load of bullshit, I would believe her. The only thing I have as evidence is his swollen face in the backseat of a car, his tremors, and that isn't proof of nothing sacred.

I couldn't tell you when I fell asleep or when Alé woke up and removed me from the place right where her lungs would be, but I know the exact moment the jury decided, miles away like it was happening right inside the apartment. It was the clatter. The not-quite-light-enough-to-call-it-morning glass shatter, Alé leaning over the broken pieces of a lamp I never really used. Then the quiet. That's when they all must have nodded their heads, signed the papers to send to the judge. Maybe they all did it solemnly, without looking each other in the eyes, like they could sidestep guilt.

The call comes an hour later. Alé sat holding me as I heaved and asked her if it was all over. She didn't say no, just squeezed me until it felt like I had a body again, until my phone rang.

I answer.

Marsha talks fast on the other end of the line, jumbling the words but not saying much, then slows.

"I'm so sorry, Kiara, but there will be no indictment."

I knew it was coming, I could feel it, but when Marsha says the words it feels like a punch, like the same sharp pain as when the metal man pushed me up against that brick wall the night it all started.

"What about Marcus?" I don't want to ask, don't even want to know, but I have to.

Marsha pauses. Silence. "I've arranged to get him a fantastic lawyer, one more fit to his case than I am, but I can't do much more than that. Not without the pressure from the indictment." She's quiet again. "I'm sorry."

I can tell her ice eyes are flooded because then she goes on some tangent about hope and I let her. It's always best to let them unravel, makes everything seem a little less cracked. I thought I'd be angry at her, want to rage, but I don't. When she hangs up the phone, almost two hours after the lamp found itself scattered across the apartment, I look up at Alé, who is back with her arm around me on the floor. She didn't bother cleaning anything up once she saw the salt streaming down my cheeks, and her hands are spotted in blood and glimmers of glass. Neither of us says nothing.

· ·

A calm hits me that I didn't think would and I rest my head back against the mattress, so I'm facing the ceiling. What did I expect but this? The sky tried to tell me everything comes in extremes, in blinding stretches of shit I can't escape. Streetwalking all the way up to the clouds. Oakland contains it all: heartbreak and yearning. Reaching for our young back. I lift my head up and turn to Alé, taking her hand, picking out each grain of glass, and lifting it to my cheek so her blood is mine. Iron for ink. Her lips move, murmur, but nothing emerges distinguishable.

She pulls me close to her chest and wraps me so tight I can cocoon in the squeeze. We both know that pretty soon we will have to contend with what it means to have lost it all and still have each other. To have lost a roof and found a home. For now, though, Alé holds me close, I wash her hands, wrap them in Marsha's black dress, and she begins to clean up the fragments of light.

I'm pulling on one of Marcus's big shirts when I hear it. I think I'm hallucinating at first, but the sound is so distinct, so visceral that I don't think my mind could make it up.

I'm walking toward the door, past Alé. "You hear that?"

She shrugs, bent over sweeping the glass up.

I open the door and step out onto the patio strip, lean over the railing, and there he is. I know from the moment I look down because he's got that same circular birthmark on the top of his head. Trevor is sitting with his feet dipped into the pool, splashing.

The sky is a soft blue and I begin the walk toward the spiral staircase, winding down to the center of my everything, that shit pool that don't never seem to stop pulling us in. I think about Soraya's first steps and some part of me that hasn't had any room to breathe misses her, wants to watch her run, watch her speak, watch her say my name, all three syllables, and learn how to shoot a hoop like Trevor.

I walk down the stairs like I'm descending straight into a fantasy, like I'm about to meet a ghost. When my bare feet hit the pavement and I'm staring at the back of his head, I know it ain't no dream. He's wearing his blue-and-yellow backpack, same one I handed Mrs. Randall. Same one I gave him for his birthday so many months ago. I walk closer, until I am standing right above him and, then, with only an oversized T-shirt draped over my body, I sit beside him, slip my own feet into the pool. My legs submerge to mid-calf.

I'm staring straight at him, but he's still looking right into the pool, like he hasn't even registered my presence beside him. His eyes are fully open now, face still discolored along the cheekbones, but the parts of him that make his face *his* are repaired. Perfectly rounded. The bulging eyes. Pouted lips.

"What you doin' here, Trev?" I touch him lightly with my shoulder, so even if he doesn't look at me, he'll be able to feel me.

He keeps his eyes on the pool, on his feet as they come up from underneath its surface and splash back under again. Then, like some timer went off in his head, he whips his head toward me, locks eyes with mine, and flashes me a smile.

"Had to come get my ball."

I can't help but beam at that, my whole body spreading into a grin 'cause both of us know it's so much more than that, but also, maybe in some ways, it's just that simple. How we grew together in the bounce of a ball, how the beginning of our collapse started with a basketball court and a beating. How we don't get to return to none of it again, but maybe we can steal this moment. Maybe this excuse is just enough to spin us into a pickup game where we'll laugh because we can, until the sun disintegrates and nighttime threatens to set us free just to capture us again, back into the things we can't escape. When I have to send him back onto whatever bus he snuck here on. Don't even matter, though, because I will send him off with a kiss to the forehead and that ball in hand, that momentum can't nobody take away.

It seems both obvious and ridiculous when Trevor stands up, takes off his backpack, and lifts his shirt up over his head, then removes his shorts, standing there an inch taller in the same baggy boxers like he did before the shoes showed up poolside.

I don't even realize I'm doing it: undressing, slipping out of the shirt; not until I am skin rimmed in markings, accented in scabs still healing from my nails. Just like that, in the bright of a morning that is deceptively calm, both of us in our underwear, Trevor grabs hold of my hand, clasps on tight. We don't even need to count down because, somehow, we can both feel when it's time to dive in. Keep diving. Shit pool turning to ocean it's so deep. Beneath the water, I open my eyes, let the chlorine stain them red, and turn my head toward Trevor. He's looking at me. His mouth is open. I open mine and we both begin to laugh, connected by the fingers, bubbles coming out our mouths and meeting in the middle of the water. Trevor and I finding our laughter just like Dee somewhere in the beyond, screeching out this moment of delirious joy, letting the water swallow us.

AUTHOR'S NOTE

In 2015, when I was a young teenager in Oakland, a story broke describing how members of the Oakland Police Department, and several other police departments in the Bay Area, had participated in the sexual exploitation of a young woman and attempted to cover it up. This case developed over months and years and, even as the news cycle moved on, I continued to wonder about this event, about this girl, and about the other girls who did not receive headlines, but nonetheless experienced the cruelty of what policing can do to a person's body, mind, and spirit. For this one case that entered the media, there were and are dozens of other cases of sex workers and young women who experience violence at the hands of police and do not have their stories told, do not see court, and do not escape these situations at all. Yet the cases we know about are few.

When I began writing *Nightcrawling,* I was seventeen and contemplating what it meant to be vulnerable, unprotected, and unseen. Like many black girls, I was often told growing up to tend to and shield my brother, my dad, the black men around me: their safety, their bodies, their dreams. In this, I learned that my own safety, body, and dreams were secondary, that there was no one and nothing that could or would protect me. Kiara is an entirely fictional character but what happens to her is a reflection of the types of violence that black and brown women face regularly: a 2010 study found that police sexual violence is the second most reported instance of police misconduct and disproportionately impacts women of color.

As I wrote and researched this book, I drew inspiration from the Oakland case and others like it, as I wanted to write a story of my city, but I also wanted to explore what it would mean for this to happen to a young black woman, for this case to be put in the narrative control of a survivor, for there to be a world beyond the headline, and for readers to have access to this world. The stories of black women, and queer and trans folks, are not often represented in the narratives of violence we see protested, written about, and amplified in most movements, but that does not erase their existence. I wanted to write a story that would reflect the fear and danger that comes with black womanhood and the adultification of black girls, while also recognizing that Kiara—like so many of us who find ourselves in circumstances that feel impossible to survive—is still capable of joy and love.

ACKNOWLEDGMENTS

First of all, I am abundantly grateful for Lucy Carson and Molly Friedrich and the rest of The Friedrich Agency for being my best advocates and cheering me on every step of the way. Thank you to Ruth Ozeki for your peerless wisdom and for introducing me to the lovely Molly and Lucy. Thank you to my editor, Diana Miller, for your constant insight and thoughtful notes through unforeseen circumstances. Thank you to the entire team at Knopf for championing Kiara's story. Thank you to Niesha for giving me insight to ground *Nightcrawling* in an authentic sex-work experience.

Thank you to Samantha Rajaram for being my Pitch Wars mentor and friend. Pitch Wars was such an incredible opportunity that gave me what I needed to revise this novel and, most important, your friendship and support. A special thank-you to Maria Dong for the generous and brilliant editing help.

Thank you to Jordan Karnes for being a reader when I desperately needed one and for years of workshops and writing that prepared me to write this in the first place. To Oakland School for the Arts, for allowing me the first space where I could exist as a writer, and to the Oakland Youth Poet Laureate program for nurturing the poet in me. To all the children I have loved and cared for, thank you for filling my days with joy so I could spend my nights with these words.

Daddy, thank you for giving me your love of writing and for all the jazz. Mama, thank you for giving me a house full of books and teaching me the value of reading. Logan, thank you for being the first person I call when I'm stuck and the best listener and brother I could ask for. Magda, thank you for being my best friend and first reader of almost everything. Thank you to Zach Wyner, for your early mentorship, writing sessions, and constancy in my life. To all my friends and family, you have given me a rich world worth writing about and a community I am endlessly thankful for.

To Oakland, for raising me and giving me the cafés, libraries, apartments, and skies to write this book inside. You will always be home.

And lastly to Mo, my love, thank you for being by my side from that first read to hours of editing to the final touches. You are my biggest support, my anchor, my solace after a day's work. Without you, I wouldn't have been able to make this book what it is. You are the Alé to my Kiara and I cannot express to you how lucky I feel to come home to your arms, your food, and your words. You are my everything.

A NOTE ON THE TYPE

This book was set in Warnock Pro, a digital typeface designed by Robert Slimbach as a personal font in honor of Adobe Systems co-founder John Warnock. It was released as a commercial font in 2000.

Typeset by Scribe, Philadelphia, Pennsylvania

Printed and bound by Berryville Graphics, Berryville, Virginia

Designed by Maggie Hinders